"The Atlantic Campaign"
A Hostage for Napoleon

Georges Carrack

Neville Burton '*Worlds Apart*' Series

Volume 5

Story   by   Georges Carrack

Cover design   by   Joshua Courtright

Print ISBN: 978-0-9968671-0-8

[E-Book ISBN: 978-0-9968671-1-5]

Carrack, Georges, 1947-

The Stillwater Conspiracy: fiction/historical

Visit our website at www.CarrackBooks.com

This is a work of fiction. It is historical fiction, however, so most ship names, captains, places and time references appearing in this work may be found in historical documents, or are set closely within the time of their existence. The protagonist and his family, friends and most close associates are fictitious. The names of all characters, historical or otherwise, are surrounded by a purely fictitious story. Any resemblance to businesses or companies is also fictional and entirely coincidental.

v1.0

A story for

Two Williams

(USA and UK)

The author wishes to recognize the efforts of, and thank people who were extremely helpful in, accomplishing the publication of this book:

My wife, Carolyn, for her continuous patience and ideas,

Joshua Courtright for cover design and proofreading

Ms. Gayle Vaughan for again being my primary "Beta Reader"

All those authors of this genre who have gone before, providing the inspiration and a basic understanding of life on a British warship in the Napoleonic era, and

The internet and its contributors, without which/whom the original research necessary to complete such a tale would have been enough to stall my effort.

The Neville Burton 'Worlds Apart' Series

Volume 1: The Glorious First of June
Volume 2: The Experiment at Jamaica
Volume 3: Mutiny at Port Maria
Volume 4: The Stillwater Conspiracy
Volume 5: The Atlantic Campaign

The Seal of the
Admiralty

"The Atlantic Campaign"
A Hostage for Napoleon
Volume 5 of the Neville Burton 'Worlds Apart' Series

1 - "13th March, 1806"

Neville Burton, captain of the 36-gun frigate HMS *La Désirée*, paced his quarterdeck in an unusually rapid fashion while he reflected upon his recent personal performance. He had not been acting toward the men in his command with his normal cheerful approach. *La Désirée* had been at sea for weeks. *I should be over my childish behavior by now*, he grumbled to himself. *I have no concern that my fiancée will be gone when I return. We will yet marry.*

"Deck, thar!" called out a small dark shape in the masthead lookout's little cage, "Signal."

"Out with it, Mr. O'Brien," the captain yelled back. As the words left his mouth, he cautioned himself again to regain his normal composure. There was no reason to make this man feel anger from his captain. He was doing his job.

Captain Burton noticed the lookout's pause. "*London*, three points off starboard bow, Sir. 'Enemy'.

"Can you see *Foudroyant*, Mr. O'Brien?" He could see O'Brien turn and look aft.

"Aye, Sir, to 'er t'gallants. Wait a minute; there's more... signals – our number and *Amazon*...."

"Chase, it is," said Midshipman Hicks, who'd taken his signals glass from its becket on the mainmast and was watching *Foudroyant* intently. The quick response surprised Neville. He'd been told when he came aboard that Hicks was a bit slow, and he hadn't yet seen any reason before this to argue with the assessment.

"Chase," yelled O'Brien.

"I suppose this is why we've been out here patrolling the Atlantic, isn't it, Lieutenant Towers? Maybe we've found that French rotter Willaumez, after all. Have Bo'sun Strugnell call all hands on deck." *There may have been a reason to put off my wedding plans after all.*

"Aye, Sir. Clear for action?"

"Belay that."

First Lieutenant Towers barked an order to Strugnell, which was immediately followed by a cacophony of pipes, calloused bare feet slapping the decks in haste, the squawking of chickens being urged to their cages, officers and petit officers bawling at the men, and myriad other noises undistinguishable. The ship shuddered from the sudden addition of thousands of pounds of moving humans swarming up the ratlines.

Compared to his appearance, the first lieutenant's voice was huge. Somewhat on the tall side, but without the burly chest one would normally associate with such a roar, his ramrod straight posture gave him a height of about five feet and eight inches. His narrow face, short nose and sad-looking eyes were offset by a swarthy complexion, resulting in an authoritative appearance.

"Where away, Mr. O'Brien?" yelled Neville.

"I cain't see nuttin' but flagship, Sir."

"I'd guess east-nor-east, then, Captain. *London's* furthest out that way," chimed in Worth, "and unless he's wrong…"

"Yes, Mr. Worth, I agree. Let's haul our wind – two points to starboard. Follow *Amazon*."

Neville leaned on the windward rail and made his own conscious study of the weather. A good strong trade wind was blowing out of the east. The decks shone white in the early morning sun, and the topgallant and topsails far above his head even whiter. With the course modified only two points higher on the wind, the four-foot waves began thumping harder on the bows, throwing spray wide to leeward. A very fine mist of windward spray from a particularly large wave found its way back to Neville, dampening his face and hands, and a few dark, wet patches began to show on the deck. There were only small puffy white clouds – none gray at the bottom. Nothing threatened a storm or anything other than what he saw now for days to come. It looked a good day for a chase – an exciting one; not one of those where they would all whistle for wind.

"Deck, thar!" hollered Mr. O'Brien in another half hour. "Two Sail. They look French. East an' comin' this way."

"They must think they are the stronger force, Lieutenant Towers. I suspect they are mistaken."

"I can see t'gallant yards from the deck here, Cap'n," said Towers. "They're still… no, not so." He grabbed the long glass from Hicks and leveled it at the oncoming ship. "Sails are shivering, Sir. Backing, now. She'll turn off in a minute, I'm sure of it. What can this mean?"

Neville thought for a moment before answering. "It's logical they thought they were stronger until they got a better look. Maybe they thought we were a convoy. There are nine of us. They shouldn't have expected to find a British squadron here."

"There goes *London*, Sir." Three fore-aft-aft sails appeared on *London*, slapping hard to the wind at almost the same moment she dropped her courses. Her courses couldn't be seen from the deck of *La Désirée*, but they were no longer furled on the yards.

"I can see, Lt. Towers." *And I'm still casting my ill will about.*

"Mr. Foyle, what's *Amazon* doing?" Neville asked of his second midshipman, a gangly, bushy blond-headed youth he had brought with him from his last ship, the American-built schooner *Superieure*. Foyle was an excellent sailor, even at fourteen years of age, and Neville considered him to be a joy to have around, now with his stutter gone.

"Same as *London*, Sir; cracking on."

"All plain sail she can handle, Mr. Worth. We'd best not let them leave us behind or they'll have me at courts-martial for delinquency and cowardice."

Lieutenant Towers, standing just feet away, suddenly howled, "Another pull on the Main t'gallant staysail sheet, if you please, Mr. Gordon!" To his captain, he said, "Excuse me, Sir."

Neville nodded to Towers. "Frenchie has lost considerable time going about, hasn't she, Mr. Worth?" he observed for no particular purpose. Captains didn't usually discuss the obvious with their subordinates, but Neville was trying to keep his mind off personal problems.

"Aye, Sir, we can see her courses now. She must be fully hull up to *London*. T'other ship has gone about, too. She looks to be a frigate. I'll be surprised if she's faster than us, or *Amazon*, either."

"We'll see, Mr. Worth. I'm going below a minute. Have Lieutenant Towers call me if anything changes."

Neville stepped into his cabin, strapped on his short-sword belt, and checked his pistol. The activity gave him a few minutes for his own thoughts in the quiet space. Not entire quiet; such a thing rarely occurred on a sailing ship. Orders were being yelled above, and the ocean thrashed its way along the hull. The squad of marines responsible for the mizzen clomped about noisily in their boots above his head.

His thoughts went to the history of this venture. "Have you been living in a cave, Captain?" Admiral Warren, Commander of the squadron with whom he now sailed, had asked of him when they first met in Jamaica, shortly after news of the British victory at the Battle of Santo Domingo just this past 6th February, 1806.

Taken aback, but not on the surface flustered, Neville had answered, "The Battle of Santo Domingo is all the recent news and gossip, of course, Sir, but we have no daily news sheet here. There are three being published in Falmouth, on the North Shore, but they are almost exclusively dedicated to the comings and goings of trade. If we do see a sheet here, it will usually be weeks old. So as you suggest, it is similar to living in the wild." He didn't mention he'd been quite caught up in the beginnings of planning for his marriage to Miss Marion Stillwater, the daughter of a local Rum tycoon. Such a claim would not have gone over well with an admiral; it would probably sound more like dereliction of duty.

"You've heard nothing of our assignment, then?"

"No, Sir. I've not received orders." *Short answers. Just answer the question an admiral asks.*

"The Southern Approaches to the Caribbean must be watched in the event Willaumez has gone into hiding in South America and decides to reappear and do damage. After one passage through that area we are to cast a wide net in the central Atlantic. We are seven ships of the line, plus your frigate and *Amazon*. Be ready to sail in a week and a half."

And here we've been ever since, patrolling back and forth in the endless ocean. It's a miracle we've found anyone at all, in my opinion. What followed was not pleasant, either.

He and Marion Stillwater stood in the shade just inside the door of her father's *Independence Hall* mansion overlooking the lane to the house; waiting for a carriage. They were a handsome couple, but looks were no advantage in this situation. Neville Burton, a sturdy young man of twenty and six years, stood a fathom of height. He would be considered a very dashing officer by most women, and his well-combed long hair and exceptionally bright blue eyes did nothing but add to his attractiveness. Marion was the quintessential 'belle of the ball', although she might have been considered by some as a spinster at her own twenty and four years. Neville dwarfed her petite five feet and two inches, even with her very straight posture. Hair of a color between brown and blond hung to just above her shoulders, set off the slight tropical tan on her clear complexion. Her small facial features included a short nose and thin lips which, at the moment, weren't smiling.

"Go off sailing about, Neville? Is that the way it will be even after we're married?" Marion had inquired. It sounded rhetorical. He didn't think she expected an answer.

"Well, Neville? The cat has your tongue?" *I guess I am expected to defend myself.*

"It's not a pleasure cruise. I am in the Navy, Marion. I must go when called." *Short answers. Just answer the question an admiral asks.*

"Well, maybe you shouldn't be in the navy, then. It's not like I haven't enough money for the two of us to live comfortably."

And it's a good job she doesn't know I have my own money at Hoare's in London, or she would be even less amused.

"The Navy is a duty, Marion. I sail for King and country, and for my family's honor." He knew his statement was a mistake as soon as the words fell out of his mouth.

"King and country can sod off, if you please!" She glared up at him, as if he had created the situation. "Pardon my English," she added. Marion might have been of English descent, but she was American. The United States was only a little older than she was. 'King and Country' were still fighting words back 'home' in the USA.

"I'm sorry for my outburst, Neville." Her tone changed. "I love you, and I understand all this, but I don't have to like it." They had embraced, and just held each other for several minutes. He'd felt her warm tears on his shoulder and the ache in his heart, but when they looked at each other again, he knew they were both resolved. He felt another pang in his chest when the carriage appeared from around back of the house.

"We sail tomorrow, Marion, as you know. Will I see you at the point?"

"You will, indeed."

A knock came at the cabin door. The sentry pushed the door open enough to allow the messenger to stick his head into the cabin. "Lieutenant Towers' compliments, Sir, and will you be joining him on quatterdeck?"

Really? I haven't even sat. "Aye, Mr. Ross. Straight away."

The time couldn't have been more than twenty minutes, but the situation had changed noticeably from when he'd gone below.

"What's this, Lieutenant Towers? How can we suddenly be so close?"

"I can't readily explain it, Sir. It's as if they have dropped sea anchors. Maybe we've just had a wind they don't enjoy, or they may also have bottoms fouled terrible with the weed as a result of being in the Indian Ocean so long. *London* has closed a great distance on that big 'un there, and we, with *Amazon*, may be within range in another hour. Do you know the name of Admiral Willaumez's ship, Sir?"

"The *Alexandre*, if memory serves, but I wouldn't wager on it. Are there but two ships? I would have expected a squadron if they dared to attack a large fleet."

"Only two."

"That would explain the sudden retreat." Neville turned to look aft. "Have we left our own behind, as well?"

"We saw *Ramillies* not long ago, and a glimpse of *Foudroyant*… or rather, the lookout did, so we know they have the signals, and we must assume word has passed along, but no more."

"Why do you call me now?"

"*Amazon* has hauled her wind another point. Do you have orders?" asked Towers. He wasn't making any suggestion to his captain, particularly given his recent testiness.

Neville took his time considering his tactical situation. "Stay on course, Lieutenant Towers. *Amazon* is making her play to climb up on the wind. Since she is obviously forereaching, she will go for the weather gage. We will spread apart if we do not follow, leaving the French frigate less opportunity to fall off and run." He paused a minute, studying the situation. "For that matter," he resumed, "if she does fall off, she might be able to cross *London* and fire a broadside as she passes. There's nothing more to do now. I'm sure it will be another hour, at least, before any shots are fired – and I assume those will be by the *London*, up there. Call me when you hear cannon fire. I shall endeavor to review the pusser's report."

When the next messenger arrived at his cabin door exactly an hour later, Neville had just stowed his quill and inkwell after finishing a letter to Marion. He hadn't taken a look at even one line of the pusser's report. "*London's* fired a chaser, Sir. We couldn't see where it went."

Neville felt the stirrings of excitement he associated with a looming battle. It was too early to tell whether this might be something dramatic, or whether Willaumez might see the writing on the wall and haul his colors. "I'll be right along!" he called to the messenger. With his letter finished, he was willing to clear his ship for action. All of his personal kit would disappear down into the hold as soon as he gave the order to clear. He wondered if he should feed the men their breakfast before the action began, but the sound of seven bells in the Morning Watch extinguished the thought. *It's almost time for breakfast, anyway.*

"Good morning again, Captain," said Midshipman Foyle as they crossed paths at the foot of the main mast. "*London's* fired a chaser." They were now close enough to see her colours wave gallantly from the mizzen.

"So I'm told, but I didn't hear a thing."

"They are off to loo'ard, Sir. Wind carried it away. But we saw the smoke and a heard a little 'pop'."

"Heads up, Mr. Foyle. We'll be calling to clear." Neville started up the quarterdeck stair, and called out before he reached the top, "It's time, Lt. Towers. Call to clear for action."

"Call to clear, Mr. Strugnell," repeated Towers.

Boatswain Strugnell, a sturdy man of average height, considered himself one of the toughest men aboard. His face, surrounded by bushy sideburns straggling down his cheeks and almost meeting at the chin, bore the scars and flat nose of a brawler. He was sharp of eye and quick to use his starter if Neville didn't watch him closely. His normal attire included a very bright red cap that he claimed to have taken from a Barbary pirate, however, which made that task easy. His pipes began almost immediately, commencing a new round of crashing and banging, running and shouting. One of the goats, being particularly obstinate about being sent to his cage, almost crashed into Neville as he ran by with a landsman after him.

"Get that animal off my quarterdeck!" Neville shouted after the man. "Time, Lieutenant?" Neville asked Towers.

"Four minutes and ten seconds, Sir. *Amazon* may be close enough to fire soon, I think, unless the frigate turns to run."

"Hmmm."

Another 'pop' issued from the two big ships, now slightly to off to larboard. Smoke appeared, clearly indicating a big gun on the French ship. *London* answered almost immediately.

"They'll be into it in a few more minutes, for sure. Look, Lieutenant Towers; just as you said, the frigate is turning down our way. We must cut her off while *Amazon* runs her down." He turned to the Sailing Master and said, "Fall down two points on the wind, Mr. Worth. Let's be sure she can't simply sail past us."

Sailing Master Worth was a weathered fellow of some indeterminate age. One could suspect him of being rather long in the tooth, with his deep tan hiding an otherwise blotchy white and red complexion. His hooded brown eyes gave an impression of being a tad slow, but he never seemed to miss a thing in the rigging – not a wiggle of a sail's clue or shiver of a sheet. Shorter than most, at about five feet and an inch, and slope-shouldered, Worth made up for stature by being very strong in his stance, and very decisive. Moreover, his trade-mark six-inch-tall purple hat with a red band and a half inch brim never blew off.

"Down, two points, aye, Captain," Worth repeated. "And forward, "Mr. Strugnell, you heard Cap'n. See to your braces, if you please!"

"She's turned far more than I expected, Mr. Worth. She's going to pass by *London* and then she'll be across our bows on this course and run away. Down another two points."

"Aye, Sir." Neville yelled again for Strugnell to urge his men to their duties, and then another order aft to the youngest of the midshipman, "Mr. MacDavin, you're officer in charge on the poop. Don't let those bloody marines slouch! Lay the mizzen sheet off about three feet. Lively now, lively. We've got a Frog to catch."

La Désirée stood taller as the force of the wind came further behind; less from her side. "If we both stay our courses, Cap'n, we have an almost-certain collision about half an hour away," observed Worth with a touch of excitement in his voice. Realizing he had stepped beyond his station, he added, "…if you don't mind my saying so, *Sir*."

Captain Burton turned away, smiling to himself. He had a good cadre of officers here, no hint of any mutinous behavior; several weeks of boredom and back-breaking work had forged them together well. He could be confident as they now hurtled into battle, but he was disappointed in himself for reading the situation wrong. The men should have been at breakfast now. They would go into battle hungry.

La Désirée now charged forward toward the Frenchman, who had *Amazon* close on her aft quarter, and the Frenchman was charging toward the battling ships of the line.

"I believe we are forereaching, Mr. Worth. We seem to have a slight advantage of the wind, and we should pass forward of her. She will pass *London* first, however. She may not be the same size, but she might do damage. *Amazon* has gone behind the smoke of the battle."

The French frigate neared *London*, and her guns began to speak. First the bow chaser; then a foredeck carronade.

"She's doing damage, Sir!" yelled Foyle. "She's at least making holes in a few sails."

"Someone's fired a broadside," remarked Towers. "Either Amazon fired at the French as she passed on the far side, or Frenchie had the strength to fight both sides and fire at *Amazon*. We'll see in a minute what condition *Amazon* is when she appears from behind them."

"We'll be clear of *London* in another fifteen minutes, Cap'n," said Worth.

The three frigates swept past the second-rates. *Amazon* appeared from behind the smoke, leaving the frigates clear for their own clash. All were soon well clear of the larger battle under way.

"I don't see a scratch on *Amazon*, Cap'n," said Miller, "Must've been her fired at the French.

"Lieutenant Towers, prepare to give them a rolling broadside as soon as we reach her. Lieutenant Carlyle, get your sharpshooters into the tops. We'll give them everything we have."

Men with red coats and long muskets began clambering up the ratlines. "They'll be thankful for the steady roll of a quartering sea, won't they, Captain?" Neville decided the remark wasn't really meant for him to answer, and ignored it. Gun crews below were sharing the excitement, shouting at each other and cheering when cannons roared. Even in the cool of the Atlantic storm, many had their shirts off; most had bandanas holding cotton stuff in their ears.

Neville motioned Lt. Towers over to Worth, and to them both he said, "If I were Frenchie in this situation, I would try very hard to keep on to the last, raking *London* as she passes – if she can –

and shooting at us as we near her, but then jibe to starboard at last chance. She'll give us a full broadside as her motion falls with the turn and we go by. So be ready on the sails to let the sheets fly and try to slow beside her if we can. Make sure every man-jack is ready on the guns to give them our broadside. Pass word. I still can't tell how many guns she has, but probably a few more than us; she looks bigger."

"Aye, Sir," they said in unison. "We'll cross in another ten minutes now, I'd wager," added Worth.

"Get your bow chaser busy, Lt. Tow…" Neville's voice was drowned by the sound of a long six-pounder blasting on the foredeck, and then a ball from the enemy removing a foot-long piece of the quarterdeck rail as it howled across the deck. One of the marines howled in pain, and Neville turned to see a three-inch splinter protruding from his left arm. Smoke was rapidly dissipating downwind from their adversary.

"They fired their stern chaser at the same time, Lieutenant Towers! I hope we aimed as well as they did."

"Can't tell, Sir. Don't see no holes."

The forward cannons on each frigate were beginning to speak; two shots came at them from the Frenchman, followed by a huge explosion from *London's* duel.

La Désirée's forward three guns fired in rolling succession; then a fourth shot from *Amazon's* bow chaser.

"If she doesn't turn, we'll sail right by, Captain!" said Second Lieutenant Miller, forgetting his place in the excitement.

"When pigs fly," said Neville. "Loose sheets on the foremast. Let him know we'll stop in front of him if we need to."

The order was passed quickly to the foremast landsmen by Tower's amazing voice and, within seconds, the roar of flailing sheets and sails arose forward.

"Thank God! He's got the message," yelled Third Lieutenant Bradley from the waist.

Neville's mind was already imagining the sound of splintering wood and the crashing of rigging as two ships collided, but the nightmare ended when he saw the French frigate begin to turn. "Forty guns," yelled Bradley, just before three of them fired. The two ships were about a cable apart by then, and would probably be as close as a half cable before the Frenchman turned fully parallel to *La Désirée*. Neville felt a crash forward that was strong enough to shake the ship, "Fire!" he yelled. *La Désirée* let loose her full broadside, and the Frenchman fired the remaining guns on her port side. Another crash above Neville's head shivered *La Désirée* yet again, though it seemed to have no consequence. The rumbling of several tons of cannons rolling in for reloading followed the crash.

"I can't believe it, Captain," said Worth, "I don't see any damage on her, save a hole in her main course. We have trouble, though," was the last thing he said before the mizzen yard crashed down across the binnacle, smashing the wheel to pieces and throwing Worth and two helmsmen ten feet aft.

"What's happened forward, Lieutenant Miller?" Neville called down into the waist.

"Jib-boom is split Sir; broken by a lucky ball."

"Two lucky shots at once?" muttered Neville, "and we're helpless? And Frenchie has got away?"

"Not got away, Captain," said Lt. Miller, who had seen Worth go down and sprinted up the quarterdeck stair to help. Foyle had beaten him there. "*Amazon* is on her now. You can hear it. *Belle Poule* is her name; forty guns by my count, as Lieutenant Bradley said."

"I'm all right. See to Worth," Neville said, refusing their aid.

Boatswain Strugnell appeared, panting from a run aft from the foredeck. Red hat in hand, he said, "Jib-boom is sprung as well as half shot away forward of the bowsprit, Captain. We've got jibs off and we'll have to take down the foremast top hamper."

"Get it done fast, Mr. Strugnell. And get Mr. Mason to work," he added, referring to the foremast midshipman.

"Aye, Sir," he called over his shoulder as he jogged forward.

"Where is Mr…" He instinctively ducked as yet another crash amidships reminded them that *Amazon's* battle with *Belle Poule* was not far away; close enough for them to be hit by errant cannonballs. "…Mr. MacDavin?"

"MacDavin here, Sir," said a very shaky little voice. When Neville turned, he was relieved to see Worth standing beside MacDavin, leaning on the young boy's shoulder. The sight was somewhat comical, nonetheless, since the weathered Worth was a half inch shorter than the twelve-year-old.

"Ah, you're fine, then?" asked Neville. "The others?"

"Alive, but one may lose an arm. T'other's got a mean gash on his leg, but Doctor Elworth will bind him up good, and he should be right as rain in a month or two, if he don't need to become a cook."

"What's the trouble up there, gentlemen?" Neville asked the two of them. They looked skyward together, like a pair of penguins.

"Mizzen yard's come down, Sir," said Worth.

Neville rolled his eyes. "My goodness. I hadn't noticed. What the dev… I'm sorry, Mr. Worth. I understand you've been knocked hard on the head. Mr. MacDavin, get your crew up there and start putting it all to rights, if you please. Haul Chips back here to work on this, not the confounded jib-boom. Mr. Worth, I suggest you just sit for a few minutes."

"*London* and t'other Frenchie 'ave been at it an hour already, Captain, and *Amazon* half of that. Are we going to try to get back into it?" asked Miller.

"That's why I brought you over from *Vanguard*, Lieutenant Miller – you're always wanting to get into the scrap. But, I think not today. I expect the battle will be over before we can sail – or steer, for that matter. We had better rig relieving tackles as fast as possible. If it doesn't go right for *Amazon*, I would think the *Belle Poule* would come back to finish us before she sails away. Whether she would sink or capture us is mere conjecture. Take charge of the relieving tackles, will you, please?"

"Fetch me a glass first, Lieutenant. Let's see if we can see what the status of *Amazon* is."

Neville swung the glass over to *London* first, wondering if he could learn anything. Nothing of interest. He then peered at the Frenchman's transom. There, below the upper gallery – or what remained of it – was the name *Marengo*.

"*Marengo*, Lieutenant Bradley. She's not *Alexandre* – not Willaumez's ship. We've caught someone else out here in the middle of the ocean. The name seems familiar to me. Does it to you?"

"No Sir. No recollection."

"Look there, Captain!" said Foyle, "*Foudroyant* is getting into it now, and *Repulse* and *Ramillies* are not far off! I can't believe *Marengo* will continue to fight!"

A cheer arose from the company as a fresh broadside from the 80-gun *Foudroyant* split the air, followed by another from the 74-gun *Repulse*. *Marengo* replied to both with sporadic fire.

"Quite a bit of damage to both. How about *Amazon*?" He swung the glass to the other battle just as *Amazon* returned one of *Belle Poule's* lucky shots, dropping her mizzen mast over the side.

The sight turned Neville's stomach as he watched the rigging go down; two men jumped from the top of it as it fell.

"Mr. Worth, I see you're up again. Have Mr. MacDavin help you forward and see to it our scrawny Midshipman Pakenham is chopping away the foremast rubbish and Mr. Clark is setting the jury bowsprit the way you want it." Another errant ball from the *Belle Poule-Amazon* battle whined high across *La Désirée*.

"Bugger! A hole in the Main tops'l. Don't we have enough to repair?" queried Worth to nobody.

"I wouldn't want to be the Frenchie in charge on *Marengo* now," said Miller. "*Ramillies* will be in range in a few minutes."

"They've seen the light," commented Neville, "Here comes her colours down now." He noted the chimes: six bells of the forenoon watch. Over three hours!

"And *Belle-Poule's* tri-colour as well," said Worth. *Ramillies*, sure to have been ready to fire, sailed regally past the battle, her huge British flag snapping proudly in the breeze.

No more smoke was rising from any ship. The noise had stopped, but Neville's ears were still ringing.

"May I suggest, Captain?" asked Worth

"Go ahead."

"Get the canvas off her, except a steadying sail astern to pull us head-to-wind. We'll ride much more smoothly while we make repairs."

"My very next order, Mr. Worth. Get on forward, now, if you would. Hold on to things and keep an eye to the splinters… Lieutenant Carlyle!" he bellowed.

"Here, Sir," answered a marine officer picking his way around the debris from astern.

"We have no immediate need for marines, I think, other than to join in repairs. Organize a band of your red-breasted brethren to rig relieving tackles on the rudder, if you please. Lieutenant Bradley will direct you. He's done it before, I believe. Where is he?"

"There, Sir, by the mainmast bitts."

"Thank you, Lieutenant Carlyle." He then bellowed for Lieutenant Bradley.

"We have relieving tackle rove, Captain, and all the men have had their dinner," reported Bradley. At the reminder, Neville's stomach growled. *Not **all** fed*, he thought.

"Damn!" Neville swore to First Lt. Towers. "We'll be called over to the flag at any moment, and we'll be ordered to supply men for the prize crews and to take some of the prisoners, despite having all we can handle here. I'll argue for a bit of mercy due to our condition, but you'd best give me a list of, say, a dozen men you can spare. Fetch a messenger, please... and be ready to accompany me."

Towers sent the nearest landsman to the quarterdeck. He stepped up nervously and knuckled his forehead, "You need me, Sir?"

"Just carry a message down to my cabin, please. Tell my steward, Hajee Ayoub... you know him, yes? Tell him I need something to eat – anything – up here as soon as he can manage it. And the large coffee I didn't have this morning."

Neville spent the next half hour roaming around the ship to check on the progress of repairs. The carpenter brought a new wheel up from the holds, and he now busied himself at fashioning a very crude binnacle. Neville knew there would be a proper new one installed by the time they made port; it would be a matter of pride for Chips. The rudder had not been shot away, or any of the normal rudder-control tackle. Only the deck components had been smashed. Repairs should be quick. He kept an eye on the flagship as he moved from one station to another. When *Foudroyant's* flailing sails began to furl, he walked back to his cabin for an much-anticipated dinner; at least he hoped he would have time to eat. The Admiral probably wouldn't call his captains before *Hope* arrived. *Courageux* and *Namur* looked to be an hour out; Neville expected Admiral Warren would not wait for them. After the last of his fish and eggs were eaten, he put on the clean uniform Hajee had laid out for him and returned to the quarterdeck amidst the sawing and hammering, to inspect progress there.

"Signal from flag, Captain," announced Lt. Miller the moment Neville's foot touched the upper deck, "Repair to flag. All captains and their first officers, Sir."

"Now, there's a surprise!" he responded sarcastically, "Have Mr. Strugnell find what he can of a boat crew and have him launch my gig, if you please. I should have thought about the boat crew earlier."

"He's got 'em ready, Captain. When I asked, he said 'it weren't his first cruise'."

Neville had not been aboard the third-rate *Foudroyant* before. He sat waiting in his gig while the senior captains of the ships of the line went up; the wait was by no means comfortable or dry, with the little rowing-boat bobbing over the six-foot seas while the wind continued to whistle about them. He was thinking what an admirable job his coxswain was doing when the curl of a larger wave broke into the gig and soaked his shoes.

By British standards, *Foudroyant* was an odd ship. Built at the Devonport yard, she carried her 80 guns on two decks in the French style; not as the typical British three-decker. When it came his turn to climb the side, he gave thanks for the missing deck.

Once piped aboard, Neville went directly aft to Admiral Warren's cabin, leaving a set of wet footprints along his way. The affair looked as if it would be convivial, at least while they waited for everyone to assemble. Most captains and their lieutenants were there before the frigate commanders were allowed up the side, and they had their rum or claret or whiskey in hand. The conversation was spirited; the excitement of the battle had not left a man in the room, except for the captured French Captain Bruilhac and his first officer. They stood unhappily on the larboard side of the cabin, speaking quietly to each other.

Admiral Warren had yet to make his entrance. Neville would be obliged to spend some time with Captain Parker of *Amazon* once he arrived. However, since Parker was also not yet there – probably tending to repairs as long as he could – he decided to show his respects to his enemy. He crossed the room to the French officers. "Bonjour," he said, touched his forehead, and extended his hand, "Captain Burton of *La Désirée*."

"*Capitain* Bruilhac of *La Belle-Poule*," said the senior man. "*Parlez-vous Français?* (Do you speak French?), asked the captain.

"*Oui, Monsieur Capitain,*"

"*Bon, Bon,*" Bruilhac replied. "My English is not the best. I may have time to improve it now. This is M. Lieutenant Pomeroy."

"I am pleased to meet you," Neville said, again in French. "You made a gallant try."

"We had not a chance once your *Ramillies* arrived, *non?*" said Bruilhac.

"It looked that way from my ship," answered Neville. "Is your Commodore here?" Neville looked about for a French Admiral, but saw none. "Who is he?"

"Admiral Linois," Captain Burton. "He might come with the captain of *London,* but we believe he was injured."

"Linois?" commented Neville.

Yes, do you know him?"

"We met once."

Bruilhac glanced at Pomeroy and raised his eyebrows slightly.

"How bad are his wounds?" asked Neville.

"I only know he was wounded and taken below with his captain – also wounded. It must be serious. I can't imagine him leaving the quarterdeck if it were not." A short conversation ensued, wherein Neville learned the situation prior to battle was exactly as he'd guessed; Linois had thought them to be a convoy when he approached to attack. The two French ships were, indeed, on their return from the Indian Ocean, where they had been since 1801, annoying British trade. The encounter was completely by chance.

A louder commotion began at the cabin door, and all faces turned to see Captain Burrard-Neale of *London* arrive; and with him the defeated Admiral Linois of *Marengo*, his arm well bandaged and in a sling. Once inside the door, Linois cast a furtive glance around the room and, seeing his frigate captain Bruilhac, crossed directly to speak with him. They exchanged informal salutes, and their conversation continued in French.

"How is Captain Vrignaud, Admiral?" asked Bruilhac.

"His wounds are not mortal, Captain Bruilhac, but he will lose an arm. Thank you for your brave efforts today. How many are lost?"

"Six, Admiral, plus twenty and four wounded. And *Marengo?*"

"A full sixty – maybe a few more, and eighty wounded."

Bruilhac sucked air between his teeth. "I am sorry, Sir."

"As am I," said Neville.

Admiral Linois turned a mildly angry glare at Neville. Though he looked ready to deride the impudent British captain, he did not speak, and stared at Neville for a moment. "Do I know you?" he finally asked.

"We met, when we were both younger, Sir. On the *Formidable*. I am pleased to see you are well. You have lost an eye, though?"

"It happened then."

"I am sorry. There was so much blood from your head wound. I didn't notice."

"Ah," he said, now with recognition; "the midshipman who saved my ship from fire! I surrendered to you, did I not?"

"Aye, Sir, but I think possibly more by accident."

"Well, here we are again," said Linois.

Admiral Warren entered from his private cabin and looked quickly about for his senior captains and, supposedly, the French. Seeing them, he nodded to his steward, and moved to his formal dining space. The steward tinkled a little glass bell, and announced dinner.

"*Oui*, Admiral," said Neville, "it would seem so. I wish you the best." He gave his sincere bow in the French style. Linois returned the honor, marking the end of any conversation with a mere captain – particularly if French were to be spoken.

Neville found himself at mid-table. First Lieutenants were seated toward the foot. The experience was still satisfying for Neville. Not long ago he would have been seated, as a commander, between the captains and lieutenants. The change wasn't much, but in the service, any advance is appreciated. As a frigate captain, he still remained rather uninvolved in the conversation, until talk of the battle gave Admiral Warren an opportunity to comment on the performance of his ships: "It seems you were not very effective, Captain Burton."

Neville had been concerned there might be some displeasure at his bad luck – being put out of service with only a broadside or two. "Admiral Warren, I…"

"Not so," interrupted Captain Parker. "His performance at delaying the enemy is one of the best I have ever seen."

"I must agree," said Captain Bruilhac of the *Belle Poule* in halting English. The way he said it, it was more of a complaint, "His interception was perfect; we would have had a collision if I did not bear off. Once I did, I could not escape the battle with your *Amazon*. I thought we would be away, but then *Ramillies* arrived and, alas, here I sit."

Prize crew arrangements were made within the day and executed by dusk. *London* had been the only other British ship damaged in the fracas, and that not extensive. As the last of the light turned their world from blues, pinks, and grays into purple and black, the squadron set sail for England.

2 - "Baltimore"

On 20th February, 1806 – almost a month before the guns of Neville's *La Désirée* would be blasting their defiance at the French – Marion Stillwater entered her father's office. It was a quiet Saturday morning. The Stillwater Rum Trading Company doors were closed. "Well, Father," she announced, "I've made up my mind."

"Um… Would you like coffee, sweetheart, or would you prefer tea?" asked Chester. He leaned back in his creaky wooden office chair and pulled a slim cigar from his humidor. He began searching his desktop for a match.

"Seriously, Father, just because I intend to marry an Englishman... You are aware it's still the fact that half the people in the United States were born in the British Isles, and most of them probably prefer tea. But here, in Jamaica, you've trained me to the coffee... and I've told you before, you should oil your annoying chair."

"Yes, yes, of course," Chester said with a smirk. "No cliché intended." He puffed on his now-lit cigar and carefully blew a smoke ring at the ceiling. In his thoughtful mode, he was obviously trying to decide whether to say something or let his daughter have the next word.

Marion took advantage of the break. "Neville will be gone for some time, I'm sure, so our wedding plans are completely on hold." Her look was pensive, if not simply pouty. "I'm going to the United States for a bit of holiday. Maybe I'll visit Ellen in Boston, and maybe I'll go on to London, as well. It's quiet here. I'm sure you can find someone to help with the sales or to run the place."

Chester sat up. His old chair groaned again. "Well, then, Marion, I guess it's time we had that chat."

"Chat?" she asked. "What chat?" Now she was the one on the defense.

"You've had the thought, I know. I knew it from your look when we rode here from the house to catch Mister Stearns some months back… when Neville preached that we must stop our efforts to sell rum to France and we must walk straight in every way or his navy would drum him out. You remember?"

"He didn't **preach**, Father."

"All right, a bit of a strong word, I suppose, but he certainly did admonish us to play it all straight, did he not? This is the rum business, for the love of…!"

"Yes," she said, "and after this little episode of sailing off when we have a wedding planned – well, not **planned**, but intended – I can't say I'd mind his being a civilian, anyway. But to answer your question, yes. I remember the very moment you mention." She returned to her defensive posture. "Why?"

"Let's do it! What better time to set it all up than when your gallant Captain Burton is off playing war games?"

She could feel her skin creep a bit despite the warm day. Surely, there would always be a bit of fear when Neville sailed off to possible battle, probable storms, and the ever-present diseases of strange lands.

"I'm sorry, Marion," Chester added quickly. "I don't mean 'playing', like there is nothing to worry about. You'll hear from him soon, I'm sure. Shall we go back to my idea?"

"Yes, Father, of course." *Now he's just trying to keep me distracted until my enthusiasm returns. I should have been ready for it.* "I'm the one with 'The Paris Plan', after all... even though it didn't work. That stupid, stupid Stearns!" she spat.

"Base a new company," Chester continued, "or just a Stillwater warehouse, if you will – in the United States. Maybe we have to make it a new company to avoid our English-Jamaica connection, I don't know. American companies can buy rum wherever they want, and there's nothing illegal about American companies trading with France. Are we not allies? I say Baltimore." Satisfied with his pitch, he blew another smoke ring at the ceiling.

"Baltimore?" she queried into the smoke ring. She felt a sudden surprised confusion, with a dozen questions in her mind at once: *Would it really be worth it? Will Neville be all right with it if we are married? Why on earth Baltimore? Should I volunteer for the job? How cold does it get in the winter, anyway?*

Her father's answer interrupted her: "Yes, Baltimore."

"Why Baltimore?"

"All the obvious reasons, my dear. Baltimore is the third largest city in the country; over thirty thousand people live there. It's bigger than Boston, for all love, and I hear it's growing like a weed. You can get anything done you can imagine. It has an excellent seaport. The weather is far better than Boston, particularly in the winter. And, for our connections in the Navy Yard in Washington, it's close! Maybe we should even think about a sales office in the warehouse to deal with those fellows. You should go set it up." He became more excited as he spoke.

"I should go?" Her confusion returned. *Me? Not live in Jamaica? Spend a winter in the snow?* "Does it snow there?" she asked.

"What? Yes, you, and yes, a bit, but they have fireplaces there, you know," answered Chester. "I thought you just said you wanted to take a bit of holiday from here. Summer is coming; it should be beautiful there soon."

"Why me, then? I know how to run this place here, but set up something new in a strange city? I don't know…"

"First, you want a change. As much as I agree with your last statement, I think you need the distraction, and you're fully capable of it. It's just a warehouse, and maybe a sales room. Have you not managed the warehouse functions here for the last five years?"

So I see, it is about distraction.

"I'll stay here to hire and train a salesman," Chester continued. "We haven't replaced Mr. Stearns yet – and I probably need a manager, so I don't have to do everything the two of us do here now so routinely. I'll have to train them both."

"Oh, yes. I don't envy you that chore." She felt more interested by the minute. *It gives me more freedom to move about without explaining everything to father.* "You're right, of course. I'll take the warehouse in the snow. I don't expect to stay there forever."

Marion walked down the gangway of the *India Star* onto a bustling waterfront boardwalk just two months later. She had armed herself with a seven-inch jewel-hilted dagger and conspicuously displayed it at her slim waist. It projected an interesting contrast to her appearance, which combined 'beautiful, rich and entitled' with 'young, confident, and impetuous'. She did not present the appearance of an easy mark for street hustlers. She immediately waved down a hack, flashed a few gold coins, and requested the driver take her to her hotel and return to find her dunnage. Marion was not new to international travel.

Once away from the chipping dark brown and green paint of the smelly waterfront, spring was in the air. Most of the trees either showed a light green hue with their new leaves or were already dazzling full green, and a full range of tree-blossoms and hedge-flowers had been in bloom for several weeks. Marion felt an air of excitement to the slight chill of the day emanating from the gay clacking of the hack-horse's hooves on the paving-stones.

"I've done considerable planning on my 'Baltimore Project', as you can see from all this, dear," Chester had said to his daughter before her departure, "but Baltimore seems to be growing so fast that any building our land agent there deems suitable for our warehouse does not stay on the market long enough for me to close the transaction by post. It's one of the reasons we need to have personal involvement."

"So you waited until Neville was gone…?"

"Well, yes."

"Hmmpf."

"It wasn't me sent him away… but now he's at sea, and your wedding plans are on hold, you need something to sink your teeth into. I think this is your cup of tea…"

Marion gave him a withering look.

"Oh, I'm sorry," he'd added. "No English reference intended." He then continued without hesitation. "Here's a few hundred American dollars. I've funded a bank account at Alexander Brown & Sons. This little black book here has all the contacts you should need. These are letters of introduction to Mr. Brown and the land agent, and there are a few extra copies for anyone else who thinks himself important enough to demand one."

Marion was determined to make all necessary Rum Company arrangements as quickly as possible without making a mess of things. Both aspects were important. She had no intention of causing her father to think, for even a moment, that she couldn't handle this endeavor, but 'quick' was important to her own plans.

Once in her room, she opened her travel case and took out a letter she'd received from Sir William Mulholland at Britain's Navy Office in Whitehall. *Just to reassure myself?* she wondered.

London,   *12 December, 1805*

Dear Marion,

I understand you might be quite busy at the moment, but if you are at all curious, I have an adventure that may interest you. I think it would suit your skills quite well.

If you have any interest, please advise me if you could join us at my offices to discuss it in mid-June of the new year. Georges will join us. I'm sure you two would like to catch up.

Uncle William

Marion had posted her letter of agreement before she had heard her father's plan for his 'Baltimore Project'; hence, her statement to Chester about taking some vacation time. Due to the nature of Mulholland's business, excessive correspondence was not appropriate. While she might normally have written to postpone, the better course, once Neville had departed, was to stick to the timing Mulholland had proposed, even when the Baltimore Project interceded.

Marion remembered very well how she had gotten herself into the present situation; she though back upon it:

"I'm old enough to go, Father," she'd pestered. "Do you not think me mature enough for a sales trip? I've been dealing with these lecherous old coots from the ships in the harbor for months… a year, maybe. I know you have a plan for Mr. Stearns to go. He could certainly chaperone me. I won't take 'no' for an answer, Father."

Chester was businessman enough to know his daughter's beauty would draw moths to the flame – moths with orders for rum – and protective enough to know he must send someone with her for security. Michael Stearns had been with the company for three years by then. He was a large, imposing figure, whom Chester had no reason to doubt, and would soon be officially dubbed Sales Manager.

The day came when Chester agreed. Marion and Mr. Michael Stearns had gone to Washington, D.C. to socialize with the Navy and worm their way into the related political circuit.

"This last series of parties has been quite profitable, hasn't it, Mr. Stearns?" she'd asked one day. He hesitated to answer immediately. It was no secret between them that, although Mr. Stearns may have written the actual orders, Marion had created most of the success. Michael often departed the party early with some woman.

"Undeniable success, yes," Stearns answered. "You seem to have a talent for this; a gift for understanding when to switch from pleasure to business and back again. I'm better at the straightforward hard sell. I find these parties tedious… You won't report that back to your father, will you?"

"No, Mr. Stearns, not as long as our partnership continues to work this well." *I know he has no idea what I'm thinking, and I'm happy to leave it the way it is. I know Father would frown on his behavior. So this is what it means to keep someone else's secret.*

Not only was Marion having the time of her life, but she was turning the heads of dozens of important men. Some were quite rich, though none of them turned hers. She often wondered why, but finally concluded the answer was merely a bit of cultural difference. She had grown up in an English community – a relatively provincial one, however. Kingston, Jamaica was no Washington, D.C., the people were more English than American, and the men she had met at home, few of which were eligible, did not puff themselves up so severely, wearing their importance and self-centeredness on their sleeves. Many here were a rugged sort, as well, boasting of their rough life in some wilderness to the west.

There had been one, though, who stood out. Not surprisingly, he was English – not formerly English, like many of the others – but ***still*** English. He seemed more... cultivated?... than most. She supposed the political necessities of his job required him to be humble in this country which had not long before split itself off from the motherland by way of revolution.

"Marion, this gentleman has asked to meet you," said Stearns at the party for the Governor of Virginia's 50th birthday (anything being a good reason for a party in D.C.). "Miss Stillwater, may I present Mr. James Looten." He leaned over to her and whispered into her ear, "I doubt you want to spend much time with him. He's just a British attaché; not likely a customer." He stood back and added, "I'll leave you, if you don't mind..."

They found each other's company enjoyable, however, and they spoke more at the party for the Kentucky governor's push to make dueling illegal at the federal level. At one of several 'Midsummer's Night' galas, where she actually met the new President Jefferson, James Looten had asked her aside to the veranda of the place – a mansion overlooking the Potomac River.

"May we have a few moments out on the veranda, Miss Stillwater," James had asked, "for a few minutes of private discussion?"

Marion was surprised to feel a rush of emotions, despite having been approached by many men in the course of her Washington adventure. Most held no interest for her, and she could sense that a few were just simply dangerous. James was far less rough than many, spoke well, and wasn't exactly an insider to Washington politics. She'd felt her heart begin to race, wondering if her feelings were the beginning of some romantic attraction. The warmth of the evening added to her emotions: uneasiness? discomfort? excitement? danger? As he spoke, a new excitement arose and grew, but it wasn't what she had expected. She met James more than once, however, and soon learned this was not an affair of the heart. He invited her to intentionally place herself in harm's way. Even now, she could not recall all the words; some about his evaluation of her strong personality; some about patriotic need; some about personal accomplishment... Would she be a spy (although he didn't use the word) for Great Britain... not against the United States, but against France?

"Will you think about it, Marion?" Looten finally asked.

"No, I will not," she'd said. "When do I start?" It wasn't about taking money; she had enough; she didn't even ask how much – or if she would be paid at all. It wasn't about patriotism for the USA; quite likely the main reason she went for it was the excitement of perceived danger – and because she felt almost as English as she did American. She assumed the 'job' involved danger... doing things women don't usually get to do; the sort of things in which Neville finds himself involved. Without knowing what it is actually like to be involved in a dangerous situation, her excitement about the concept grew. Mt. Looten promised to get back to her very soon.

Marion needed to talk to someone; to tell someone of her excitement. When Michael Stearns stopped by her room rather late in the evening, telling her in a slurred voice that he was just checking to confirm she had safely returned to her room, she thought, *Mr. Stearns! I can tell him... some of it, at least.* She invited him in. The visit did not go well. Stearns' inebriated state caused him to misunderstand her intentions, although being allowed in may have been what he'd had in mind. After entering, he pushed her into a corner, took her in his arms, and began his attempts to kiss her. His inebriation was also what saved her from worse.

"Mr. Stearns, what do you take me for – one of your trysts? Get out! Out his minute! Father will hear of this!" She shoved his large but slow-thinking body out the door and slammed it in his dumbfounded face. She slumped to the floor and cried. What was worse – that she had narrowly missed being raped, or that she had no one to talk to... about this, or the British thing, either?

She didn't have to face Stearns the next morning. A bellboy appeared very early, with a note from a visitor in the lobby – one Mr. Looten. "Would she join him for breakfast?"

By mid-afternoon of the very same day, a half-panicked Michael Stearns received the very same bell-boy carrying a note:

Mr. Stearns,

For now, we will forget your unspeakable behavior of last night. In compensation, you will NOT tell my Father that I have gone to Boston for a couple weeks on personal business. I assure you it is NOT with a man, but it also not yours to know.   Keep up your sales!

M.S.

So, here she was, five years later, in Baltimore. She was older and far wiser now, and without the rascal Stearns who had fled from certain arrest back home in Jamaica. Again, she had the 'cover' of a business trip to the United States, but this time she had a plan to visit London.

Yes, Baltimore was big enough to get anything done one needed. Finding people with the time, skills, and inclination to do it, however, was a problem. This fact became evident immediately upon her arrival. Wagons carrying lumber and foundation stones for building, fish from the wharves, crates of dry goods from England and France, and every other imaginable package choked their path more than once on the short trip to the Harford Inn, her rooming house on Pratt St. She needed an assistant first, even before the land-agent.

Marion's luck held. Mr. Alexander Brown, the banker, loaned her a man he described as 'honest'. She had learned early that 'honest' did not necessarily coincide with 'reliable'. Coming from Jamaica, where many were honest, but not reliable, she immediately recognized the type. Nevertheless, she soon found him exceptionally efficient when allowed to operate on his own schedule – not banker's hours.

"Here 'tis, ma'am," he announced one morning a week later, after he arrived at half ten in the morning. He dropped a large envelope on her desk.

"What's this, then?" she asked.

"Papers for that warehouse up on East Pratt Street, Ma'am, near the corner wi' Patapsco. Th'owner says you're to have 'em signed and give him a deposit by three today or he's got another buyer will be there at four. Anything else, Ma'am?"

She stared at him for a few seconds before saying, "Everything's here, Mr. Arnold? You've done this before?"

"Yes, Ma'am, nigh on a hunnert times. All there."

"No, Mr. Arnold. Nothing else now. You may take as long a lunch as you need, as long as you're here to carry this up at half three."

"I'll see to wagons, then, ma'am. And you'll be wanting barrows?"

"Yes, Mr. Arnold, yes…and…and…some locks for the doors?"

"Yes, Ma'am." He left.

She wanted to dance about the office and skip back to her hotel room. Her thoughts raced; she pulled out the small bottle of rum her father had given her for little celebrations and poured herself a shot. She sipped it while she wrote a new list of things to do; a shorter list, with hiring Mr. Arnold away from the banker, at the top.

Next, Marion's set herself a deadline for completion of the start-up project by booking herself passage to England on the *Isle of Wight*, sailing from Baltimore for London on 2nd June, 1806.

The fastest six weeks of Marion's life then followed. By the time she climbed the *Isle of Wight's* gangway, she had immense feelings of both accomplishment and exhaustion.

Baltimore, Maryland　　　　　　　　　*1st June, 1806*
Dear Father,

Send rum.

The Stillwater Baltimore warehouse is ready for business. Your manager is Mr. Arnold. He has arranged for everything we need, including six warehousemen.

I depart tomorrow for London on the Isle of Wight, a fast transporter of perishable goods. I know I owe you a better explanation, but it's a business trip. It does not involve a man, including Neville, although I pray he might be there.

It is my intention to stay at the Saxon Arms, as before, so write to me there. If the Saxon Arms is not available, or if I must stay for some time, I can use Neville's flat. I'll write.

Your loving daughter,

Marion

3 - "At Sea: March, 1806"

Four days following the battle between Admiral Warren's squadron and Admiral Linois' ships at sea in the Eastern Atlantic, the recovering ships of both squadrons were mostl;y recovered. The weather at noon was fair, with a light breeze from the northeast. A breeze from the northeast forced them to sail to the northwest, hoping for a more favorable wind. Neville had stopped his pacing of the weather quarterdeck for a few minutes to observe the spouting of a pod of whales close abroad to windward.

"If I might ask, Captain?" said Lt. Miller.

"Amazing creatures, aren't they, Lieutenant?" Neville mused. "Yes, go ahead."

"Are we the only British squadron out here? Are we leaving the whole of the Central Atlantic unguarded?"

"I have no idea, Lieutenant. The Admiral has not taken me into his confidence, and he's made no informative announcement. I find your question a bit superficial, however, I must admit. How much of a defense is one squadron in this vast sea, anyway. The blockade of a port, however, is another matter. He may have orders to patrol, but just between you and me, I expect he sees the excuse to accompany prize ships to port as being a valid reason to quit this drudgery. I'm perfectly pleased to comply."

"As am I, Captain. Bo'sun Strugnell says he should have the bowsprit and jib-booms set to rights by this afternoon and we can begin with the foretopmast and jibs. What do you think of that cloud?"

"I looked at it, Lieutenant Miller, but I think it's too early to tell. It's a strip of cirrus from the nor-east, to be sure, but it has no curl to it – at least not yet. If there is a blow to come we should know better tomorrow."

Cold rivulets of rainwater dribbled down inside their tarpaulin jackets whenever they turned their heads. The brims of their hats were slapped up by the wind, allowing the water into their collars. The cirrus cloud had gone to mare's tails three days ago, and in those three days the cumulus began piling up and up over a sea that slowly transformed from blue to steel gray. On the 22nd of March, the clouds gained thick black undersides and began to spit rain fitfully. The wind rose, too, forcing *La Désirée* to furl her courses and outer jibs. The fleet she sailed with did the same. The sea grew larger.

"I expect we'll see a signal to fall off inside the hour, Mr. Worth," yelled Neville above the noise of the oncoming storm. "*Marengo* looks to be having trouble already. She's probably light in ballast with most of her stores gone on the last leg to home, and still with all her guns on deck. What did MacDavin and Chips tell you about the mizzen yard repair?"

"No sail on it now, as you see, Cap'n." He paused to blow rainwater off his lip. "They said it might not hold in a blow, and it looks like that's what we've got comin' at us. *Ramillies* is rolling more than I would expect, too."

"I noticed. It's just as well we can't use the mizzen, methinks. We may be down to the foretops'l in another hour. I'll pass word for Lt. Towers and t'others to be ready for the order."

A very dirty night followed, during which the squadron spread wider to avoid collisions in the dark. Morning didn't dawn, in the normal sense. The ocean became less black, and sails became visible in the distance.

"Well, we haven't lost sight of everyone, have we Cap'n?" observed Lt. Towers when Neville climbed the quarterdeck stair. The rain had become more horizontal than vertical, it seemed. It had also become more difficult to distinguish between rain and spray from a sea now running consistently above fifteen feet. "Tops'l holding, Sir, but sailmaker says it won't take it much longer. Can we go to bare poles without the Admiral orders it?"

"Is that her for'ard there?"

"No, Sir. That's *Marengo*. Haven't seen flag this hour gone past. She's fallen down more south."

"Set a t'garns'l on the tops'l yard, then, with a set of loose sheets. *Marengo* doesn't look to be faring well; rolling something awful today, and she's got nary a sail up to steady herself."

After a time on deck, Neville decided he had nothing useful he could do there. He went below to ask 'Cookie' personally about his plans for dinner. It would probably be cold pork for a few days. He'd no sooner gotten confirmation of it than Seaman Barnes trotted his way, hat in hand.

"Pardon me sir, an' First Lieutenant Towers' compliments, Sir, and he sends a message, Sir could you come on deck, Sir… there's something bad gone wrong with *Mango*, Sir. Aye."

"*Marengo*, you mean? The ship?"

"Aye Sir. *Marengo*," he said, "Sir, aye, Sir."

The wind had gotten up. Neville could hear it below decks. He wasn't looking forward to climbing the stair into the nasty weather, particularly with his old leg injury barking because of the cold, but he assumed it to be serious, or he wouldn't have been called.

"Look there, Captain," yelled Towers when Neville had approached to within earshot – which, under the conditions, meant about two feet away.

"I can see there's a ship there, Lieutenant, but that's about all I can make out in the rain." A wave boomed on the starboard quarter, spray flying high and across the entire quarterdeck. Neville took a tighter grip on the binnacle handrail.

"You saw her rolling before you went down. It looks to me she's lost a mast because of serious rigging damage. I'm not sure which one in this rain; might be the mainmast."

Neville's stomach churned. *I wouldn't want to be in charge over there right now*, he thought. *So, what's our condition?* "Do you believe we, ourselves, are in danger of foundering, Lieutenant?"

"No, Sir, and I've spoke with Mr. Worth on it. He thinks same as me. We're weathering well…might lose a stick or two, and other things as might not be tied…" Another boom from a wave aft. This one tore the signal swivel gun, with a piece of the stern rail, loose of its mounts. The water carried it forward, narrowly missing the helmsmen's feet, to where it took a small chunk out of the binnacle at deck level before it crashed against the foot of the mainmast. As luck would have it, quick-thinking Midshipman Foyle jumped on it with a bit of rope, tying it securely to the mast before it could slide to leeward with the next heave of the ship's deck.

"Sorry, Sir. I missed that one," said Towers. It was his job to keep everything aboard in order.

Neville gave Towers his best 'withering glare', which was difficult in the weather, but said nothing other than, "Maybe *Marengo* is a crank old thing. And, there is no doubt she suffers extremely from having her captain a prisoner aboard *Foudroyant*, unable to do more than watch. There's naught we can do other than try to stay nearby. We may have to fish some men if she gets worse, but not in this."

Just before the next dawn, a set of studdingsail booms, improperly lashed for such weather, worked loose and began thumping holes in the ship's boats. The noise would have been noticed in any lesser a storm, but not this day. The poles continued unattended until one of them stove a hole in the barge and then destroyed its lashings on the weather side. Once loose, a large boarding wave smashed it cruelly, and then took more than half of it overboard. Four of the studdingsail yards and a man working his way along the leeward manrope to the foredeck went with it.

"I saw it go, Captain," offered Midshipman Hicks. "Tweren't nuthin' anyone coulda done once the barge came loose."

"It shouldn't have come to that, should it, Mr. Hicks? I see Lieutenant Towers has a crew on it. Pass word for Bo'sun Strugnell, if you would, please."

In one more day, the storm began to abate. It was far from done, however, but the waves decreased to ten feet, and the clouds were letting more light through.

"*Marengo's* lost all her masts, now, Captain," observed Worth, who had just returned from balancing the big signals glass on the poopdeck rail.

"Aye. The visibility is much better now with only this light rain falling. You've slowed us well, but we've gone past her, I see."

"Aye, Sir. *Marengo* couldn't move much with all her rubbish hanging over the side, and she'd be bashed all the harder by the waves. Whatever went over first would have ripped away the other masts if it couldn't be cut away."

"I'd say they've cut most of it off, wouldn't you, Mr. Worth? Did you see any men in the water?"

"None I could see, between waves and rain, Sir, no." He continued absentmindedly, "Even if there were, setting out boats would be extremely risky."

"That's not your decision, is it?" responded Neville. *My irritable behavior hasn't gone away, has it?*

"I'm sorry, Sir. I didn't mean to…"

"No, I'm sorry, Mr. Worth. You made a fair observation, and we've all been beaten down by this storm."

Not much changed during the day, but the wind dropped considerably with the sundown. Captain Burton joined Towers, Miller, Bradley and Foyle on the poopdeck for an observation of *Marengo* before the light of day went completely. "After a storm, a fresh breeze feels like a summer zephyr, doesn't it?" remarked Neville, "*Marengo's* motion is much better, too. She may live through this, after all."

"We might see a nice morning tomorrow," said Worth, "and if this wind stays quiet, the seas should be down almost to normal. We can send a boat over."

"Have one ready at first light, if you would, please, Lt. Towers," said Neville.

The fourth morning after the storm began was a joy to behold. The wind was still a fresh breeze, and the sky still overcast, but the seas were down in the six to eight foot range, and the rain had ceased. Bright spots in the clouds gave a promise of some blue sky to be seen during the afternoon watch. After his breakfast, Neville took time to write. He could feel the calm flow into himself as he wrote to his beloved Marion:

Dear Marion,   27th April, 1806

At Sea in the Atlantic off the Canary Islands

I will post this the moment we are arrived in England, for there is where we are now bound.

I have Suffered no Injury, nor any other thing but the typical Discomforts of being at Sea. Our Squadron under Admiral Warren did not spend muche tyme off Southe America. We have been Patrolling the Central Atlantic, expecting we might cross remnants of the French Squadron under Willaumez after his thrashing at Santo Domingo, so as to take them home as prizes. You can Imagine our Surprise when we encountered a very different French Enemy – "Contre-Admiral" Linois. Do you remember I have told you of taking his sword when we captured Formidable when I was but a Midshipman? I met him, and he has himself Remembered me.

Our 80-gun London (Captain Sir Harry Burrard-Neale) fought Linois' ship Marengo – a 74 – in a Great Battle. Linois hauled his colours when aid came to London from Foudroyant, Repulse, and Ramillies.

Our Frigate Amazon and my Brave La Désirée made our attack on their Frigate Belle-Poule (there being but two French ships). We cut off Belle Poule, but saw very little action. Her first few shots were lucky, indeed, and Dis-Abled us to float away while Amazon engaged in another great long Battle. Losses were terrible – over 80 men amongst the four main ships of the Battles (just 13 of ours), and many Wounded (27 of ours, and only 3 minor things on La Désirée).

We had only just done our repairs when the lot of us were hit by a Great Storme of almost Hurrican Windes and waves of *five Fathoms or more, that lasted four days and did even more Terrible Damage to Marengo, who lost all masts, and Ramillies, who lost her Main and Foremast. Our damages were not major in this, either, Except for two men who fell from the Rigging and one man who was swept over the side when we lost some Studdings'l booms and our Barge.*

We have collected the Squadron again, and are Under Way now for Spithead, with Marengo and Ramillies under Jury Masts. We should arrive about Portsmouth first June, I should think.

I shall pray Jamaica befalls no such Stormes this Yeare.

Pray that I find a Way to Return very, very soon to Wed. We will need to… &ct, &ct…

Your devoted fiancé,

Nv. Burton, Captain, HMS La Désirée

"*Marengo* is keeping station well for a ship so badly damaged, isn't she, Mr. Worth?" queried Neville.

"Aye, Sir, and it appears the pumping has stopped. There's been water coming over the side constantly these three days past."

"So I noted. And *Ramillies* has a topmast up. They're making progress."

"I calculate we'll round Ushant tomorrow, Captain."

"I agree. We've had good sights these last two days, so I expect we have little error."

Another small blow struck them East of Ushant. It would have been nothing of any consequence if it hadn't included a mishap.

"I'm sorry to interrupt, Captain," said Lt. Towers, "but it seems we've lost a man."

"Who, Lieutenant Towers, and how?" asked Neville. He looked up quickly from his desk, unhappy to be interrupted from his reading of the Bo'sun's stores request, and even more displeased to hear the news at hand.

"Connors, fell, Sir – our youngest foremast seaman, if you remember. He lost his holding when the men were shortening the forecourse, and fell to the deck. Doctor Elworth says he might have survived with only a few broken bones, but his head hit the leeward carronade on the way down. The right side of it split open like a melon, spilling his brains across the foredeck. Mr. Pakenham fainted dead away at the sight, and they had to lash him to the bitts to keep him from washing away while they completed the sail change."

"He's gone through all our time at sea, only to die two days from home. It's a sad thing, indeed. We'll have a service tomorrow, then; four bells in the forenoon watch."

"Aye, Sir."

"Just be happy you're not in battle or the middle of a storm, Lieutenant Miller," Neville said on their second morning in the Portsmouth Dockyard. "This place is amazing, isn't it?"

"I've never seen such a huge factory, Sir. It goes on a mile or more, I'm told. But I'm not sure I wouldn't just as soon be out in a storm… a mild one, anyway, rather than in a stinking harbor."

"What's making all the mist, there, Sirs?" asked Midshipman Foyle. They were all standing on the poop, looking landward at the sprawling yard while they enjoyed a morning tankard of coffee without fear of spilling due to sea motion.

"I'm told it's steam. They are using a machine to make rigging blocks, and the steam powers it."

"Steam? Like from the kettle?"

"Aye, steam. I dunno. We'll be here several weeks to make repairs all proper. Chips will have new spars for the bits that *Belle Poule* shot away. Lieutenant Towers, you be sure to keep Bo'sun Strugnell on the cordage, and maybe he can get a few new blocks from the steaming thing over there. Go see it for yourself."

"Aye, Sir, of course."

"Work out your own shore leaves. I'll leave you a list from what everyone's reported. I have business in London, so I'll be gone for at least two weeks."

"The post, Sir. How do we find ours?"

"I'm going to the Navy Office, so I'll check there, but I think our arrival has already been reported to London via the semaphore thing you see on the tower over there." He pointed to a conspicuous tower to the east topped by a whirling pair of painted blades. "If there's post for us, it should be here in a week, I should think. If there's any for me, send it straightaway back to London, to this address, if you please." He handed Lt. Towers a scrap of paper with his scribblings on it.

"I'll be looking for my orders. I am hoping we are ordered to return to Jamaica. We weren't originally assigned to Admiral Warren's squadron, and *London* will be here for some time. I don't wish to spend months in here, either, Lieutenant Miller."

"The miracles of a modern age," wondered Foyle aloud.

4 - "Michael"

I thought I had it all covered. I did, really, until that damned Brit captain Burton started poking into things. Late in January of 1806 Michael Stearns was sitting at a little writing desk in his boarding house in Norfolk, Virginia, ruminating about his experience in Jamaica. *It was good for a few years, except for Chester Stillwater. What a fool. No ambition, really, except about the money. He deserved to be made the fall guy...and it almost worked. I could have explained it to Marion, and I would have her in my bed. What now?*

Who could have put that obnoxious captain onto me... some clever fellow in England? Surely, Burton didn't smoke it himself. He's not bright enough on his own.

That's it! I have the idea! I will kidnap one of those clever fellows in England's 'snoop shop'. I don't care which one. I'll take him to France personally to show America's commitment to her allies... and make a name for myself in the process; maybe some money, too. Then, those toadies in Washington will pay more attention to me. I know they have such an organization. I learned about it when I was in France. That fool Georges Cadoudal let it slip. He just had to show me how clever he is.

Stearns picked up his pen and began to write, but he didn't get far before realizing he didn't know whom to write. He put the pen down and went out, and down to the docks. He knew the process of handling men at the docks from his days as the Stillwater Rum Trading Company's sales manager.

I'll find a man to do the job and explain the whole thing to him. I have the name of the perfect idiot in England for him to use… Otto Ames.

A month of poking around the docks, thought Michael. *It has taken far too long, but I think I have my man. He seems to understand what I'm telling him. Finding a ship won't be so difficult, I'm sure.*

Two more weeks of watching the shipping schedules and he found his ship: the *Spirit of Concord.* He arranged to hire the ship for a return trip from England with a cargo of only one man. The ship would leave Norfolk once the captain loaded a suitable cargo for England. Purely by accident, he also discovered some exciting information.

"Where are you bound?" Michael had asked a man at the end of his negotiations with *Spirit's* master. He had thought only to make some conversation while he ate his lunch at a small pub he favored near the docks. The man he sat by turned out to be first mate on a trading ship.

"Baltimore," the man answered, but offered no more.

Then, for a salesman, the man became a challenge. Michael would make him talk. "What's your cargo?"

"Rum."

"I used to be in the rum business," said Michael, "rum from where?"

"Where it all comes from, boy," said the man, "Jamaica."

"Jamaica's where I worked in the rum business. Whose rum is it?"

"Stillwater, they call it." The man began to open up. "We're the first shipment in to a new warehouse they're settin' up in Baltimore. There will be more behind me."

"Did you meet the girl there who runs the place with her father?"

"No, but I've heard she's quite a beauty. I'll be makin' sure to look for her."

"Look for her? Wasn't she in Jamaica when you loaded the rum?"

"No, big fellah, she's in Baltimore where I'm takin' it. Why such interest?"

Michael felt as if he'd been kicked in the chest. His head began to spin, but before he unsteadily pushed himself out of his seat, he replied, "She'll be my fiancée soon..." He turned and began shuffling out.

Over his shoulder, the man said, "Then you ought keep better track of her, I'd say."

I must go to Baltimore. This changes everything... or maybe not. I can work from Baltimore, just as well, although I will have less time. I'm sure my social calendar with Marion will be much busier than anything I have enjoyed here. Marion — just up the river in Baltimore, I can scarcely believe it. What do I need to do? There's packing, and I must change my instruction... and maybe the Spirit can take me to Baltimore and find a cargo there. I hear the city is booming. Be still, my heart!

Michael Stearns walked down the gangway of the *Spirit of Concord* a week later with a happy and hopeful heart. He immediately began his search for the Stillwater Rum Company's new warehouse. He expected no problem, which proved correct. Finding it open, he walked in.

"Hello!" Michael called into the cavernous space. *Odd,* he thought. *There's nobody about.*

"In here, Sir!" a voice cried from behind a wall to his left, "Come on back."

Michael walked across the large room, his footsteps echoing around the wood-paneled walls. Certainly, this would become the sales hall, with waiting chairs and visitor booths. He found a man in the back sitting at an old desk with a neat pile of files. He looked up from his scribblings.

"Hello, I'm Ralph Arnold, and I'm sorry about all this. We're not really open yet. I should have locked the door, but you're here… have a seat. May I know your name, sir?"

"Michael Stearns, formerly an employee with this company in Jamaica," he said, and sat staring at Mr. Arnold.

"Really," said Mr. Arnold. Michael thought he detected interest. "Stearns… Stearns. I'm sure I've seen your name on all sorts of bits of paper here."

"I would expect so. I put in several years. Nothing's been said of me?"

"No, but this has all been quick, quick. Miss Stillwater…"

"Yes, she's here?" Michael interrupted.

"No, she's not. She set all this up, put me in charge and wrote her father about it, and off she went to England. I have some men lined up to work the warehouse as soon as we have rum, so…"

"Gone…?"

"Yes, I'm sorry. You know her, then?"

He knows nothing about me. Marion is not here. They haven't started up yet. I should play my role very carefully regarding Marion… and Chester, of course.

"Yes. And her father. Will Chester be coming?"

"I've not been informed of any such visit."

"Will you be needing a salesman? I moved back home to care for aging parents, and I've just got in. Do you know where Miss Stillwater roomed?"

"Yes, she took her lodgings at the Harford Inn on Pratt Street. I can give you directions, if you need a place."

5 - "Cornwall"

Sir William Mulholland, in the course of his profession, rarely had a need to leave his comfortable office in Whitehall and travel into less secure territory. When an opportunity of sufficient merit presented itself, however, he would occasionally venture out. Such was the case in mid-May of 1806, when he received a note suggesting he meet an informant near Falmouth.

"Mr. Gregory, where did this note come from?" he asked his assistant.

"I don't know, Sir William. It has been here at least a day. Possibly, it simply came in with the post... but I see it has no receiving stamp. I'm sorry, Sir. I've no idea."

Mulholland turned the envelope over. Being one of those crude things available at any printer's, it had sloppy folds, very cheap paper with wood splinters embedded in it, and a seal of the cheapest green wax. The writing, even, was done with some charcoal pencil, not ink. Shuffling in the stack of paper, however, had not rubbed it so badly enough to remove Mulholland's name.

"Wait a moment, Mr. Gregory."

He prized off the wax and opened it. Unlike the envelope, the paper inside was fine linen, and the writing in good ink. He recognized the handwriting as a man he trusted; a man stationed in France these last three years. While he wondered why the message had come thus, he remembered the man's nature. He would relish such drama, so the letter's appearance was therefore not overly concerning; and it was most likely genuine:

My dearest William,

Please come visit. Your friend N.B. on the continent has modified his intentions in a very interesting manner. I have a detailed book on the subject you might very much enjoy reading. I should like you to have it, but I doubt there is anybody remaining in your employ I would recognize. It should be delivered to you discreetly, but you know my health would not allow me the pleasure of a visit to London. Would you mind meeting me for tea on the 12th of June in the King's Arms at Penryn? Just take a packet to Falmouth and pop in. I'm sure a breath of salt air would do you good. It cures all, you know.

Please R.S.V.P. to the desk at the hotel, attn. Otto.

My best regards,   Otto A.

Mulholland handed the note to Mr. Gregory. "What do you think? He makes it sound easy: 'just take your packet to Falmouth and meet me in Penryn for a spot of tea...' It's three hundred miles, for all love! Five days or more in one direction."

"Yes, Sir, but it does sound like the package you've been waiting for, and the trip could be a comfortable jaunt aboard ship. The Good Lord knows, we have packets aplenty. No dirty, awkward mail coaches and miserable roadhouses. Sail down, pick up the package, *"et voilà",* you're back inside two weeks, easy. If the weather is nice, you can write under way; catch up on your letters."

"You make it sound like a holiday."

"It almost does. I think I envy you, Sir."

"Maybe you're right," he agreed. Then, referring to his marine corporal driver and personal guard, he added, "Tell Corporal Truett to ready himself for the same trip, and not to forget his knife and pistol, but to leave his uniform in the barracks. We'll plan to leave on, say, 6th June, and travel as light as we can manage. Put it on my calendar. Oh, and send a note to my house in Bury-St. Edmunds asking Mr. Spencer to pack a case for me."

"Aye, Sir," said Gregory, conforming to the etiquette of the Navy Office in which they stood.

The sail to Falmouth, aboard *HMS Pilchard,* was uneventful. The affable Lieutenant Samuel Crew acted as commander of the almost-new Royal Navy Bermuda schooner. She proved to be fast and comfortable, weathering a one day 'near gale' blowing in off the Atlantic on her second day out beyond the Nore. In addition to Mulholland, she carried four 12-pounders, two carronades, and a crew of 20. She short-tacked into the Falmouth anchorage at the mouth of the Penryn River and dropped anchor in the afternoon of a lovely late spring day.

"It's the tenth, Sir," stated Lt. Crew, "I trust the date will agree with your schedule."

Mulholland recognized the statement for what it was – as close to bragging as the lieutenant would dare go.

"Yes Lieutenant, thank you. Well done. I shall go into town tomorrow to stretch my legs and investigate the town. I can find my meeting place and, perhaps, a nice place to eat. No offense intended. Please give my regards to your cook."

"Only a couple blocks to walk, Sir," said Corporal Truett. "Up Broad Street, the man says."

"No need for a carriage, then. After five days on a boat, a stretch of the legs is a good idea."

"Just there on the right, Sir," said Truett, a few minutes later. "Quite a fine sign: Unicorn and Lion holding the shield."

"It is, yes. My meeting isn't until tomorrow, but it won't hurt to drop in and take a look 'round, will it? I'll inquire of the desk clark if he has a note. Keep an eye here in the street, please."

Mulholland opened the door, which rang a small bell. A very thin young man walked out from a door behind the reception desk. "Yes?"

"Do you perhaps have a note here for a Mister Mulholland?" he asked.

The clerk looked him over carefully. "Yes, I do. Came just yestidy. Do you require a room?"

"It depends on the note, I suppose. May I?" He placed a sixpence on the counter.

"Man said you'd gimme a shilling… Sir."

"Oh, did he?" Mulholland raised his eyebrows.

"It don't mind, Sir. This is good."

"Hmmm." Mulholland turned his attention to the envelope. It was almost identical to the one he'd found on his desk. Rough paper, charcoal writing… and fine linen inside:

W-m,

Thank you for coming, but we'll not be meeting here. Have a nice dinner, if you have time. I hope you are here early. The pot roast is quite good.

After your cheese, go to the fishmonger a bit farther up Broad. Ask for pound of wing of skate; a man there will give you instruction.

My best regards,   *Otto A.*

"Thank you, boy," said Mulholland. "I'll stay aboard one more night." He wagged the note at the clerk and went out the door.

"It's a bloody game of treasure hunt, Corporal… I should expect such from Mr. Ames. Come along. Now we've to walk up the street to some fishmonger, who will probably send us somewhere else."

They arrived at the fishmonger to find a three-woman queue to add to Mulholland's annoyance. When it came his turn, he found he had the shop correct. No instructions were offered, though. "You're a day early," said the surly counter man. Come back at half nine tomorrow. We got no skate today. Next!"

The two men walked back down Broad Street to the King's Arms. Mulholland went in for a plate of the pot roast, and Corporal Truett went across the road for a pint at a little pub he had spotted on the way up. They were back at the fishmonger promptly at half nine the next morning.

"You again?" said the counter man. "Here's your skate; and a note. That'll be a half crown."

"I'm not…" began Mulholland, but stopped his speech when the man gave him a withering stare. "Here's your half crown. Keep the fish," he said.

Another identical envelope contained the message:

Wm,

Get a carriage and run up the road to Redruth. It's about ten miles. Go to the Queen's Grace Hotel on Green Lane for tea."

Have patience, Otto A.

"I'm tempted to get back on the ship and go home, Corporal Truett, and if it were farther than ten miles, I would. Let's go, though. We can be back before dark."

It took them most of an hour to hire a carriage and horse, and wait for the stable boy to harness the animal.

"Groom, do you know the Queen's Grace Hotel on Green Lane in Redruth? We're supposed to meet someone there for tea."

Unlike the fishmonger, he was a cheery fellow, full of information. "Yes, I know it, Sir. It's a very nice tea, and good rooms if you need to stop for a night. It's a bit less than ten mile, and a good road once you get up the hill. Just ask someone when you get into town. 'Ave a wonderful day, and enjoy all this sunshine. God bless you both."

The day did, indeed, turn out to be a good day for a ride in the country. With a relatively smooth road added to the good weather, Mulholland's aching neck received few jarring bumps. Copper ore from the mines around Redruth was returning the little city to prosperity, which resulted in heavy wagon traffic toward the port at Falmouth. Despite the wagon traffic being in the opposite direction, it created a constant cloud of thin dust and caused frequest delays to allow wagons to pass on the narrow lanes. They had no difficulty finding the hotel once they reached Redruth, and Mulholland went in to the desk. He rolled his eyes as he was handed yet another little rough envelope.

My dear William,

"You're almost there, Sir William. I very strongly recommend you stop now to have a tea before you come out the last mile and a half to a little cottage on the Portreach Road to the norwest. Stone, standing between two large oaks. Blue sign: Donegal.

"As much as I would like to just get on with it, Corporal Truett, I am going to take Mr. Ames' advice and have my dinner. It's what, about half one in the afternoon?"

"Yes, Sir."

"Mr. Ames says it's a mile and a half more to a cottage where we'll meet. I'd say we have time to eat, go there, have our meeting, and trot all the way back to Penryn before it goes dark today, wouldn't you?"

"Aye, Sir, I'd say so. We've long days this time o' year. We just passed a pub I'd like to try, if I might, Sir."

"Go on, then. I'll see you in an hour."

Sir William Mulholland dabbed his lips with his dining cloth and tossed it on the table. His action caused the waiter to appear promptly by his side, so he asked for his check. Five minutes later he waited by the door, squinting into the bright June sun, when the carriage and Corporal Truett came trotting up the road. Truett was nothing, if not prompt.

Mulholland showed Truett the note. "Just out the Portreach Road, it says… a small cottage," he said.

Truett pulled out one of his pistols. He checked it, and then slid it into a holster he had strapped to the seatback.

"Expecting trouble, Corporal?" Mulholland asked.

"Always," Truett answered, "even though we haven't seen so much as a man interested in us. They seem happier when we leave."

"This is quite possibly Mr. Ames' dramatic nature," said Mulholland. "He's always been this way. He thinks the butcher keeps knives just to carve him up, and the birds fly off with news of his movements. It's what's kept him alive so long, though, I suppose."

"One can't be too careful, can they?"

"Thank you, Corporal, but let's get on."

Redruth being a small town, they passed the last of its houses a mere fifteen minutes later. Nothing but rural landscape, including a few sheep and cows, presented itself before a small white cottage appeared just around a bend in the lane.

"Here it is, Sir Mulholland," Truett called down, "Cottage between two oaks. There's the blue sign."

At his call, a large tree limb crashed down across the road several yards ahead of their horse, and a pistol fired behind the carriage. Truett could not reach for his pistol. His hands were busy with the reins, working to keep the horse from bolting. Before he had the horse in check, there were four men in front by the limb, all pointing muskets at him, and three off to the sides behind.

An eighth man, who now appeared to be in charge, yelled to him: "Throw down your pistol, Mr. Truett, and you'll be allowed to walk away! We don't want you. Climb down!"

Mulholland was instantly ready to move. He'd seen action with the horse guard in his earlier years, and, without his own weapon, his instinct was to evade the enemy. He jumped out of the carriage, saw the musketeers ahead, and crouched down. Then his world went dark, as a black bag slipped quickly over his head and the three men from behind knocked him into the dirt, sat on him, and bundled his hands and feet. They were talking excitedly, but in some foreign language… Welsh, perhaps?

Despite his writhing, his captors quickly carried him a short distance. Without sight, he tried to determine his situation by sounds, smells, and feeling. He heard no further gunshot, nor the sound of a man – Truett – being knifed or knocked on the head. A door creaked open. It must be the cottage. They picked him up and carried him a few more feet. Musty smelling air enveloped him. It must certainly be the cottage. They sat him on the ground with his back to a cold wall, and left. The door creaked again, and then slammed. There was the noise of a chain rattling, as though being pulled through an iron ring, and the clack of a lock.

6 - "Atlantic Passage - Eastbound"

The *Isle of Wight,* a British-flagged, full-rigged, two-masted brig, left Baltimore in May, carrying on this occasion a cargo of rice, cherries, sheep cheeses and brined beef. She was a relatively fast ship, acceptable for carrying these perishables on the short passage from America to England. She boasted one hundred and fifteen feet of deck and comfortable seaworthiness. She could attract passengers because she sailed directly to London – the major market for her cargo in England.

The *Isle of Wight's* first officer yelled first forward, "Topsails, Mr. Bliss," and then leaned over the dockside rail to yell down, "Wharf, there. Cast us off!"

Marion, standing with the three other passengers on the poopdeck to observe one of the two most interesting moments of the ship's passage, felt the slight jolt of the ship as the topsail sheets hardened and the water below them resisted sideward motion.

"On schedule, Master Dunne," she heard the first officer say to the ship's commander. "We have a fine day for it."

"We do, don't we Miss?" the passenger to Marion's left said to her, "We'll have worse out in the Atlantic... Your first trip abroad?" She had hoped to hear the Master's response, but this man's inquiry drowned it out. She turned to face him. He was a middle-aged fellow with a full beard; not tall – maybe five feet and eight inches. Twinkling eyes looked out at her through a cheery expression. A sensible suit of civilian clothes and a well-tanned face indicated more a well-to-do farmer than some city banker or merchantman.

"Yes, it's a beautiful day, Mister..."

"Riggs, Miss. Mark Riggs, at your service. Tobacco – Virginia. I mean no offense, Miss, but you look tired."

"Hello, then, Mr. Riggs, tobacco, Virginia. I'm Stillwater, Marion, rum, Jamaica, and yes, very tired. It's nice to meet you, and no, not my first time aboard ship." She held out her hand, and he bowed to give it the customary greeting kiss.

"Jamaica, how interesting," he said, thus beginning the usual getting-to-know-you conversations of people who find themselves in unfamiliar, but close, quarters.

The day was perfect to begin a sail down the Chesapeake Bay. No nasty weather to act as omen for a bad passage; a good fresh westerly breeze moved the small ship smoothly but spryly away from the pier. Marion put her hip against the rail to steady herself – rather than lean over, both hands on it, as she saw the men do, to watch Baltimore, and then Dundalk, recede. They passed out the Patapsco River to the upper Chesapeake, while Marion returned to her thoughts; trying to remember more of the etiquette of passengers at sea.

One-foot undulations gossiped along the sides of the *Isle*, slapping happily on the windward hull before passing her by as she slid downwind at three knots, and then four. The breeze tilted the decks slightly. The angle was not startling to the two first-time passengers, yet gave the notion of a proper ship at sea.

It had rained three days ago, which cleared and cooled the air and left puffy sheep's-wool clouds to wander about the blue sky. The peacefulness of the circumstances made an impression on

Marion – a great contrast to her last weeks. Her day – perhaps her next week or two – would not be devoted to the demands of man; they would be ladled out to her by God; by the winds and waves of the great Atlantic. She would undergo the metamorphosis from active to passive.

Marion slept for most of the next day – an easy thing to do in the calm waters of the Chesapeake. The ships' first officer greeted her when she went topside to view the scenery after dinner, "Why, good morning, Miss. I've been looking forward to meeting you."

After they introduced themselves, she asked, "Where are we now? We obviously haven't left the Bay yet, and it looks like quite a big harbor over there." She was aware of his close attention.

"It is; one of our largest: Norfolk. That's the navy anchorage."

"My fiancé is in the Navy. I hope to see him in London, but there's no reason why I should expect to."

"Fiancé?" he said in a rather surprised, possibly disappointed tone. "Why, Miss? What does he do for the Navy? Why would he be in England?"

"Oh, I'm sorry… the British Navy. He's captain of the frigate *La Désirée*. Have you heard of it?"

He presented her with a somewhat crooked smile, and said, " 'Her', Miss, not 'it', and I am most… humbled."

"I don't understand."

"Your fiancé would not appreciate your reference to a ship as 'it'. It's almost always 'she' or 'her'. And to be a captain of one of our frigates…" He blew a puff out through rounded lips… "I'm awe-struck with the thought. I may be the first officer, but this is a mere merchant vessel. Excuse me, but I thought you to be American, although you have an odd accent."

"Odd? I suppose. I am American, but I grew up in English Jamaica…"

"And you'll marry an English Navy officer… 'There but for the grace'… excuse me." He turned and walked a few feet forward, when he met the second mate and gave instruction to begin changing course from southerly, as they had been in the Bay for the last couple days, to easterly – to leave the Bay and enter the Atlantic.

Marion did not find the passage uncomfortably rough, in general. The worst they encountered were confused seas and a near gale while crossing the Great Stream of warm water from the Caribbean as it coursed northward along the East Coast of the USA. In eleven days, the master announced their arrival at the 'Western Approaches' to Britain. A few glimpses of land were seen to the northeast, but nothing more until Old Grimsby and St. Martin's Island appeared to Starboard.

"We'll pass the Lizard in the night, my friends," said the First Mate at supper, "and should be in to London in two days, particularly if this west wind holds. You've had a fast crossing."

"And you'll still have your cherries, won't you?"

"We will indeed."

"Where will you stop in London, Miss Marion?" asked Riggs (tobacco, Virginia). "I know a lovely place on Russell Square."

"I've booked a suite at the *Saxon Arms*, downtown," she answered. "It's quite nice, and close enough to where I need to go."

"Relatives? Certainly not business."

Oh, I've put my foot in my mouth. I had better start thinking a little more clearly. This one I can slip out of quite easily, though. "Not rum business, right off, of course. My first steps will be to Whitehall, to see what is known of my fiancé."

"Ah, right. A Navy captain. I shall pray all is well."

June 16, *Saxon Arms*, London: "Hello, Miss Stillwater!" gushed the elderly reception clerk. "How nice to see you. It's been what… two years? And your handsome fiancé… have you married him yet? Is Miss Ellen with you?" he asked, craning his neck over to peer into the lobby and out the door to see if Ellen had accompanied her. "Certainly you're not alone! Tsk, tsk."

Oh, that's right, Marion thought, *He had quite the eye for Ellen.* "No, not this trip. No Ellen. She married Captain Dagleishe. Do you remember him? He's always at sea, so she's still living in Boston.

"Boston! It would be better if she stayed here in England to cheer us all up, I say."

"She would be flattered to hear you say it, too."

"Room 317, just as before," he said, holding a key out for the bellboy. "Has everything come with you?"

"It's all in the hack, yes. I'll go up straight away, if you don't mind."

"Yes, yes, go on. It's all ready. Charlie here will come back down for your trunks."

Having the same room at the same hotel as her previous visit to London carried good news and bad news. On the good side was familiarity, and happy memories of a wonderful few months with Neville, Ellen Aughton, Joseph Dagleishe, oh, so very much, the time with Neville… On the bad side was the emptiness of the place, with none of them here. And then, somewhere toward worrisome, was the clerk. He remembered a great deal, and he obviously knew more than she thought he did. *Desk clarks are discreet, if nothing else, though. I wouldn't want any of his observations to slip back to Father. Neville and I weren't actually bespoke then, and neither were Ellen and Joseph.*

Marion looked about the rooms. The door to the 'lock-off room', where Ellen had stayed when attending, was locked now, probably in use by a handmaiden for the next suite over. *The clark knew that. Why was he looking for Ellen when he knew she wasn't coming? Interesting.* Her mind wandered back to her first meeting with Ellen – in Boston, after Marion had first met the British attaché, Mr. Looten, in Washington some years ago.

Marion had arrived at a large brownstone townhouse in downtown Boston on a warm late-spring day. The trees in front were in full bloom, with white blossoms on the limbs, as well as all over the sidewalk. She'd rapped at the door twice, but nobody had answered. She took the scrap of paper with the address out of her pocket and checked it again. This should be the place. Then she noticed another scrap of paper sticking out of the door jamb, so she'd pulled it out and opened it:

Marion,

If it's you, please come in. I'm in the basement.

If you're not Marion, don't dare try it, unless you have a very big dog.

Marion swung her small travelling case through the door into the ample foyer and dropped it on the small Persian rug. This is a strange greeting, indeed... "Hello," she yelled. "Ellen?"

She noticed a door on the right at the far side of the foyer. Either it was a door to a basement or she would find a number of coats there. She crossed the foyer and grabbed the handle. It creaked open, displaying a narrow staircase downward. A light emanated from below – some oil lamp – she could hear a rhythmic creaking and panting, and wondered for a moment if she should continue.

"Hello," she yelled again. The panting stopped. "Ellen?"

"Marion?" a female voice called from below, "Is that you?"

Marion continued down the last few steps, to where she found a slim girl dressed very strangely, in something like a man's bathing costume. She was drenched with sweat, and had her mid-length hair tied back in a bun. She jumped to her feet in front of some contraption resembling the inner workings of a rowing boat – without the boat. Ropes went from it to pulleys on the wall and – weights, Marion guessed.

"Hello," the girl said enthusiastically, and walked across the small room. "Welcome to Boston, I..." She extended her hand, but acted unsure of the proper action. She pulled it back and wiped it dry on her legging.

They both remember the air going still, or quiet, or something, when Ellen came close enough to shake hands. They both stared, dumbfounded, into each other's eyes, and both raised an arm; halfway, and then full up to touch the other's face.

"You're beautiful," said Marion, touching Ellen's oval white face. "White as a china doll, with pink cheeks from your exercise. Stunning. Are you Ellen? I didn't expect…"

"You…," interrupted Ellen. "You must be Marion. Such a gorgeous creature. Your eyes set off your satin brown complexion. Such eyes… and these," she added, touching Marion's lips.

A dog barked outside – loudly – the moment was gone.

"I… I'm sorry," said Marion. "I should never… I never…"

"Nor me," said Ellen, now with a stronger blush of pink than before. "You are not at all what I expected. I don't mean…"

They had both laughed, but it was the beginning of a very close friendship, both personal and professional. Ellen had been asked to take an assignment as assistant to some girl in Jamaica. She had not liked the idea at all, and had told her contact she would only consider it if she could meet the girl in person and decide for herself. Their week in Boston had sealed their fate; Ellen began Marion's orientation to the world of spycraft on the spot, with assurances it would continue more rigorously, once home in Jamaica, and that they would certainly have grand adventures in the future.

7 - "Atlantic Passage - Westbound"

Mid-June, 1806: Sir William Mulholland waited in the musty dampness of a small cottage he could not see – owing to the bag over his head – for several hours. He heard noises that sounded to him like rats. *Yes, rats for sure, I hear the squeaking now. No, maybe squirrels in the thatch above.*

Shortly, he heard the sound of a horse and wagon outside, followed by the jangling of keys and the rapping of a chain being pulled out of a ring. The door creaked open, but he detected no change in the light. *It must be dark outside now*, he thought. "Where's my driver?" he asked

"Don't panic, Mister Mulholland. He will be held until it's safe for us to release him. Then, he can find his own way home from wherever in hell we leave him... unless he does something stupid, of course."

"And what happens to me, now?"

"Just a boat ride, as far as I know," the voice said. It said more, but returned to Welsh.

Two men lifted him to his feet and began dragging him forward. Dragging was necessary because his legs, after sitting on the hard floor for several hours, were partially numb and not working well. By the time they had regained their feeling and began to work, they threw him forward onto some other hard floor. This floor was not stone or dirt, though; certainly wood, and not as hard as the four-inch-thick deck of a ship. A sudden jerk, followed by a jouncing of the floor he had been thrown upon, the jangling of horse harness, and a driver's command, gave him understanding.

I'm being moved in a wagon. I should try to estimate how far.

Thankfully, the ride was neither fast, causing excessive jarring, nor far. It lasted, by his estimation, about forty-five minutes, ending finally with a very smooth ride for the last five minutes. *What road could be so smooth*, he wondered. The wagon stopped. He heard nothing other than hushed voices, of which he could discern no word at all, for another ten minutes or more, and then the back of the wagon... *opened? A door? What wagon has a door? A hearse!*

Someone grabbed him by the feet and dragged him out. Again, he was assisted by two large onion-smelling men to walk through soft sand, and then small wet stones... *it's not ground. It's the 'smooth road'; a strand. I'm at the water's edge.* His shin hit something hard, and he cried out.

"You call out again, and I'll knock you on the head myself, gov," said his 'interpreter'. "Get in."

The only sympathy he received was two more men lifting his feet and tossing him up and... *definitely into a small boat. I'm being taken out to a ship, no doubt. I must be at the strand in Portreach. It's perfectly clear now. I can feel the bow of the little craft bobbing with each wave that comes ashore, and I can hear the little surf lapping at the tiny stones of the beach.*

The boat sat still for a few minutes more, and then men clambered aboard – four, he thought – and then the boat lurched out into the water. The sounds and jerkiness of rowing followed for fifteen minutes or so, on a relatively calm sea. After the small boat thumped against the side of a ship, they threatened him again not to call out, and removed his hood so he could see his way to climb up a short ladder into a middling-sized ship… *a schooner, maybe.* He didn't get much time to look.

Once aboard, the lights of a nearby town were visible, as were the small boat with the Welshmen departing upon the sea, shimmering with starlight. He assumed the lights to be Portreach. They weren't far away, but he didn't have much time to study them (not that he knew the place anyway), before being led to a cabin below-decks and locked in. By the commands, sounds of men running and heaving on lines, and then the clunking of windlass pawls, it soon became clear the ship had weighed anchor.

The cabin appeared to be comfortable, despite its diminutive size. Mulholland soon spied a niche on the bulkhead. It was apparently to be his cabinet, for it containing a bottle of scotch whiskey, a glass, a small bottle of tooth powder, and a note written in French. *Apparently, they know I speak French, even though the one has spoken to me only in English. Possibly, he doesn't know French.* He unfolded the note.

(in French)

M. Mulholland,

> *Make yourself comfortable. I am sorry there is no food, but I'm told you had time for a nice tea. There will be breakfast, once we are well out to sea.*

Someone planned this whole thing very well. I wonder what part Mr. Ames played… notes every step of the way… and I wouldn't have come if not for him. Maybe he was an unwilling accomplice?

For two days his food was delivered, but he spoke to no one. As well as he could put it together, the date was 15th June. *I had assumed we were bound for France, but we cannot be simply crossing the channel, or we'd be there by now... maybe farther south, or into some port in the Med. Why would they do this? Would I not be taken directly to Napoleon and questioned; or traded for someone of great importance to him?*

On the third day, his door opened. "Would you care to meet the Master?" the visitor asked.

"Yes, very much," responded Mulholland. "Must I be in irons?"

"No. There is nowhere for you to go, and many to watch you. Come along."

The bright light from above began to hurt his eyes even before he reached the companion stair. The fresh salt air was an improvement to the stale air of his cabin, but he had to squint his eyes tightly to discern handholds. "Wait a moment," he said at the top of the stair... "my eyes." They cleared in another minute or two, but still he could see nothing but blue. It was blue above, save one huge cloud formation in the distance and the sails and masts above his head, and blue below. He scanned the horizon around him, but saw nothing but more blue. No land.

"It's a grand day, Monsieur. The Master bids you sit there on the poop." The man pointed to a chair set by the taffrail. Mulholland was no sailor, but he could manage the ship's easy motion today. He walked to the chair and sat. After another five minutes of enjoying the sun and breeze, a man appeared from below and walked to him.

"Good day, sir," he said in English. "I am John Fielding, Master of this ship."

"Good day, Master Fielding," said Mulholland. "You know who I am. Where are we bound?"

Fielding thought for a few seconds before answering, "I suppose it makes little difference what you know. There's no way to escape, other than into the hands of the Lord. We are bound for

Norfolk, with a cargo of trading goods for the Indians. There I will pass you into the hands of another."

"Norfolk? In the colonies?"

"Colonies?" puffed Fielding. "We're not your colonies. You might remember something of a revolution thirty years ago. We are the United States of America now, your highness."

"I'm sorry. I'm quite aware of it, and I meant no offense. The destination was just such a surprise. Whose vessel is this?"

"The *Spirit of Concord* is mine, sir. She's an American-built schooner; as fast as they come. But never mind. Nobody will be looking for you yet."

"It's the seventeenth, yes?"

"Aye."

"Must I remain locked in my cabin?"

"No, I suppose not. As long as you stay out of the way when there's work to be done, you may wander about as you wish. No climbing, though, ho, ho," he concluded with a laugh at his own joke, and walked away.

I have no cloak, so I expect I'll stay mostly below out of the weather, unless we're in the tropics. "You're being paid to deliver me?"

"Aye," he said again. "You are a paying cargo. I mean you no harm, but we'll not be friends, either. My uncle was killed in the war we just spoke of."

"I see. I'm sorry."

8 - "Spy"

Having planned repairs in detail, Captain Neville Burton took up his small travelling-pack on the 16th of June and swung over the rail into the chains to wait while oarsmen were filling his gig.

"I'm at Whitehall, Lieutenant, or the address I gave you, if you need anything. If it's an emergency, don't forget the semaphore contrivance over there."

"Aye, Sir. I'm sure all will be fine."

Neville hopped the last few feet into his gig, and the coxswain, yelled, "Oars out…" The boat's crew acted smartly. Filled with enthusiasm, they would be the only ones with shore leave this day.

The thought of travelling the ninety miles to London by coach was encouragement enough to cause Neville to look very hard to find a ship going his way. As luck would have it, he found friends, although he had to wait a few days for them. The advice-boat *Spy*, with Lieutenant Goss now in command, had arrived a few days earlier. Neville had a special eye for this particular small ship, since he had been primarily responsible for her capture from the French back in '95. He crossed over to say hello.

"Ahoy, *Spy*," the Coxswain called out to the advice boat as she neared.

"Ahoy, who goes?"

"*La Désirée*," responded the coxswain. That response, meaning the captain of another ship (specifically, *La Désirée*), created an instant alarm aboard. The lookout turned and yelled something into his ship. Before the gig came much closer, a man came bounding out from below, still trying to get into his jacket, with his hair all a-fly and an unfastened collar. Neville could see him gesture this way and that, and issue a few orders. Another man handed him a short glass, and he swung it up to his eye, pointing it straight at Neville.

Now close enough to see more detail, Neville could watch Goss's mouth say, "Oh, my," before he turned to issue even more frantic orders.

In the remaining three minutes it took to guide Neville's gig alongside *Spy*, Goss did a commendable job of gathering enough men to pipe Neville aboard. The step from the gig's gunnel to *Spy's* little chains being small, Neville was up on deck the moment the two boats touched.

Neville saluted the colours, stepped forward and touched his hat to Commander Goss, pushed aside Goss's offered hand, and embraced him warmly. They slapped backs before stepping back to view each other.

"You look well, Lieutenant... Oh, I see, it's Commander Goss."

"As do you, Captain Burton," said Goss. "Did you really need to appear un-announced?"

"I couldn't take the chance you'd dash off. You un-rateds are always dashing off. I know; I've been one. So, where are you on the List, Commander?" Neville asked, "And where's Commander Dinning?"

"Gone many months now... on to be Captain of the frigate *Caroline*. And I'll be on top of the List in just weeks now, God willing and Peace not declared," said Goss. "I have such luck; maybe it's because you're in the harbor, Neville. There is nothing I want more than to go check the Captain's List at Whitehall, and here I have a packet from a French prize... that one, over there," he said, pointing to *Marengo*, "to take up to London. And you... how do you come to be here?"

"The French prize over there. We've come in with her."

"Of course you did!"

"You'll never guess her captain's name. It's a whole story I can tell you if you'll do me a favor."

"Anything, Neville. You've but to ask."

Spy stood from Portsmouth the following morning, and in two days had managed to round the Nore Lightship and set anchor in the mouth of the Medway.

"This is almost exactly where my naval career began, Commander Goss," commented Neville. "You still have Mr. Acton aboard, I see."

"He is indeed, or I might not try this next bit. With him as pilot, we can reach the Pool in two or three days. If you remember, he knows the Thames as almost none other. He's learned the bit beyond Gravesend here aboard *Spy*, as we've had numerous occasions to sail upstream."

Before low water of the next morning, Neville awoke to someone rapping at his cabin door. "Beg pardon, Sir. Commander's compliments; could you step up topside?"

Finding his way about in the darkness below took Neville several minutes, despite *Spy* being a small ship, but he eventually found his way up. Goss had warped *Spy* out of the Medway in time to catch to the tide. His excitement was obvious.

"What is it, Commander?" Neville asked, "Do we have an invasion?"

"No, Captain; a wind shift. You really are the lucky omen who walks. Wind's usually sou-west here, but it's gone into the south, and steady. Mr. Acton thinks it'll hold, and if it does, we might be to the Pool in one tide. One tide, Neville!"

Grain Edge appeared from the mist of a new day. They passed the marshes of Kent with no incident, as well, but the meanders of the river had the fore-and-aft rigged *Spy* close-hauled as she could go on most occasions. At some times she cheated her main boom to windward with an extra line to a larboard stern chaser ringbolt. The south wind and tide pushed them past Gravesend, although the wind began flagging as the overcast sky began spitting on the decks. They did, in the end, make their way to the Pool of London on a single tide, although rowing boats were needed to lay aside a quay as the tide began its inevitable ebb and the south wind died away with the beginning of a heavy rain.

"It's been a lovely walk down 'Memory Lane', Commander," said Neville when they finally had a moment to sit in Goss's tiny cabin with a tot of rum, listening to the rain drum on deck above. "Most enjoyable, and I thank you for it."

"Aye, it has, Captain," said Goss, "Now, let's go look to our future at Whitehall. We can hack it from here in the morning. It's just across the bridge and 'round the Embankment. Or, we could walk, if you like… if the rain stops."

9 - "Whitehall 1"

Marion woke early, excited about the adventure in which she expected to participate. *Besides*, she rationalized, *I have nothing better to do today.* She dressed simply and, once again, opened her note from Mulholland:

Dear Marion,

I understand you might be quite busy at the moment, but if you are at all curious, I have an adventure that may interest you. I think it would suit your skills quite well.

If you have any interest, please advise me if you could join us at my offices to discuss it in mid-June of the new year. Georges will join us. I'm sure you two would like to catch up.

Uncle William

She went alone to the hotel dining area for breakfast, wondering where Georges Cadoudal, the man Mulholland had referenced, would stay in London. *Even if Sir Mulholland is not in, or is unavailable today*, she thought, *someone there might be able to help me contact Georges.*

Marion was hungry. She easily devoured a plate of fried eggs, with a boiled tomato on top, and a piece of cold English toast. *This is such a treat after two weeks of the food aboard the Isle of Wight, despite that the cook tried hard to please me, but why the English bother with this cold, dried bread they call toast, I'll never understand. The tea is exceptional, though.*

Her breakfast concluded, she asked the waiter to put the food charge on the bill for her room. "Also," she asked him, "will you please call me a hack for half an hour from now. I have only to go to Whitehall, and I'll have no baggage."

"Yes, Miss, but it looks as if it will rain this morning, as you may have noticed. Don't forget your brolly."

Marion needed no umbrella when she departed the hotel a half hour later, because the front door opened under a wide portico that protected guests and their carriages from the often-inclement weather of London. She carried the brolly, however, expecting it would be needed at Whitehall. Inside the coach, she directed the driver: "The Admiralty building at Whitehall, please."

"Admiralty," he said with some surprise. "That's not usually a woman's destination."

"Off we go, anyway, my good man," she said.

They arrived in twelve short minutes, allowing for some traffic delay that appeared to have something to do with an overturned wagon of Spanish oranges. "Here 'tis, Miss, on the right: Admiralty portico."

"Not here, driver… next door there; the yellow one."

"It's not a public building, Miss. They'll not let you just walk in there. You're not English, are you?"

"You just wait for me, then, please, whether I'm English or not. If they let me in, I should not be long, but if I'm detained, I'll have someone bring you a note and your fare, will that do?"

"Detained, Miss?... All right, yes, I'll wait." He hopped down from his seat and opened her door, then took her hand to help her down.

She still didn't need the umbrella. The rain – more of a falling damp – had stopped for the moment, but the sky was still overcast, indicating more to come. Two red-coated marines stood at attention by the door, but they made no move to open it for her. She pulled the big wooden slab open and went in.

Another marine met her inside: "I'm sorry Miss. You may have been mis-directed. This is not the Admiralty; it's not a public building."

"May I have an audience with Sir William Mulholland?" she asked.

The marine's face gave no hint of recognition. "There's no one here by the name you've given, Miss. Maybe the Admiralty can assist you. It's just next door."

"In room four?" she asked.

This time the marine paused a moment before responding, "Go back there," and gesturing towards the back of the spacious room. "Vestibule on the right; the clark there will inquire, Miss." After watching her walk there, he made an abrupt about-face and returned to his post at the side of the large foyer.

"Letter," said the clerk, holding out his hand. *This one's an odd duck*, she thought. *A poor skinny thing with a wig that looks more like a woolen winter cap.*

"No proper letter," she said, "Only this." She handed him the note, well-creased by then, but signed 'Uncle William', and in his handwriting, for anyone who knew him.

The clerk very noticeably raised his eyebrows. "Oh, you must be…" He looked at her more closely. Studied her, one might say. "Please have a seat there. It may be a minute."

He returned in five minutes. "Sir Mulholland is not available today," he said. "Nor tomorrow. He's away." He held the letter as if it might transmit the pox: "You're early. The note plainly says 'late June'. I will place this in his tray."

"No, I'll keep it," she said, snatching the note back. "Will you please leave him a note with my name and hotel? Marion Stillwater at the *Saxon Arms*." Again he raised his eyebrows, but said nothing more.

Realizing there was probably no lie about 'Uncle William' being away, Marion resolved to write a few letters, visit a bookseller, and wait patiently for a message from Mulholland. Surely, it couldn't be too long.

"Oh, one more thing, sir," she said. "Do you know where I might find a M. Georges Cadoudal?"

Again, the eyebrows went up, but the clerk answered, "I really can't help you, Miss. The name is quite unfamiliar to me."

So I would expect him to say, but it was worth a try. I'll check next door for Neville's ship before I return to the hotel, though.

"Yoo hoo, there," she said to the driver of the hack out front. "You were right. I'm to go next door. Please continue to wait." She snapped the umbrella up to guard against a mist that was gathering itself into a fine rain, and walked through the great portico of the Admiralty into the busy foyer.

At this building, she couldn't touch a door handle for the attention of any officer within a few feet of her, regardless of rank.

"May I be of assistance, Miss? It's not often we see the likes of you in this place," said a dashing, yet senior-looking captain, within a matter of minutes. He apparently had assigned himself as her escort and protector.

"It would be most appreciated, Captain," she said, "I…"

"So, you know the Navy ranks then. Why is that?"

"My fiancé is a Captain, Sir, of the frigate *La Désirée*, so yes, I know the ranks. *In the rum business, it doesn't pay to be ignorant.* "I don't know where he is, and I've come to find out."

"A captain with a ship. A lucky man, and a frigate, as well. And you. He certainly is a lucky man. Come with me. There's a list."

He walked her up the stairs to a room with the walls full of lists. Lists of men lost, ships captured, ships lost, and finally, the current station list.

"The name again, Miss…?"

"Stillwater. Soon to be Burton."

"I am very pleased to meet you, Miss Stillwater. I'm Captain Sinter… but the ship name, again."

"*La Désirée*, good sir… assigned to Jamaica Station, the last I knew."

"Here's the alphabetical listing, here… La… La, La… Des… She's here in England, Miss; in Portsmouth since twelve June. If I were him, I would have contacted you immediately!"

"He doesn't know I'm here – thinks I'm home in Jamaica. I just got in yesterday from Baltimore."

"Baltimore? Not from…? Never mind. Now that you know, you can send him a message there at the Navy Yard."

Marion's heart skipped and beat faster. Her thoughts raced. *How fast can I contact him? Should I go there? What if he leaves? Certainly, Sir William would know… where is he? Could he be here at his flat? He doesn't know I'm here. I must write! Where could Georges be?"*

"Excuse me, Captain Sinter; does it say how long he will stay?"

"There is nothing written in the 'orders' column, Miss, sorry."

"No mind. Thank you so much for your help. Oh, thank you!" She threw her arms around him, gave him a kiss on the cheek, and fairly ran down the stair and out to find the waiting hack, leaving Captain Sinter with his biggest grin of the week.

"Driver, 42 Bedford Avenue, please."

"You're wet, Miss. You should use the brolly." The rain was coming down steadily now, creating puddles on the street and running in little rivers into the gutters. She hadn't noticed.

"Oh, yes, yes. How silly of me. But drive on. I'm in a hurry, now. It's not far." *Damn! Damn! The key is in my room. I can knock on the door. He'll come out if he's there. But if he doesn't come out, I still won't know if he's in town without peeking in to see if his things are there. I could go to the hotel first... no, I won't waste the time.*

The hack clattered to a halt in front of the big apartment building, the horses snorting rainwater out of their nostrils, and shaking their heads to remove more water and jangle the reins. Marion wasn't waiting for the driver to open the door. She hopped out and walked off, again without the umbrella, before the driver set the brake, tied the reins, and climbed down. He stood in the rain and shook his head as she disappeared into the door.

Inside, she ran straight into Mrs. Brown, Head of Housekeeping for the building. "Oh, what luck. Mrs. Brown! Mrs. Brown, is he here? Is he in? Is Neville Burton at home?"

"You're all wet, Dear," she said, but her alarm grew quickly as she realized Marion's state of concern. "What's wrong? Are you all right? Is the Captain well?"

"He's here then?"

"No. No, he's not. I haven't seen him in a month of Sundays, Miss. It's been quiet forever."

Marion wasn't used to such emotions in herself. She burst into great sobbing tears. Maybe she was far more tired than she realized.

"There, there, Dear," said Mrs. Brown. The motherly woman stepped forward and took Marion in her arms; she waited until Marion calmed. "Everything will turn out, you'll see. You have a place to stay, don't you?"

"Yes, of course. I've just found out his ship is in Portsmouth. I so hoped he'd be here. I have to catch him before he sails off again; and I've come for a meeting, but I just found out I'll have to wait for... for someone. I could move over here from the hotel. I can come here, yes? I have a key."

"Certainly, Dear. And you'll feel much better tomorrow. But you're drenched, Miss. I'll fetch a towel for your head. Just bring it back when you come. You should carry a brolly here in London, Miss."

If I'm going to move over to Neville's flat, I'm going to do it without delay. I'll just get more comfortable if I stay here, thought Marion. "Mr. Herbert, your accommodation has been excellent," she said to the desk clerk. "I mean no offense whatever, but I am going to move out today. I find my fiancé's flat sitting idle while he is away, so I shall stay there. *And I won't mind knowing you don't watch my every move.*

"Yes, Miss, I'll send Charlie up in an hour."

By noon, Marion had managed her move as efficiently as she had managed the set-up of the Stillwater warehouse in Baltimore. Her key worked the door exactly as it should, and the hack driver had helped bring her trunks in. Mrs. Brown was out shopping, but no matter; she had been advised. Marion only needed some time to make the bachelor's abode more to her liking. She began by moving a few small things.

She needed space in the armoire. She moved a shirt she found hanging, and thought, *How long it's been here, and yet it still carries the smell of him...* She hung her dresses and moved on to the sitting room.

What's this, she wondered, when she found a paper on Neville's little writing desk. *How sweet; a draft of a letter to me:*

> *42D Bedford*   *June 20, 1806*
> *London, England*
>
> *My Dearest Marion,*
>
> > *There is so much I want to tell you - so much has happened. But first I must write of my love for you - of how much I am sorry not to be by your side, and how*

It ended there. Half-way down the paper a huge ink-blob had been wiped up quickly, as though Neville had spilled the ink-pot. If he'd finished the letter, it was on a fresh sheet of paper, and probably sent away. *How old must this be? The date is... yesterday? Could this be right? He was here yesterday? Why would Mrs. Brown not tell me? Surely, he's not playing... where's Mrs. Brown? Oh, where's Mrs. Brown? Neville couldn't possibly betray me... could he? I didn't see her on my way in....*

Marion walked rapidly to the door, jerked it open, and ran down the hallway toward the building foyer. Before she got there, the outer door opened to reveal a man carrying sacks of something. *Groceries. They are groceries; and Mrs. Brown is behind him.* "Mrs. Brown!" she called out, and again, "Mrs. Brown!"

Mrs. Brown looked up from her bags, startled, "Oh, my dear," she said, "Oh, Oh. I couldn't catch him. He was here just one night. He came in late, and I didn't see him until this morning when he left. I was in the window and he waved as he walked to the hack stand."

Marion was becoming aware that Mrs. Brown was almost as upset as she was, which now changed her feelings from curious and angry to great worry; "What, Mrs. Brown? Catch him? And why would he be here for only one night?"

"I don't know, but I ran into the street just as his hack went by. I waved my kerchief, and he just waved a friendly good-bye. Oh, I'm so sorry. I couldn't tell him, and I couldn't tell you. I didn't know where you were staying."

Marion regained her composure quickly. She felt herself steam up with anger. *That creature at Whitehall in Sir Mulholland's office. He's it. He's at the bottom of this rotten barrel...* "It's all right, Mrs. Brown. I've got it now. Thank you for your help." She smiled as sweetly as she could, turned, and walked back to her flat.

10 - "Whitehall 2"

The June morning dawned dim. It wasn't raining, though it looked as if it might.

"Come along, Captain," said Goss. "Finish those collops and seize the day!"

"Ha, ha! Who's excited about a little trip to town? All right, but you'll have to wait for me to drink the coffee, as well."

"Arrrgh."

Since it wasn't raining, they walked. "We said we'd walk, Commander Goss, not trot," admonished Neville about half way to their destination. "Walk. I have my digestion to consider."

The walk took but a half hour, all said and done. Neville had no question where Goss would go first… straight to the posted Captain's List.

"I don't see it, Commander," Neville said. "I've run my finger up and down, and your name's just not here."

"Ha," said Goss, "You can read as well as I can. I'm the top name." He tapped his finger against the board about six times. "Top!" he repeated.

"Ha, ha, ha!" laughed Neville. "Celebration! A celebration is called for. I must go next door and stop in to see my Godfather. It's a well-guarded building, though, and they don't allow general visitors or tourists, sorry. When I come out, we'll find a pub and drink more than we should, and we can stay in my flat tonight."

"You have a London flat? My God, Neville, what…"

"Another story for another time…"

"I'll go check on my orders. It's not often I'm here in person. You run along and we'll meet… where? At the flat: 42D Bedford Ave. It's not far. Mrs. Brown will let you in."

Neville arrived where Marion had been just the day before, at Sir William Mulholland's office building to discover it under heavy guard.

The duty of the two sentries who stood outside the door was apparently to dissuade any obvious organized attacks on the building – not to stop individuals from entering. Since he was alone and unarmed with anything other than the formal Navy officers' sword, they allowed him to enter. The reception inside was different.

"Your name, Sir?" asked the marine. It struck Neville as unusual that the marine's rank was lieutenant, not private or corporal.

"Burton. Captain Neville Burton."

"Appointment?"

"No, I…"

"Why would you come here with no appointment?" the marine asked. He turned and yelled, "Corporal!"

"I'm here to see Sir William Mullholland."

"Exactly what I expected," said the marine lieutenant. "Please follow the corporal."

Neville followed the marine through a narrow door in the side wall of the visitors' foyer, down a short hallway to a doorway on the left. The corporal gestured for him to enter. Within, he found nothing but a small table and a pair of chairs facing each other.

"Please, have a seat," said the corporal. It sounded more like a command, so Neville sat. He saw no reason not to. He waited there at least five minutes before anyone else came in.

A man Neville did not recognize, wearing civilian attire, entered the room and sat opposite him. "Good morning," he said.

"Good morning," Neville responded. "Has there been some problem with Sir Mulholland?"

"Why would you ask?"

"Because when I said I was here to see him, I was led in here. Who are you?"

"I work here. Why would you…"

"You work here, but you have no name?" asked Neville, beginning to sense a definite belligerence.

"Captain, it's not your place here to ask questions."

"It is beginning to appear that it is. Your name…?"

The man paused. "Chapman… Roger. Why did you come?"

"Sir Mulholland is my Godfather. *He's not, really, but it's always worked for me before.* I always come in when I'm in London. I'm sure he would be offended if I did not."

"Godfather?" queried Chapman. "There is no record of you."

"It's not a Navy rank, sir. Why have you asked me in here? Is Sir William not well?"

Chapman paused again. "Sir William… such familiarity."

"Godfather, remember? What's going on here?"

The door opened, and a man walked in and handed Chapman a folder… a dossier.

"Just a moment, if you please, Captain," said Chapman, and he took a minute or two to page through the file. Then he looked up at Neville, paused for another minute, and said, "He's missing."

"Missing? Who's missing?"

"Sir Mulholland. Do you swear you know nothing of it?"

"Me? Why would I? I've just got in from Jamaica. Have you checked his home?"

"We…ah…we don't know where he lives."

"How could you not know? It's not a secret."

"Apparently it is; at least from us, but it's…"

"Should I have my mother drop by? Or my sister, perhaps, to see if he's all right, and post us a note?"

"Thank you, Captain, but we don't need sarcasm at the moment."

"It's only partly sarcastic. Either would do, if it would help."

Chapman stared Neville in the eye, and he did not appear to be at all amused. "It may be worse than 'missing', as I began to say. He went down to Cornwall almost three weeks ago, and hasn't been heard from since." He waited until he thought Neville had taken in the information, and then added, "But his driver's been found… dead; drowned. The horse was a-wander; no carriage. On the Atlantic Coast at Portreach; it's a small town."

"Kidnapped, you think? On the way to France?"

"It's likely. But it's not something I should discuss with you until we know more."

"If you can't discuss it with me, who can you discuss it with?" Neville could feel his anger rising.

"We must keep it very close for now. There's not much in your file. It doesn't appear you had much official communication, so there's nothing negative, either."

What? Not much in my file? He must have another file somewhere. I should keep my mouth shut, I think, if I want to help. "So I'm free to go?"

"Unless there is something you can add… but you say you're just in from Jamaica?"

"Aye, with Admiral Warren's squadron."

Chapman hesitated again. "Oh, nice job, that. We've just had some good information from *Marengo*."

"I assume so. I carried it in." *Or rather, Goss did, but I was aboard.*

Chapman gave Neville a queer look, and then said, "I think you'd best go, before we find a reason you shouldn't."

I am not sure how I would dig into Sir William's disappearance at the moment. Rather than waste time, however, I should go find my sailing orders. After walking to the side of the building where he expected to find the office with his orders, the door he opened presented a waiting room for young lieutenants who were apparently looking for their first assignments. *This place gets worse every time I come in. Now where?* "Excuse me there, can you direct me…"

Having found the proper office, he was handed the envelope he sought. "Here you are, Captain. You're just in time. This would have been in the afternoon post." *What? That fast? I'm going straight back out? How do I help find Sir William?* He opened the envelope. *Yes, that fast. Sail on the 27th for Jamaica? Alone… no squadron…I'll have only tonight at home here, and I'll need to find a ship back to Portsmouth. I'd better hurry back to my flat to get some rest, then. Ohhh, the celebrating with Goss!*

The rain had paused again. There were puddles, and everywhere the most magnificent shades of green in the trees and bushes. Traffic was light, probably due to people avoiding the rain, so it was not long before Neville reached 42 Bedford and found a note tacked to his door:

Captain Burton,

We'll celebrate at the first opportunity, but I'm off. When they saw me, they immediately wrote me orders to carry a Captain to a ship in the Channel Fleet, and from thence a packet for another in the Med, so I must fly.

All my best,   Cmdr. Goss

It's for the best, thought Neville. *Celebrating before the success is always bad luck.*

Before going to bed, he went out 'round the corner to a little carvery he'd noticed for a quick dinner, returned to his flat, and dashed off a letter to Marion – in Jamaica.

Morning brought very welcome sunshine. The rain had washed the soot out of the air, leaving it wonderfully clear. Neville had not slept well, worrying about Sir William, and so packed and hurried out the door early. He hoped to find *Spy* still at the Pool, or another similar vessel bound for Portsmouth. As much as he wanted to help with the search for Sir William, he was loath to forsake his position as Captain of *La Désirée*, which is exactly what might happen if he did not appear on time; and of time, he had little. He caught Mrs. Brown's eye in her window as he left, and gave her a quick smile and wave.

He found a hack driver leaning against his coach wheel and enjoying a smoke at the first corner. They were off as soon as he could climb in. Looking down Bedford Avenue, he noticed Mrs. Brown waving a kerchief his way, and so waved back. *She's such a nice lady*, he thought. *I'm sorry I didn't have time to visit.*

Owing to the sheer volume of traffic from London out to England's major ports, finding a ship going to Portsmouth did not present a particular problem. The *Rose of Devon*, a coastal trading sloop, departed before noon, and was more than happy to carry him for the right price. After all, it cost the Master almost nothing. They settled on five pounds sterling.

I feel like a bloody turncoat, thought Neville. *How could I leave Sir William behind, after all he's done for me? I should stop at the Yard office and see if our departure can be postponed. I should have gone to the Admiralty and asked today. But what would I say? That Chapman fellow doesn't want the word out, and I suspect Sir William would not want the Admiralty aware of any connection between us. I suppose I have no choice but to act like a Navy officer and do as I'm ordered. Is there nothing I can do? The thought of Marion makes it the worse. I so look forward to seeing her!*

11 - "Chapman's Research"

"**W**hat have we got, Mr. Franz?" asked Chapman, a medium tall man of average build. He was not as fit as the average seafaring lieutenant, but he was a desk-sailor, after all, sporting a slight bulge at the waist. His thick, bushy brown hair was cropped shorter than sailors, probably because he spent considerable time beneath a wig.

"Not much, I'm afraid. Sir Mulholland didn't tell anyone where he planned to go, or why... at least none we know of; but we've learned a little. We assume he went to meet someone for intelligence... to receive some package he thought very important. And he wouldn't have gone unless he knew the person he went to see. We know where he went - first, at least. He took a ship to Falmouth. And we know he took his guard, Corporal Truett, because we found him dead on the North Coast - a small town named Portreach. I'm sorry to put it this way, but we assume, therefore, that Truett wasn't involved. And he was a man I wouldn't want to try taking on alone, so we assume there were several attackers.

"They found another man found dead as well... in Penryn, just there by Falmouth. The police believe he's been dead more than two weeks. Quite a stir in the area – two dead bodies. They don't know of any connection between the two, but we do. A shopkeeper in town says Sir Mulholland knew the second dead man. His name is Otto Ames, and he's the man Sir Mulholland went to see, according to Mr. Gregory - who knows nothing more, really. Because of this second murder victim, we believe Sir Mulholland traveled only to Penrhyn before being lured toward the Atlantic Coast somehow. Since we haven't found a trace of him, we assume he's been abducted."

"No note? No requests for ransom or other demands?"

"No, sir. Nothing."

"Where did he go, then, and why, Mr. Franz?"

"Our best supposition, sir, is France. He would be taken there simply for interrogation, maybe for Boney to make a spectacle of him and embarrass Britain, or for exchange"

"Possible, but in my mind, not likely. Britain doesn't even admit the man works for the military. Our story is   he's just a bureaucrat. What else do we have?"

"The only other strange thing is his visitors. There have been three people in to visit with Sir Mulholland in the last few days - not the normal people - two foreigners, and now Captain Burton this morning."

"I saw nothing suspicious about Caaptain Burton, and he says he just got in from Jamaica with Admiral Warren. Check that out, if you would please, Mr. Franz, and bring in those other two… Who were they, again?

"A Frenchman, who might be one of Sir Mulholland's… umm… associates, and the pretty little American girl, Miss Stillwater, who seems to have no connection to anything, except that she asked if anyone knew how to contact the Frenchman."

"Why would an American - particularly a woman, whether she is pretty or not - want to contact one of Sir Mulholland's 'associates' - unless she is another 'associate' that we know nothing about? Are we sure we have all of Sir Mulholland's records? Does he keep personal dossiers anywhere?"

"Not that I know of, but we can look again."

"Please do, Mr. Franz, and find those two visitors. They have something to do with this, I'm sure of it now. Let's have them in for tea and a little chat."

"Tea, sir?"

"Of course I don't mean tea, Mr. Franz - just the chat. Really..."

"Aye, Sir. I'll send our men to the addresses they gave us."

By half three Mr. Chapman heard talking and the stamping of marines' boots in the hallways outside his office, and a few seconds afterward there came a knock at his door. Franz stuck his head in and said, "Mister Cadoudal is in room eight, Sir."

"And Miss Stillwater?"

"Dunno, Sir. We haven't heard back yet."

Chapman walked to room eight, tapped a couple times on the door, and walked in. "Hello," he said in the cheeriest tone he could manage. "I'm so very glad to see you back. How can I help you?"

"Help me? I didn't think you gave me a choice about returning. How do you think I can help you? I am just a journalist."

"Ah, yes, but journalists have such freedom to move about these days, don't they?" He stopped there.

"*Oui, oui.* Yes, I suppose. So...?"

"So, I am wondering if you are doing a story about the bureaucrats of London... Sir Mulholland, in particular."

The farcical conversation lasted another five minutes, until Chapman said, "Possibly you cannot help me after all, Mr. Cadoudal. Would you mind waiting a minute more?"

Georges squirmed a bit in his seat, but replied nonchalantly, "No, no. It is no problem. I have no deadline today." He remained sitting while Chapman exited the room.

Chapman returned to his office, where Franz awaited him. "The messenger sent to Miss Stillwater's hotel has returned without her, Sir. She has moved out of the Saxon Arms - suddenly - and did not advise the clerk of her destination, except to mention her fiancé's flat being available to her."

"Some man who is away, then? Or maybe not? Some man she expected would not be away? Captain Burton? I don't think I will get anywhere with this Frenchman, unless we go to more serious questioning, either. Have you found any more dossiers?"

The hallway became alive with noise again, but this time louder, and from the outer foyer, not the little hallway by the offices. It sounded like the fracas included a woman's voice, which was quite unusual, and it continued for three or four minutes. It suddenly became quite loud, but only for the time it would take for someone to open a door and pass through it. Franz and Chapman looked at each other. Marine boots came tramping down the hall toward them. There was a knock at the door.

"Yes?"

A marine sentry from the outer foyer tramped in and stamped his feet. "There is a woman in the lobby, Sirs. She's quite unruly, as you might have heard, and insists on speaking to you."

"To whom?" asked Franz.

"Either of you, Sirs, or both, she said. She's demanding to know what you've done with some captain."

"Short... pretty?"

"Very, Sir... and very angry."

"Hmm, Mr. Franz," said Chapman, "So here she is. Fetch her in, sentry. Let's get on," said Chapman.

The sentry left, but returned shortly, with Marion a polite few steps behind. She had achieved her objective of getting inside, and would now play the subservient and demure young lady.

"Ah, Miss... Still...?"

"Water, Mr. Chapman. Stillwater. Thank you for seeing me. I appreciate you giving me a bit of your valuable time."

"Certainly, Miss Stillwater, but my sentry didn't seem to think you gave him a choice."

"We always have choices, don't we, Mr. Chapman?'

"Yes, of course. Would you do me the favor of sitting here in this little room for a moment? You weren't expected, you know, and I have another guest to entertain..."

Chapman 'parked' her in room ten, and left.

"Oh, my goodness, Mr. Franz. I will certainly agree she is angry. It flows out her pores. Have you found any dossiers?"

"I have, yes. Sir Mulholland had his own little collection in the wall unit behind his desk. Look at these!"

Mr. Chapman thumbed quickly through the stack, selected three of immediate interest, removed them from the stack, and went into room ten.

"How do you know the Frenchman?" he asked Marion, brusquely.

"There are many Frenchmen, even here in England. You haven't yet said which Frenchman."

"Mr. Georges Cadoudal." He opened one of the folders he'd brought in, looked down, and began to read.

"He's here? Why wouldn't you tell me how to contact him?"

"We are not a 'lost persons bureau', Miss Stillwater, as I assume you know." He went further out the limb: "Would you like us to divulge, to anyone who demanded entrance, where you are?"

Marion squirmed in her seat.

"How do you know him?"

Since she was in Mulholland's office, she decided it would be safe to answer the question as directly as she could, and briefly described her trip to France some time before.

"So, you do, indeed, know my Frenchman. I see another name in Sir Mulholland's dossiers, Marion: Ellen Aughton. It says she is an American, as you are, I see - where is she?"

"She lives in Boston. Why do you ask?"

"Would she help us?"

"She would do anything for me, as I would for her, and she is fond of Sir Mulholland, too, I believe... and because she is married to an English Navy Captain who is a particular friend of Captain Burton. I cannot guarantee anything, of course. For all I know she may be with child... or have a small child; it's been long enough. Again, why do you ask?"

"Mr. Franz slipped me another note just now, you may have noticed. His... people... have the idea this whole affair was a plot to abduct Sir Mulholland, and with great probability, they took him aboard a ship. Furthermore, it appears the ship is not French, but the American cutter *Spirit of Concord,* bound for your city of Baltimore."

"And?"

"And we need all the help we can get. These dossiers," Chapman said, holding up the folders he'd been reading, "lead me to a very different conclusion than I had come to earlier. Rather than suspect you, the Frenchman, and Captain Burton - although Burton is unlikely, having just arrived from Jamaica - I now think you are the team we need to get him back. You can identify him, he knows what you know, apparently, every one of you speaks French - and I still think France is where someone intends to take him at some point - and you have your own personal reasons for wanting him safe. I don't believe I could assemble another such team on short notice. This would be an entirely voluntary assignment, and dangerous. Will you help?"

"I came here to help with something, as did Georges, although I doubt this has anything at all to do with it. We were supposed to meet with Sir William about it."

"Sir William?"

"Excuse me; I meant Sir Mulholland... my fiancé's Godfather."

"Oh, yes, of course. As I said, 'personal reasons' for wanting him back."

Chapman pulled a bell cord, and the door opened almost immediately. "Mr. Franz, will you escort the Frenchman here, please?"

They waited another minute, the door creaked open again, and Georges stepped in. He had a very French look to him, particularly when he wore his cravat, as he did now. He was a heavy fellow of average height; not fat, but strong-looking, with a clean-shaven square chin, curly hair, wide-set brown eyes, and bushy eyebrows. His eyes lit up when he saw Marion, and he crossed the room as she stood for his embrace and the expected kiss. "Oh, Georges, it is so good to see you," Marion said. "I've been here just three days and I haven't seen Neville at all. These fellows," she said, waving her hand at Chapman and Franz, "wouldn't tell me where you were, and now Neville's been sent off to Jamaica by the Admiralty, I'm sure he has. I just missed him at his flat. He's probably sailing any day." She began to tremble, and a tear or two escaped her eyes.

"Neville? Why is Captain Burton 'Neville' to this Frenchman?" Chapman demanded. He seemed to be more annoyed with the familiarity of this group than anything.

Georges began, "We met in Toulon some years ago, at the behest of..."

"Toulon? Toulon is French. What was a British Captain doing in France?"

"He was a midshipman then."

Chapman stared at him. "That's supposed to explain it?" he asked. "He was a midshipman."

"Well, no," said Georges, "but then we met again," following his usual process of avoiding answering direct questions by changing the subject, "aboard the *Sans Pareil* at the great battle of the Glorious First of June, I believe you call it..."

"You were both there, aboard an English Third-rate?"

"Yes, but... no, she was French then..."

"Then what was a British midshipman doing on a French ship?"

"Because his ship, the *Castor*... This is not a short story, Mr. Chapman. What would you have me say?"

"Oh, bother it. You're right. Let's get on with it. Here's my plan: I will send a message to Portsmouth by telegraph, ordering Captain Burton's ship to be delayed, and asking him to report back here."

"Ohhh," shuddered Marion, plumping down in her chair.

"Then," Chapman continued, "I will write a letter to this Ellen Aughton..."

"Dagleishe," corrected Marion. "She married a British Captain, remember?"

Chapman politely said, "Oh, yes, thank you," although he gave Marion a glare. "I will ask her - assuming she is still 'available' - if she could either find a way to clear us diplomatically to poke around in Baltimore, or whether she, herself, could travel to Baltimore to see if she can find anything about an oddly-treated passenger on the *Spirit of Concord*. I'll have it sent on the fastest available advice boat, and it might even be there before the *Spirit of Concord*. I'll ask you two to think about something else," said Chapman. "I'll send the letter to Mrs. Dagleishe, but we have no idea if anything will ever come of it. We can have Captain Burton establish a small 'chase squadron' in the hope it could catch the return of the *Spirit of Concord* to France, but we must decide if it is necessary to make some 'excursion' into Napoleon's very backyard to catch them if they slip past by sea. Captain Burton should return in three to four days. Be ready for my call. I have things to do, now. Mr. Franz will see you out."

The advice boat *Stork*, Archibald Mewes commanding, stood from Spithead that very afternoon, carrying light ballast and a single letter to Boston. She sailed in the best of conditions for a fast passage: a full gale blasting down the English Channel from the North Sea.

12 - "The End of the Active"

The *Rose of Devon,* Neville's transport from London, waited for the sunrise before entering the anchorage, but dropped her best bower shortly thereafter, concluding a sail of three days. She chose a spot near the commercial quays of Portsmouth. The harbor was already busy with small boats carrying freight and people from the many merchants anchored about, so it did not take long to hail one of them for a ride to shore. Neville had no sea chest to transport – only a small bag of clothes and toiletries – and so decided to walk the two or three miles to the navy facilities. After only fifteen minutes walk, however, he had the surprise of discovering someone familiar preparing to launch a boat.

Midshipman Foyle and Lieutenant Miller stood at the poop railing with their morning coffee – lounging, really, without much planned for the day – watching the harbor's boat traffic and considering the weather.

"Something's amiss today, Lieutenant Miller," said Foyle. "Look at those clouds there. And the wind's out of the East. My grandmother always said, 'An east wind blows no good'," and I can't say I would disagree."

"Aye, Mr. Foyle. I would wager we'll see a blow in two to three days, if not sooner. But why do you worry? We'll not be out in it. It might be quite nice for a day below with a new book or an ale by the fire in some pub ashore. I favor the latter, myself."

"I'll go in with you, even if it means a wet ride in the boat. What's this, here?"

"It's the launch coming home. Why now, I wonder? First Lieutenant Towers said he might be gone a couple days."

"First Lieutenant Towers spouted a load of shite, I think," said Foyle. "He told me had relatives in the area, and he was going to go look 'em up. It sounded fishy to me, and then the next day he says he's going to buy some bits and bobs for his personal stores before he loses the chance… yeah, it's our boat, and it's coming at us… I think it all were lies, though. You just see if he's carrying any 'personal stores' when he climbs out of the boat. I say he went 'looking for love', if you get my meaning." He gave Miller three silly big-eyed winks.

"Hand me the glass, if you would, Mr. Foyle," said Miller. "I don't think Lieutenant Towers is alone."

Foyle gave his coffee a loud slurp before walking over to get the glass from its mainmast becket. "Here you are, Sir."

Miller raised the glass toward the oncoming boat, and suddenly stiffened. "Towers ain't alone. There's two in the stern sheets. Cap'n's with him. Call out, Mr. Foyle! Wake 'em up down there!"

Foyle trotted the few steps forward to the quarterdeck rail. He spotted Boatswain Strugnell lounging on bundle of canvas that was a jib sail under repair. With time to kill, he held a fat roll of smoking tobacco and sat talking with his mates. "Mr. Strugnell, prepare to pipe the side! Captain's on his way out!"

Strugnell didn't move. He continued to lie there, giving Foyle a vapid stare.

"Mr. Strugnell, get lively, man!"

Strugnell sat up and hollered back, "What are you about, Mr. Foyle? You gave me quite a start. I thought you said the Captain is on his way out. He's in London, you know."

"Not now he ain't. He's in the boat with Lieutenant Towers." Now Foyle wagged his arm back and forth in a point-point-point gesture, and waved the glass for effect.

"Shite," yelled Strugnell, jumping to his feet. He started blowing his pipe immediately following, and running forward. The response to his pipe was the rumbling noise of running marines and others with ceremonial duties associated with the captain's return. Several of the marines were still buckling belts and pulling on boots by the time Mr. Foyle hailed the boat: "Who goes?"

"*La Désirée*," came the proper response, and the drummer boy, who had only at the last moment found his drumsticks, began beating. To the ship's credit, they managed a proper reception.

Neville stepped quickly up into the main chains and onto the deck, saluted the colors, and turned to cast his eyes quickly across the decks. He gave Strugnell an unfriendly glance, but said nothing, except, "What's this, here?"

The others followed his gaze shoreward, to where another small launch crawled its way across the water toward them. There were many boats about, but this one had the look of navy and approached from the direction of the yard. They all watched quietly as it came.

"Who goes?" cried Mr. Foyle again.

"Message for Captain Burton," called the Coxswain. The little boat soon came alongside, where its painter was handed to Foyle. The message followed. Foyle handed it up to Neville directly.

Neville would normally have taken a message below to read in his cabin, but since this one had no packet, or even an envelope, he simply unfolded the terse telegraph message there and read it.

PORTSMOUTH:

CAPTAIN BURTON / LA DESIREE

DO NOT SAIL. RETURN TO LONDON.

CHAPMAN

"Does God love a duck?" He queried aloud. He turned to his men, and said, "Good morning, everyone. Hello and good-bye. I'm going to London as soon as Mr. Foyle can find me a ship." He went below.

Neville's sentry knocked shortly before noon. Neville assumed it to be the customary call to declare the new day, but when he looked up from his little desk, Foyle stood in the door. "I've found you one, Sir," he said. The brig *Active*, leaving tomorrow for Chatham, the master says, 'despite the weather'."

"What's wrong with the weather?"

"Looks dodgy, Sir."

Active stood for London on the late-morning tide, with Neville standing beside Master Joshua Pincus as she worked her way past Southsea.

"If it were up to me, I'd stay in port this morning, Captain," said Pincus. I don't like this much east in the wind, and the clouds are odd."

"It is a bit strange, I'll admit," Neville said, "but I have orders to go."

"As do I. The owners are quite clear that if this cargo of herrings can't go on *Active*, they'll go on some other ship. It's Beachy Head I'm worried about. If this picks up, we'll be trying to weather the head at high current, and just go nowhere."

The weather did prove to be troublesome; the little ship worked its way east into the wind, while the seas grew higher and the wind veered south.

"I'll not go farther out tonight, Captain," declared Pincus. "We'll tack for shore in the middle of the night and come away again when we see something. The seas are beyond my liking."

At dawn, they tacked away from shore, and were making very little headway. "This is a miserable passage, Captain. I've a mind to put in somewhere."

"It is, for sure. Look. There comes a small ship, cracking on. Do you have a glass handy?"

"Aye. There under the binnacle. Why do you care?"

"A navy habit, I suppose. She'll pass quite close, if we stay on our tacks. I should be able to read her name. She looks Navy."

Twenty minutes later the small sail had grown. The ship passed close, indeed, and Neville could read her name: *Stork. My word*, thought Neville, *It's Commander Archibald Mewes. I wish I were on his mission today. He's getting quite a ride!*

The seas had grown to five feet and more, with an occasional standing wave of two or three feet caused by the strong tidal flow. "I'm not sure we're stemming this tide," said Master Pincus, "and it's becoming extremely uncomfortable." As if the ocean had heard him, the next large wave pounded the bows hard, sending green water rushing down the foredeck and spray completely over the ship. They had not yet switched to tarpaulin jackets, and now their boat cloaks were wet; soaked through in patches. Another similar wave hit only two minutes later.

"Pfft," uttered Pincus, blowing saltwater off his mustache. "That's enough for me. We're going in to Cuckmere Haven."

"Where?" Neville asked.

"Just behind Beachy Head – to our North, here. A small river comes out there, and there's a break in these great white cliffs. We can anchor and wait. There should be some protection from Beachy Head herself."

"This doesn't look to be the best harbor for a storm," Neville said when he saw the little open roadstead.

"Maybe not, but it's what we've got. We've ducked in here before, and my men are familiar with it."

"Two anchors, Mr. Stokes," Pincus said to his first mate.

Active had her anchors down twenty minutes later, but Neville and Pincus did not go immediately below. "I'll stay on deck and watch fifteen minutes or so to be sure we're well anchored," said Pincus. "We're closer to the surf line than I'd like, but there's not much choice here."

"So I see. I'll stay with you. I have a line between a rock on the beach and a small tree inland. I haven't seen us drag yet."

"Mr. Stokes," Pincus yelled over the din of the remaining sails and sheets being tied down, "Be sure to keep the jib and main stays'l very handy."

"Aye, sir," he answered.

"It's been twenty minutes, Captain," said Pincus. "I think we're holding. May I offer you a whiskey?"

"Aye, Sir, I agree. Let's go below."

Neville followed Pincus below to his tiny cabin, where Pincus found a jar of brown liquid and a couple little metal cups. He poured each of them a couple fingers of the liquid, and they sat on his little stools.

"Ah, a very nice thing for a day… Did you feel that?" asked Neville.

"I think not. I was just sitting."

"Maybe I'm imagining. I thought I felt a very slight thump, as if we'd touched bottom."

The two sat motionless for a moment, hearing and feeling nothing disturbing. Pincus timed his first sip with a large wave that rolled beneath the ship. The bow rose first, then the whole ship came up on it, and finally the stern. The wave had gone when Pincus took his sip, and the stern continued to fall. At the very trough of the departing wave, the ship trembled heavily and they heard the crack of wood.

"The rudder struck!" shouted Pincus. The two men leaped to their feet, splashing whiskey about the little room as they raced for the door. Pincus was up and out first, yelling for Stokes before his head even reached deck level.

Men were running about in near panic by the time Neville reached the deck. He looked to shore. His rock and tree were no longer in line. "We've dragged anchor, sure!" he yelled to Pincus.

"Sails up, sails up!" Pincus screamed at Stokes, who already had men on the job. "Aye, dragged," yelled Pincus. "Lend us a hand, Captain. Clap on that halyard."

Another large wave rolled slowly beneath *Active*, culminating with another hard thump on the bottom. The sails were up.

"Sheets, there, man! Sheet 'er home," Pincus howled. The roar of flogging sails ended with two distinct cracks when each sail filled with wind, and the ship heeled hard to starboard. She began to move toward the open sea. "Get ready on the anchors, Mr. Stokes. She should tear them out of the bottom as we pass over."

Another wave stuck the heeled ship, sending green water across the deck and down the companion where Pincus and Neville had just climbed out. Pincus was calming, however. "We might make it, Captain. It won't be the first time we've had a little water below."

But the fates conspired. *Active* moved thirty feet toward safety when she came up hard against the first anchor cable. Pincus had no time to scream any order like 'cut the cable', for the ship was struck at the same moment, hard on the starboard bow, by another wave. Stokes and Neville were both thrown off their feet. The force of the wave spun the ship to larboard – not all 'round, but just enough to put her in irons. The roar of flailing sails and sheet renewed, and the ship slid sideways thirty feet to larboard in seconds. With this second yank, the anchor did not hold. *Active* landed cruelly, the length of her hull on rock and sand beneath the water.

Pincus knew it was done. "Abandon ship!" he bellowed, after a moment of sincere disbelief, "Abandon ship. Get yourselves to the beach, every one 'o you!"

A man stood unsteadily on the rail for a moment, and then jumped and began swimming. Two more jumped. *I see,* thought Neville. *The ones who can swim are first to go. They'll make an example for the others, though.* Four men jumped off the bow, two from the stern. One stood shaking at the rail. Pincus threw him over, and followed.

Active had been shoved even closer to the beach, each wave hitting her harder as more of her tilted hull became exposed; each wave dropping her harder onto the bottom with sickening cracking noises. Neville stood on the rail, holding onto a main shroud for steadiness.

I must time it so the ship is not pitched over on me when I go in, he thought. *Ready, Now!*

Neville's first awareness was the cold. It stopped his breath for a minute after his head came above the frothing surface. His leg, where it had been broken by a cannon explosion years ago, screamed at his brain, threatening to incapacitate him. It was frigid; not warm, comforting Jamaica. He was next aware of being thrown toward shore, then thinking his feet were above his head. His mind played tricks: *'Come up, Neville, swim to the surface'*, cried Maria, his first Jamaican fiancée, *'this is water, not sand. You can swim'*. Then down again. *Maria, which way is up? Can I come see you?*

She answered his aching brain: *No, Neville. It's not your time. Go back and love Marion. Have children with her.* His face met something hard, yet forgiving. Sand, pebbles... both; beach. The tumbling surf jerked his left arm behind his head, and then sat him in two feet of cold water. A wave knocked hard on his back, bending him so far forward that he smacked his lip on one knee. Before the next one, he pulled his screaming leg inward and under him with his hands, and rolled forward to stand. Another wave kicked him forward; his face thrust into the sand and pebbles again, so he crawled, spitting blood from his split lip, and salt, sand, and pebbles. Waves hit him twice more before he reached a place where the waves were small enough to allow him to get to his feet. He dragged those recalcitrant feet one after the other through two feet of water; then one foot, six inches, and none. He stood numbly on the strand, beginning to realize he'd survived. *My goodness*, he thought, *I have both my shoes.*

Most men seemed to have made it ashore, but a couple were rolling, lifeless or near so, in the surf. Several showed small injuries, like Neville's split lip. Pincus lay there too, half in the water a few yards away. Neville watched two men sit him up; he retched out salt water and began looking around.

Recovery did not go quickly, but by an hour later, most of the men were gathered in the lee of large clumps of grasses and low banks at the east end of the strand. Master Pincus, with Neville's help, began to create some organization.

"We need to gather everything we can save, men," he announced. "The more the better, and I promise I'll get you at least some of your pay somehow. Have we got everyone?"

Someone in the back said, "Thomas has run. He'll not be back… nor Edgar. They're both from 'round here. Just as well. I got sick of hearing 'em complain."

"William's gone too. I'm sure he's not in the water, but he'll be back," said another. "He's from 'round here, too, and he'll bring us help."

"None dead, then?"

"We don't think so. Some swallowed a barrel of water, but we've pumped 'em dry."

The men set themselves to gathering flotsam from the ship. "Pile it here, men," Pincus ordered. "Keep it tight together, and we'll post a watch. We'll have vultures here soon enough."

"There's a barrel, Mr. Stokes. Grab that, if you please, and Mr. Thompson, there's a hatch cover floating over there. It might serve nicely for a table. There's some rope over there to pull in, Mr. Jay. We'll have that to help gather other bits." And so it went for the next hour, as the pile of flotsam grew. Ship's planks, line and blocks, barrels of water, herrings, and even butter were hauled in as the ship went slowly to pieces. The masts were off her by then, and she was in half, but the ocean did not stop pounding her bones.

"If it don't go quiet soon, there will be very little left by morning," said Pincus, with a genuine tear in his eye.

"Here's young William now," somebody announced. "He's got a wagon."

"Yeah, and he's got vultures behind him," said another. Several townspeople from Seaford had followed William. A small knot of them gathered at the far end of the strand.

"Haloo, William," said Pincus. "We can't thank you enough for coming back. Should we expect ill from these people you have behind you?"

"Not unless you leave all this unguarded. Shipwrecks are not uncommon along this coast, and they're a welcome source of extras for the people of the area. Sometimes the ship's company just walks away from it. If they do, the townsmen have it all faster than you can say 'Queen Anne'."

"And where do we take our goods in the wagon?"

"My uncle has a large barn to the north of town. He was happy to hear you might pay a small storage fee. If I didn't tell a lie when I said you would, we should start loading."

"It sounds like your best option, Master Pincus," said Neville. "I'll go with William on the first load, as his guard. I must go. I have orders to be at Whitehall yesterday, and there's not much more I can do here. I'll leave you my knife. I'm sure there are several more amongst the men. You can defend."

"Aye. We'd better be loading. I'll choose the most valuable things first, and I'll send another man along to learn the way, since you're not coming back."

"Will we pass a stable on the way, William?" Neville asked the young man after the loaded wagon began clattering along the sand road toward town.

"Aye, Sir. Jacob Landon's. It's a fair big 'un. He's got horses, donkeys and mules, three hauling wagons and a four-horse coach. He cares for the parson's chaise, too."

"Excellent. Take me there. I'll buy a horse for my ride to London. Do you know the way?"

"To London? No. I ain't never been so far north by land. Jacob will know."

Jacob did, indeed, know most of the way. "I can't give good directions into the center of London," he said, "but from here, I think you should simply take the road north to Lewes, then Lickfield and Maresfield, and from there on to Croyden. Then you'd better ask some local for the next part. You'll be pretty close in to London by then. It's nigh on seventy mile," he volunteered.

Ugh, Neville thought. *That will mean at least three days on a horse – probably four. I do dislike horses! But it looks like the bad weather is done for a while.* "And a knife? Do you have something I can use for my defense on the road?"

Should I go straight in to Whitehall? Neville wondered in a moment when the horse refused to go farther without grazing. The horse moved to the next patch of green grass. *How silly. I simply cannot appear at Whitehall looking – oh, no, smelling – like this. I've never seen anyone appear there in anything but their best, regardless of how poor their best is. To the flat, then. I must go there first, and clean up. I have no idea why my summons was so urgent. Perhaps Chapman has decided I'm guilty of abducting Sir William. If that's correct, then I would need to defend myself at a courts-*

martial. I cannot look and smell like this. They have no idea what time I arrive in London, anyway.

The horse began plodding forward. *He's looking for water, now, I'm sure. How I do detest horses.*

The rural lanes became small roads, then larger roads, and the buildings began to crowd in. Soon the distance between buildings decreased to naught; they became row houses, increasingly covered with soot. The horse could find nothing to eat, although there were occasional fountains to drink from, and so it just plodded forward.

Neville had reached the point, as many travelers do, when he decided that another day in an inn – or lying in a field – was not worth the trouble. He plodded on, finally arriving at 42 Bedford Avenue at about ten in the morning. He knocked at Mrs. Brown's door, and waited patiently. After a couple minutes, he knocked again. The second knock caused some noise inside, and shortly a voice within called out, "Who is it?"

"Captain Burton," he replied.

Her little peephole opened. An eye appeared, and then the whole door opened suddenly. "Oh, my dear Captain," she blurted, beginning to step forward to hug him. She stopped short. Her face wrinkled up.

"I know, Mrs. Brown. I must look a sight – and smell worse. I need a key. I'm afraid mine is at the bottom of the Channel."

"The bottom of... oh, my..." She bustled off. When she returned, she had his key. "I tried to catch you," she began.

"Catch me? When?"

"When you left last. I went into the street and waved my kerchief. I know you saw me. You waved back."

"Ah, yes, I remember; very sweet of you. I should love to hear the whole story later, but right now, I'm truly knackered. After noon, then?" he said.

Mrs. Brown said no more as Neville walked quickly down the hall.

Neville noticed a slight but delicate aroma at the door to his flat, but it rang no bells in his brain. The key worked. When he opened the door, the aroma flowed over him. There was no mistaking Marion's presence. *She's here? How could she be here?* "Marion?" He cried. "Are you here?" He rushed from one room to the next, but no person appeared. *She has been here, though. Her things are here — everywhere. The closet... has her dresses. What did Mrs. Brown try to tell me?* Neville ran back the hall to Mrs. Brown's door, and rapped impatiently. She soon returned to the threshold.

"Mrs. Brown, is Marion here?"

"Yes, she is. I tried to tell you, but when you walked off, I decided you must know."

"How could I have known?"

"I don't know." She began to ramble, "She visited the day before you left, but you weren't here. Then you were, but you left early. That's when I waved in the street, as you remember. I didn't know her hotel, so I couldn't contact her there, but then she moved in the next day... the day after you left, but you never came back, and she was angry with me for not telling you, but you left in the hack, and then I have no way to contact you, and..."

"I'm very sorry, Mrs. Brown. I don't mean to upset you. Where might she be now?"

"If she's not in, I would guess she's out on errands. She seems to be out quite a bit, but she must be quite a window shopper, because she rarely comes in with packages."

Not errands, then, is it? She goes to Whitehall, I'd bet on it. Well, I can't run over there like this. Marion's here! She's really here! Is Sir William back, for all love?

"Mrs. Brown, will you give me an hour's rest, but then run a bath? Oh, and there's a horse out front. You may have the animal. You may ride him or make horse porridge, for all I care.

Precisely at noon, Captain Burton stepped out the door of number 42 into Bedford Street, and turned right to walk down to the Strand and over to Whitehall. He felt considerably better, notwithstanding only an hour's sleep. The thought of meeting Marion far overpowered his concern of a court-martial. *If Marion is, indeed, working in some way with Whitehall, then there is far less chance I am in trouble, too. I doubt she would play any part against me.* As gray cloud passed overhead, dropping rain. Not much rain, but more than a drizzle, and the sun reappeared, accompanied by a light breeze. *In all, a very nice day for a walk. And far better than riding a bloody horse!*

Arriving at the familiar door, he brushed off a few drops of water remaining on his epaulettes and stepped inside. The usual marine guard greeted him, now with a hint of recognition, and the guard did not suggest that he might be in the wrong building. He was escorted to the wig-hat fellow in the back vestibule, and there asked to sit. Mr. wig-hat opened the door to the office, but did not enter.

Neville heard voices inside, and footsteps approaching… and he recognized at least one voice: Georges! Mr. wig-hat stepped aside, and Georges emerged, suddenly finding himself face-to-face with Neville, who had jumped to his feet.

"Captain Burton, I declare!" bellowed Georges. "Here you are at last." He reached forward instinctively; quickly grabbing hold of Neville's shoulders and jerking him forward to plant a kiss on each cheek in the French style, but then shoving him back to arms' length to add, "You look well, except you've done something to your face. Where have you been?"

Through the entire greeting, Neville strained to see behind Georges to get a better look at something else he'd just had a glimpse of: Marion.

A gray and blue blur then elbowed Georges aside and threw itself at Neville. "Oof," he said, as Marion's firm body thumped against his chest. She didn't let go, either, for at least a minute. Chapman watched the whole scene with obvious amusement, including waving off the marine sentry who had come at a trot when he heard the disturbance.

"Back inside, everyone," Chapman ordered. "Now we have business to attend to."

Neville had so worried himself over the idea of being arrested, that this nonchalance about his arrival – except Marion's concern for his face – left him befuddled. *The concern is not for me. And what is Marion's concentration on my face?*

"I've sent a packet to Boston," began Chapman, once they were back in his office…"

"Ahh, Commander Mewes, I expect."

"How on earth? How do you people always know…? Oh, bother. Yes, yes… Mewes. And why are you so late? You should have been here days ago."

"Truly, Neville," said Marion. "I've been quite worried."

"*Stork* sailed past us – the merchant ship *Alert* – just before we went on the beach at Cuckmere Haven."

"On the beach? As in… shipwrecked?" spluttered Chapman.

"Ahem… Yes, shipwrecked… not quite sailing ourselves onto the rocks…" *I must make this seem not so dangerous, or Marion will certainly fly off.* "The anchors drug, and we quickly found ourselves within the surf line. A simple mishap; nothing more."

"Any hands lost?"

"No; some injuries. Two run off."

"And that's what happened to your face, isn't it, Neville?" queried Marion. "No danger at all, despite almost being killed."

"One tumbles about in the surf, is all," he said, "But there is land beneath, and one simply walks out. See? Here I am."

"With a fat, split lip, yes. Hrmmph... sailors." Marion crossed her arms and sat waiting for Chapman to continue.

He did, outlining the plans they had created, including the formation of a 'chase squadron' to intercept the *Spirit of Concord* when she made her expected return. Neville's part was to organize the squadron in Portsmouth, and then return to be on watch within easy contact in London.

Neville and Marion were not unhappy with the plan.

13 - "Stillwater of Baltimore"

The bell jingled when Michael Stearns opened the door to the little lobby of the Harford Inn on Pratt Street in Baltimore. The clerk behind the desk looked up from his Bible to greet him with a simple "Hello."

"Do you have a room available for a few months?" Michael asked.

"We certainly do. It's your lucky day. With all the goings-on in this city, we have been as busy as the proverbial beaver, but one has just opened up."

"I know a Miss Stillwater who stayed here for a while a month or so back. Do you remember her?"

"I certainly do. Most cheerful thing, and quite pretty, yes?"

"Most likely her, yes. Is her room available? She told me it was particularly delightful."

"Hmmm…" The clerk began paging through his guest book. "Room Four," he said. "No. Our best room, but not available."

"I'll take whatever you have, but will you make a note to move me as soon as room four comes open?" *I really must stay where she slept.*

"Why certainly, sir. Sign here, please." He pushed the book across the desk.

Michael stayed there while he waited for the delivery of his 'man from London'. He moved to room 4 when it came available. He didn't know when a second room would be needed for his 'guest', but, given time for sailing back and forth, he estimated it would be sometime after mid-August. When the time came, he booked the second room, as well.

He also took a sales job with the Stillwater Rum Trading Company. The job would keep him busy and highly amused, as well as affording him weekly pay. Even better, he would be paid by Chester Stillwater. He assumed if Mr. Arnold did write Chester and tell him of it, there would be no response from Jamaica ordering him to be removed from the premises, before he left of his own accord. He prepared himself to receive his hostage by buying a child's toy constable badge (who knows what one looks like, anyway?), a pistol like the police carried, and a modern set of handcuffs.

14 - "Stork's Beat Westward"

The *Spirit of Concord*, having no time-sensitive cargo, took the longer and easier route to Baltimore, south past the Canary Islands and across to a point in the Ocean near the Bahamas Islands, before she turned north. She may have taken the high end of the sixty to eighty days typical sailing time westward, but not so long as to concern her owners. She appeared in Baltimore roughly on schedule. Before entering the harbor, Mulholland was again locked in his cabin... with apologies from the Master.

'Constable' Michael Stearns appeared to take custody of his prisoner very shortly after the shore crew came to unload cargo. He arrived, copper badge displayed prominently on his jacket lapel, within half an hour of *Spirit's* tying alongside the quay. He also wore a police sidearm, and brought a shiny set of handcuffs.

Mulholland knew he had arrived in Baltimore. Even locked below, no one could miss the sounds and movements of arrival... thumping alongside the pier, shouting of the line handlers, absence of sea motion, the running about as sails came down... and then relative quiet for the half hour before a polite knock came at the door. *How ridiculous*, he thought, *I'm locked in, and this fellow knocks at my door?*

The lock clicked over, and the door opened. In front of Mulholland stood a robust man about six feet tall, with a square jaw suggestive of a marine sergeant. He appeared to be near forty years of age, confident, and wearing a great grin and a fine suit of civilian clothes, the police accoutrement notwithstanding. "Hello, Sir Mulholland. I am your host for now. Stearns, Sir. Michael Stearns. I'm much honored to meet you; a pleasure, sir; a pleasure." The 'constable' spoke with a flat accent containing a hint of – what did they call it – an 'American southern drawl'? He extended his hand. Mulholland did not take it.

"Why am I here?" Mulholland asked.

"In good time, good sir; all in good time. First, I offer you a choice. You may give me your parole not to attempt escape, and we can walk out of here as.... ummm... 'associates', or I can take you out in handcuffs and find a small barred room in which to hold you until we ship out. Which will it be?"

"Ship out? To where?"

"Oh, not a question I will answer, sorry." He still grinned, and Mulholland thought to poke him in the face with his fist, but he refrained.

"I will say that I intend to enjoy some very nice meals while you're here, and I invite you to join me. My treat, of course, since you didn't bring any money. Baltimore has some very nice restaurants. We're not in the back woods, as the English would have you believe... no offense intended."

Mulholland thought about it for a minute before concluding that he had nobody in the USA to turn to, no idea where he might run from Baltimore, no idea why he had been taken there, no American money, and no idea who this person was. "My parole, then," he said at last. *At least until I can learn something.*

* * * * *   * * * * *   * * * * *

Aboard the advice-packet *Stork*, Commander Mewes decided not to follow in the wake of the *Spirit of Concord*, but rather beat into the westerlies above the high pressure zone surrounding the Azores. It is a much shorter route, but fraught with the dangers of gales and icebergs. Commander Archibald Mewes was willing to take the risks; they were the keys to advancement... and he lived for the excitement. If *Stork* survived, she had an excellent chance to beat *Spirit*, not by days, but by weeks. She made the passage in sixty-one days, arriving in Boston on the 25th of August.

Archibald personally took the letter ashore, hoping to quickly find the address provided, as soon as *Stork* docked. He found the address – Ellen's house; the same place where Marion had gone to visit – to be a brown-brick row house on a quiet tree-lined street. He thought this an unlikely place to be delivering a letter which he understood to be of great importance to his country, but this was the address given. If a woman of the name written neatly on the envelope matched an inhabitant, then the address must be correct. He walked up the seven stone steps and knocked at the door. He waited. Nothing happened, and then he noticed a bell cord to the side, and pulled it. He knocked again and waited another three of four minutes. He had about decided to leave and try back later, when the door opened. In front of him stood a slender woman in strange form-fitting garb, wet with sweat, peering at him through pretty gray eyes from an oval white face. Her countenance struck him as beautiful. He reminded himself to be most formal, regardless of his assumption that the woman was American, and not English.

"Good morning, Commander," the woman said.

"Oh, you know British naval ranks on short glance? Your name, Miss...?"

"Aughton," she said.

"Might there be another name, Ma'am, or another woman at this address?" *Surely, this woman must be house staff.*

"I suppose I am Mrs. Captain Joseph Dagleishe, to you. You look disappointed. Aughton is my maiden name. They know me by that, around here."

He'd been told she was married to a British captain. "Ah, yes, I forget... This is for you, then," said Archibald, pulling the letter out from inside his jacket. "I am Commander Archibald Mewes of the advice packet *Stork*. I've been sent with this message from someone I am told you will know, and I am to wait for your response, which may be immediate - or I can return in a day for your answer. I am also at your disposal to convey you to any other port you require."

Ellen took the letter from his hand, opened it, and skimmed the contents quickly. "Come back tomorrow, please, Commander; say ten in the morning? I must discuss this with my husband." Joseph was at sea, but she preferred never to tell strangers, even an unusual visitor such as Commander Mewes, that she was alone in the house. Besides, she needed to do some calculations on sailing times and dates before she could agree to the suggestion in the letter.

"Ten it is, Mrs. Dagleishe." He took another gaze into the pretty gray eyes and gave a slight bow before turning to leave.

* * * * *   * * * * *   * * * * *

Inside the house, Ellen studied Mr. Chapman's letter carefully. It explained his suspicion of foul play regarding Mulholland, the reason for his letter to her, and presenting what facts they had. It concluded with a note on the involvement of Neville, Marion and Georges. The letter gave her to know that she must help if she could. She pulled out her calendar and a page of sailing times she had taken from a shipping company a year or two before, when she had considered a visit to Joseph's home town in England. She decided, given the dates written in the letter, that it might be possible to catch Mulholland if he did, indeed, sail for Baltimore on 14th June. If his ship did sail slowly, it might take as long as eighty days, which could therefore be as late as September third.

If, if, if... This Stork may have beaten them across, but I still have to get to Baltimore. What do they think? This isn't England. I can't just call for the Royal Mail coach. Commander Mewes did say he would wait for me, and transport me anywhere, though, did he not? Joseph is away on Galitea. He won't be back for months, I'm sure of it. I can leave a note here at home, as well as write him at any time, and I'm bored here! She packed.

Commander Mewes appeared promptly at ten the next morning. Ellen heard the knock, since she had been waiting for it for an hour. She swung the door open to see a very damp commander standing on the porch this very dreary summer's day. She smiled, partly at knowing this was the beginning of an adventure, and partly at the sight of the bedraggled officer. "Shall we go, Commander? My trunk is there, if you could have your driver carry it out."

"Go, Madam? Where?" asked the astonished Mewes.

"Baltimore, Sir, as quickly as ever we can."

"Aye, aye, Si... Ma'am," Mewes responded. "Driver!" he yelled.

Ellen waited for the driver to come gather her trunk, locked the house door behind them, marched to the carriage, and climbed aboard. Now Mewes smirked... at the audacity of this little powerhouse. He climbed in opposite.

Stork did not stand for Baltimore until the next day, however. They had missed the day's best tide, and they needed water and firewood. Mewes agreed to send a boy to shop for a short list of specialties Ellen requested. He insisted that he could not allow a woman to walk about in the waterfront. He knew he was treading on dangerous ground to offer any sort of compliment to a captain's wife without him present, but he added, "...especially one as fetching as you, Ma'am."

"Ten days, Commander," Ellen said to Mewes when *Stork* opened the mouth of the Patapsco River. "Excellent! Would you be willing to help me find a man... an Englishman visiting this city? It's all in a rush, and if I don't find him quickly, it may be all for naught. What must you do after carrying me to another port?"

"Return to England, of course, but we will be here several days, at the very least, to reprovision. I can leave supplies to my First Officer, and assist you, yes."

"We'll begin in the morning, then, with a search of hotels. I assume he would be kept in a reasonable one, though I could be wrong."

" 'Kept', Ma'am?"

"A possible abduction, Sir. I'll explain in the morning, since you have agreed to assist."

In the morning, they began with a rooming house where she knew Marion had stayed. The address of the Harford Inn on Pratt Street had been on her correspondence. Why not start with something familiar? Archibald and Ellen dismounted the carriage and walked in to the desk. "Excuse me, kind sir," Ellen began, 'We are looking for a friend who may have stayed here. Could you help us?"

"Certainly, Miss. Name?"

"Mulholland," she said. "Mr. William Mulholland."

Mewes coughed. His jaw dropped. He regained his composure quickly, and whispered to Ellen as the clerk began to speak, "I know him!"

"I'm sorry, Miss. You've just missed him. He was..."

"Here? He was *here*? Until when?"

She turned to Mewes. The clerk looked down at his book again.

"Know him from where?" She asked Mewes.

"He stayed here," said the clerk, "together with a Mr. Michael Stearns, until just yesterday."

Ellen's head snapped 'round to face the clerk. "Stearns?" she asked. "Michael Stearns?" *If I know of this place because Marion stayed here, then the reprobate Stearns probably knew it, too.*

"From... From... I can't say," stammered Mewes. "Mrs. Dagleishe... I don't think..."

"Yes, Miss, with Mr. Stearns," the clerk said, giving Mewes a glare. "Three weeks until yesterday, Miss... waiting for a ship. You would think in this town of commerce it wouldn't take long, but they were here for three weeks. Anything else, Miss... Mrs. Dagleishe, did I hear?"

"Correct. Yes, If you could tell us where they've gone?"

"I shouldn't pry into others' affairs, Ma'am, but I believe it's fair to say they were taking the *Pride of Maryland* to France; Le Havre, I believe, with a cargo of wheat. She sailed yesterday, ninth September."

"Do you know what sort of ship, Sir?"

"I think they call it a ship-sloop, Miss, and I hear the local shipbuilders make a joke of her speed. I really don't know more, Miss, sorry. I'm not much on ships."

"Thank you ever so much, Sir. Good Day to you."

Ellen stepped outside. The drizzle had stopped falling, and the summer humidity was increasing. Mewes followed her out. "Commander Mewes, Sir. What caused you such anguish?"

"I know him, if it is indeed *Sir* William Mulholland you seek. It would be a grave thing if he were abducted! What do we do now?"

"How do you know him?"

"I told you... I don't think I'm at liberty to say."

"What rubbish, Commander, why would you not... unless you do the same sorts of things I do..." she trailed off, giving him a crooked look.

"Things you...?"

"Like this, right here today," she said. "Here, read your letter. I don't think there's any danger in it." She pulled it out of her small handbag and handed it to him. A drop of water fell from the eaves into the center of it.

"Let's move to the carriage first," he said. "It's got wet, but not destroyed," Mewes said in the carriage. "This is amazing. Who are these people Mr. Chapman has referenced here at the bottom?"

"I won't say anything about Georges, but Neville Burton is a British Navy Captain..."

"Captain Neville Burton?" Mewes blurted, almost aghast. "I've met him. Carried him from the Med to England... well, not all the way to England... they took him off my *Stork*, herself, and..."

"Yes, yes. Another time, Commander. My husband is a special friend of his, and Marion - that name in the letter, there, is his fiancée, and a very special friend of mine."

"My word," said Mewes, "I'm in the middle of it. I must admit, Mrs. Dagleishe, that I hold Captain Burton as a personal hero. He smoked it that I was on special assignment - from Sir Mulholland - when I picked him up from the *USS Boston* in the Med. I met Sir Mulholland once, but mostly I see this Chapman fellow."

"So what do you say, then, Commander? Chase the *Pride of Maryland?* Writing a letter would be nonsense. It would not get there sooner. We'll have plenty of time for chat."

Mewes smiled wide, "There's nothing I like better than a good chase," he said, "and a ship-sloop cannot ever outrun my *Stork*. We must have tomorrow for provisions, if we don't wish to starve under way, but then..."

15 - "Atlantic Crossing - Eastbound"

"**B**altimore is lovely, is it not, Mr. Mulholland?" Michael asked when the *Pride of Maryland* sailed past Fort McHenry on the bright morning of September 9, 1806. "It was the right time of year to visit. I am pleased we found this ship, too, despite her poor sailing qualities. There aren't many going to France these days."

"Simply lovely," replied Mulholland.

"Has my hospitality not been over the top, Sir? Fine restaurants and an excellent room?"

"But not free to leave."

"No, your wandering off wouldn't work well for me. But, there is no lock on your door aboard ship, you see?"

"Why bother? There's nowhere to go."

"True. Once we arrive in France, you will be given over to our French allies as a show of the commitment of the USA to France. They can do as they wish with you."

"Just how do you plan to convince the French I am of any use to them at all… or if I am who you say I am?"

"That will be my business. But I expect your government will assist me. Once we are there, they will undoubtedly demand your release, which will be proof on its own."

The passage aboard the *Pride of Maryland* was uneventful, save a half gale northeast of Boston and a few days of rain north of the Azores. Mulholland avoided Stearns as much as possible, and made his distaste as obvious as he could. He became reclusive, after about eighteen days, as the ship neared the Western Approaches to the English Channel. The behavior began to worry Stearns.

"Sails, ho!" cried *Pride's* lookout at some point Stearns estimated to be south of Penzance.

"Who would we expect to see, Master Shutwell?"

"The British Channel Fleet, of course, on blockade of the French ports. We are American, so they must allow us to pass, but it doesn't mean they won't stop us and be extremely rude during a search of my ship. It would appear your 'guest' has heard the call, as well. He's gone up there, on the forecastle, to have a look, you see?"

"So he has – and we haven't seen him in three days…"

Mulholland stood on the bow observing the fleet for a few minutes, and then went below again.

"Not only will they search, but they may very well conscript any sailor they believe to be English."

"Oh?"

"Yes, it would probably include your Mr. Mulholland. You don't want him standing there when they come aboard."

By morning, after a rain shower passed, the fleet was again visible; and now very close. Two ships appeared to be sailing to cut off the *Pride of Maryland*, but Master Shutwell did not alter course. Mulholland went on the bow again, and then below. An hour later, the first of the British ships, the frigate *Galatea*, fired a signal gun.

"She expects us to let fly our sheets and prepare to be boarded for an inspection, Mr. Stearns. You see, just as I said. There's your Mr. Mulholland, going for another walk on the bow, too. You might not want him to be up there." He turned to his first mate: "Let fly, Mr. Rolland, we can't argue with these buggers. Get the topmen up to furl. We could be here for hours."

The noise of flapping sails and sheets overrode all conversation for another ten minutes, while the three ships slowly slowed near each other, and finally sat rolling gently on a low mounding sea. Shore birds began to swoop curiously.

"The frigate's lowering a boat, you see? They'll be here in a minute. What's that? Smoke?"

"Fire!" someone forward yelled, "Fire below!" The cries cause instant panic. Nothing on a wooden ship is worse than fire.

"Fire crews! Fire crews!" bellowed the first mate, "Get below!"

Thick white smoke began to billow from the hatches, yet some men had the nerve and fortitude to venture below pulling hoses.

"Man the pumps," yelled the first mate. "Get over there, you lubber, and start pumping your arse off!" he yelled at one man.

The smoke increased. Master Shutwell looked up to see the progress of the frigate's boarding boat. They were close, now, looking like a water beetle bobbing through the waves. "Damn!" he swore. "I don't need those buggers offering help, unless we can't stop this and need to be fished from the water. Hey, what's your idiot man doing on the bow? He's jumping up and down and waving! That English dung-heap set the fire, he did. Mr. Rolland," he yelled, "get that fool off the bow. And you'd best go help him, Mr. Stearns, real quick-like."

Stearns and Rolland began running for the bow, but were hampered by the pandemonium before them. Men were running in all directions, pulling hoses and yelling. Most did not seem to have much purpose or direction. Stearns had the impression, as he ran past the companion, that the smoke was already decreasing. He focused, however, on stopping Mulholland's alarming actions. Mulholland wasn't looking when both Stearns and Mr. Rolland jumped on him from behind, knocking him to the deck. His head hit something, and he seemed to go limp for a minute, so they took the opportunity to carry him amidships. Mr. Rolland found a bit of rope and bound his hands before he woke up in a groggy state.

The cook suddenly appeared. "Fire's out, Mr. Rolland. It were mostly stuff in a barrel. We had some flames for a while, but mostly the smoke."

"Thank the Lord," said Mr. Georges. "Mr. Stearns, I'll send you some men to help you carry this fool below. Bag him in some canvas and stuff him under some sails until these British twits are gone, and we'll worry about him later." He gave Stearns a very angry look, and added, "Don't you dare let him get loose again."

Mr. Rolland stood and looked for the frigate's boat. He walked over to receive the coxswain as it neared the main chains.

"Trouble, Mister?" yelled a midshipman. The little boat held off a bit, making sure not to be caught up in a fire.

"No, Mr. Midshipman. We've got it now. A galley fire in a slush tub. No more. Smoke's gone, see?"

"You're sure? Captain Dagleishe would offer assistance…"

"No. It's out. Can we get on?"

"Where bound?"

"Le Havre, Sir. Our cargo is corn."

"Sorry, then. We must do our duty and inspect for contraband. We'll come alongside now. Take our painter, if you please, Sir."

16 - "Atlantic Chase - Eastbound"

Commander Mewes returned to *Stork* the following day, eleventh September, after shopping for personal supplies, in time for supper with Ellen. He was in an excitable state. He was a thin man of average height, with cat-like features and cat-like movements, and normally an affable, talkative fellow. When excited, however, he constantly glanced about, enhancing the cat analogy, and his movements changed from stealthy stalking to quick reflex actions one could describe as pouncing – up stairs or into a coach for example; he became truly amusing to watch.

"How long do you estimate our crossing will take?" Ellen asked.

Mewes jumped to his feet, snatched open a drawer, and pulled out a chart of the North Atlantic Ocean. Somehow, he spread it on the table without disturbing a thing. He was never clumsy. "Here," he said, pointing at New York City, "to here," he continued, pointing at Portsmouth, "in a fortnight!" He beamed. "I've not met but one who's done better!"

Ellen was amused. "How long for a ship-sloop hauling wheat?" she asked.

"Ohh," said Mewes, wrapping the chart to put it away. He rolled his eyes and spoke slowly, as though the question was beneath his dignity to answer, after the previous one. "At least five days more... maybe a week."

"We need all the speed we can manage," Ellen said. "We cannot simply chase the *Pride of Maryland*. We must beat her to England and raise an alarm for ships to go intercept her before she reaches Le Havre. If *Pride* left on the eighth, and *Stork* could leave on the tenth, making Plymouth by, say, the twenty-sixth, then maybe we could send a semaphore message to Mr. Chapman in time to get an intercept ship out in the next day or two, the twenty-seventh or eighth, and the *Pride* would be... where? In the Western Approaches, at least, or nearing Le Havre."

"And after we send a message, we could go out ourselves," suggested Mewes enthusiastically. "*Stork* may not be a full warship, but we should be able to take on a merchant vessel." It also occurred to Ellen that she might ask to stay ashore before Mewes sought his cat-fight with *Pride*. She wasn't sure her interest in naval affairs went so far as to include a cannon battle, and Mewes could identify Mulholland without her, if need be. For now, she kept those thoughts to herself. It seemed spiteful to rain on Commander Mewes' exuberance.

Stork stood for Plymouth the following day, just before the full tide at eleven o'clock in the morning, despite the grumbling of the boatswain responsible for storing the new supplies. A nice west wind was blowing, allowing her to move forward despite the flood tide. The incoming tide had almost released its choke of the river's flow, however, and by the time they reached the Chesapeake itself, *Stork* would be able to present her beam to the breeze and reach south at her maximum speed. The expanse of Atlantic beckoned her, and she leaped happily over the little waves of the 'Peake' in anticipation of the salt-water beyond Cape Charles. Once in the ocean, however, the effects of Southern Stream became apparent. Commander Mewes made apologies for the rough passage, but not for *Stork's* speed. He would stay in the unsettled weather of the

Stream 'for the winds and the current', he said, until reaching the Western Approaches. There he would drop off the warm current and tack for the Channel. Mewes did his best to dispel any of Ellen's concerns: "We should not fear gales, even in his small ship," he bragged. "Gales should not be expected before November, in any case."

"Here we are, Ellen," Archibald announced as they opened the entrance to Plymouth harbor. "We're more than a day early," he boasted: "...my new record of thirteen days!" After days of stories and chatting, their comfort with each other had improved to the point where they used their given names.

"At the very first moment we can, Archibald," said Ellen, "we must go ashore and find the telegraph office. It will go much better if you are with me. It might take me hours to explain who I am and why I want to send a message, but I should think there will be no trouble at all with you present to order them."

"I know a fast way in. We must go where we are not allowed, but it may save hours...," said Archibald, grinning another of his cat-like grins. "Have your message ready. Make it short, Ellen, and terse. I have sent dozens of these... no extra words at all, at all, or they will argue about it for hours before sending; it's most frustrating. They must send almost every letter by itself."

Archibald sailed *Stork* into the ordinary yard and docked her crossway in front of a dry dock. Yard workers came and yelled, but by the time marines were running over to push the little ship away or threaten other mischief, Archibald and Ellen were 'ashore', rushing down the dock walls, leaving *Stork* to the capable hands of her petty officers. They found the telegraph office and sent the message within half an hour.

TO: NAVY AT WHITEHALL

ATTN: CHAPMAN

INTERCEPT SLOOP SHIP
PRIDE OF MARYLAND
BOUND LE HAVRE 2 DAYS

ELLEN / STORK

"When might we expect a reply?" asked Ellen.

The two telegraph operators looked at each other, and then burst out laughing. "We mean no offense, Miss, but you've sent a message to Whitehall. You may have your answer in a fortnight, a month, or never."

"I wouldn't hold my breath," said the other. "Excuse us, though. Please step outside. We've got to go to work... message coming in."

Archibald opened the door of the little wooden building for Ellen, and she walked out.

"Hold on, you," one of the operators said to Archibald over his shoulder. "It's for your lady friend. I've never seen such a thing! *Stork*... are you *Stork*?"

"Aye, we are," replied Archibald.

" 'Stork Proceed to Portsmouth', it says. Wait... two more words: 'weigh now'."

Ellen and Archibald opened the door and stepped outside. Before the door closed, Ellen heard from inside, "Who the bloody hell were they?"

17 - "Bar Fight"

Neville strode confidently into the yellow building adjacent the Admiralty, accepted the nod of the sentry, and walked directly through the door opening to the hallway passing Mr. Chapman's office. He knocked on the door frame and waited for his invitation.

"Who is it?" The voice, definitely Chapman's, sounded annoyed.

"Burton," Neville said.

"Come in," Chapman ordered. "Come, come." He didn't wait any longer than seeing Neville's face. Before the door fully opened, he began, "I've received a message from Mrs. Dagleishe – from Plymouth."

"Plymouth?" Neville wondered aloud, and taken completely aback; "She's in Plymouth?"

"Here's the message," said Chapman, handing Neville the scrap of paper from the telegraph room. "I've answered it, ordering them to Portsmouth. They should be well under way by now." The last statement sounded to Neville as if Chapman were complaining about how long it had taken Neville to be summoned from home. " 'Two days', it says, you see? What do we do now, with you **here**? We should have thought this through."

"I came back on your schedule, if you remember, to discuss our next action." His response would have been considered insubordinate by almost any naval superior, but Chapman, technically, was not navy at all.

Chapman glared at him, but didn't rise to an argument, except to say, "I sent the messenger an hour ago."

"He wasn't very quick, then, was he?"

The two stared at each other for a minute before Neville began, "You said 'them'. Who is with her?"

"She's aboard *Stork*, my packet."

"Excellent. Commander Mewes I can use. Our 'chase squadron' is ready, Sir, as we agreed, and we could add *Stork*."

"Possibly, but you're here. How does a squadron go to sea without its commander?"

"That's it, Mr. Chapman; you've solved it in one question. It just does. My First Lieutenant Towers is more than capable, and my second, Miller, will step up easily. The other ships will follow; I'll just send the order. Le Havre is almost directly across the channel from Portsmouth, and they know what they're looking for.

"The squadron can spread out to try to intercept, but they could simply miss the *Pride of Maryland* - or she could pass in the night, of course. There is another storm beginning to roll down the Channel, as well." Neville shuddered, remembering his recent experience. "On the one hand, the storm might delay the *Pride of Maryland*. On the other, it might make her impossible to see. But, with this news today, our chances are improved."

"Yes, it is excellent to know the ship's name."

"Excellent, yes, but it's better to know Commander Mewes and Mrs. Dagleishe are here."

"The Commander I understand, but the woman? Why?"

"Mr. Chapman, how long have you been in this...? Never mind... We shall set the squadron out in the channel, and watch for a day, but no more. If we don't find the *Pride of Maryland*, then, it will be my recommendation to enact 'Option B'. We can't risk losing Sir Mulholland! Ellen will be smuggled across the Channel with Georges. If anyone can find Sir Mulholland, they can. Georges knows all the resistance leaders. Marion and I will go in directly, as she did before, under the guise of selling rum. I'll just play the foppish husband. We've brought the clothes for it. Marion knows where she's going and who to contact in the Napoleon naval organization for rum sales - in order to appear legitimate -- and she might know a few of the resistance people she met through Georges."

"How do you and Miss Stillwater go to France? No English ship can put in to Le Havre, and no French ship can put in here. Must we smuggle you across, too? Such activity would appear rather questionable to the French, I would think."

"*Stork* should do."

"May I point out, Captain, that you are not aboard *Stork*; and also, that *Stork* is British, not French."

"True enough, but not an insurmountable problem. With your permission, we can add to the squadron's orders. *Stork* should proceed with them, and carry American colours. Marion and I will go aboard some small ship here in London, and take Georges to find a smuggler on the South Coast. We will all rendezvous with the squadron in the Channel. There, Marion and I will go aboard *Stork*, and Ellen will go with Georges to the smuggler. The ship from London can go home. We can disguise *Stork* as American well enough. And, she won't stay in Le Havre, only discharge us and depart. The biggest problem will probably be to find a smuggler who will go anywhere near the navy, but Georges may know the ways of such nefarious work."

"Begin the deception, Captain, send the messages. But remember, this is a 'volunteer cruise'. I could not have the Navy order you to go, but I believe I can get them to allow you sufficient furlough – although there will be questions. I have told the same to your fiancée."

Finding a small ship willing to do little more than convey three passengers to a destination only half-way across the English Channel and pass them off to others was not difficult. Money would quickly solve the problem. *Minerva* departed London with the evening ebb tide, enjoying a light southwestern breeze and a three-quarter waning moon.

"If all goes well, Captain," said the ship's master, one Emil Jonsson, "we should see your frigate tomorrow – late afternoon."

This is all taking too much time, thought Neville. "This delay probably means," Neville said to Marion and Georges, who were standing with Neville and the master watching the lights of London grow fewer and fewer, "that 'Option B' must be used. Ellen's message allowed us only two days, and those days will be gone by the time I see *La Désirée*." The current of the Thames River gurgled past the ship's stern, quietly suggesting a very romantic evening. "I suggest a slight change of plans. If we don't stop the *Pride of Maryland* once we have met with *La Désirée* and *Stork*, this ship can take Georges and Ellen to some place Georges knows – ummm – 'alternative transportation' can be found. Marion and I will go aboard *Stork*, and leave *La Désirée* in the hands of Lt. Towers." *I prefer this master does not learn what we are about.*

"I agree," said Georges. "We don't need to... leave the country... at the same time you and Marion go."

"**T**he weather is getting worse quickly, Captain," said Master Jonsson when Neville came up from taking a few hours nap.

"So I see," said Neville. He shuddered again at the thought of being driven ashore in a storm. "Where are we? How long until we pass the lightship at the Nore?"

"There's the mouth of the Medway, there. You can see the lights of Chatham." Neville could barely see him point. The moon was closing on the horizon by then, and mostly obscured by clouds.

"Aye," said Neville. "…and the Nore?"

"We're at slack water. If it weren't for the rising wind, we'd anchor now. If we can stem the tide... three hours... dawn, maybe."

"And Margate?"

"With God's blessing and the wind holds, the middle of the morning watch."

Neville sucked air through his front teeth. *Late*, he thought. *My squadron might catch the Pride of Maryland, but we are a day behind.*

The night passed while *Minerva* pressed on, and the day dawned gray, rainy, and windy. Marion, clad in Neville's boat cloak, came on deck clutching a tankard of coffee that seemed to dwarf her. "When will we see them, Neville?" she asked.

"Not today, I'm afraid. We can hope they will present a cordon around Le Havre by this evening, yet don't get crossways with the Channel Fleet. We must also pray *Stork* understood our messages and is coming our way."

"I hope so. I am so looking forward to seeing Ellen," said Marion. "I can scarcely believe it: first I see you when I never expected it, and now Ellen. This is a wonderful week, it is."

"Nevertheless, you may soon wish to stay below. This weather will turn worse beyond Margate. The seas will certainly be rougher. I suppose I should go down, too, and try to get some sleep."

"**F**inally!" exclaimed Neville in early morning of the next day. "I worried we might pass *Stork* in the night, but she's there to larboard, I'm sure of it. May I use your long glass, please, Master Jonsson?"

"Here it is, Captain. It's a good glass, if you can hold it steady enough to see anything." The storm had blown hard the previous day, and made a lumpy mess of the Channel, but it would soon die down. The rain had decreased also, but was still heavy enough to make for poor visibility.

"Thank you, Master Jonsson. She should be quite close soon, and we can signal." Within the hour, they had confirmed the oncoming ship as *Stork*, and began maneuvering for a transfer of people and dunnage.

"Out of the question, Captain," said Master Jonsson. We c'nay use the chair or the boats in these confused seas. We must either wait or find more protected water."

"Is there a place you'd suggest?"

"Closest thing I see on the chart is a small river outlet with a protected cove... Cuckmere Haven, just behind Beachy Head, there," he said, pointing to a high point along the white cliffs to their north.

"Ohhh," said Neville. He shuddered.

"Do you know it?" asked Jonsson.

"Water's cold there," said Neville, which earned him a quizzical look from Jonsson. Recovering from his memories, he added, "Well enough for this. We'll not anchor."

"Time is getting away from us, you know, Georges," said Neville. "It has taken us two hours to work in toward shore where it is calm. You must still find a smuggler to take you across; you'll be a day behind Marion and me."

"I know, I know, but have hope. Things do not always work smoothly in France these days. This is not a bad place though. Seaford, just around the bend, is a town sure to have a smuggler or two."

"I know it is; look, there." He pointed to a section of the bow of *Active* that remained trapped in the surf. A few of her ribs farther aft still poked from the strand, but the beach was clean. Anything of value had been removed, or had since simply washed away.

"Is that...?

"Yes, it's where I went ashore."

"You see, Neville? Things work out." Georges walked away.

"Sway out the launch!" yelled *Minerva's* boatswain just then, and the noise of the activity soon took all attention on deck. Neville and Marion's heavy trunks went across to *Stork* first.

Ellen returned in the boat, carrying only a small leather satchel. She was lifted to the deck in a chair, and Marion gathered her into her arms the moment her foot touched the deck. Neville hugged her, and Georges gave his kisses.

"Georges can fill you in on everything we know, Ellen, and outline our plans," said Neville. "Do you need anything? Where is your trunk? And how is Joseph?"

"You suppose I should carry a trunk on my back, Neville? This is all I can manage, I think," Ellen said, lifting the leather satchel. "I'll be going in as Georges' errand boy, but I've left out a few dresses for France on *Stork*, Marion. If you could pack those with your things…? My trunk itself will stay aboard *Stork*, I suppose. Joseph is at sea, as he always seems to be, Neville, but you know how it is. It's the curse of being married to a sea captain, right, Marion?" she queried.

"I know what you mean," said Marion, "but I'm not married to a sea captain. I will certainly bring your things…"

"Not married yet? Why ever not…?"

"Come, Marion," interrupted Neville. "They're calling us into the boat. We must make all haste if we hope to land in Le Havre before dark."

Neville was properly piped up the side of *Stork* while Marion waited below. Naval custom preceded chivalry in this instance, but it also allowed Neville to order quick preparations for her recovery from the little boat.

Neville and Commander Mewes managed their salutations formally before turning to a friendlier greeting. "You're looking well, Archibald," commented Neville. "May I request you fish my fiancée with all haste?"

"Yes, Sir," said Mewes. "We have the chair ready." He turned enough to wag his head at his first officer.

"You look well yourself, Sir," said Archibald. "Someday you'll have to tell me what happened on the Spanish Coast."

"Certainly, Archibald," Neville said, "but I'm afraid we must now get straight to business. What do you know of the squadron?"

"Very little, Commodore, except that they sailed for Le Havre, in accord with your orders. I came here. I doubt they could have found the *Pride of Maryland* in this weather, though."

Commodore? I suppose I am, although I don't believe my orders say any such thing... "I understand. It is likely she is into Le Havre already."

"We tried to catch her, Sir. I had my best Atlantic crossing ever, at thirteen days. We sent a message as soon as we got in."

"Yes, of course, of course. Our next step, then, is to disguise this ship as American, and you will take Marion and me into Le Havre. There, we will help you make the best pretense of being in a great hurry to drop off two 'annoying passengers' and be off to some other destination."

Commander Mewes gave Neville a concerned look, saying only, "Oh?"

"Here is your other 'annoying passenger', Commander. May I introduce my fiancée, Marion Stillwater?" Marion had arrived on deck, but not at her most radiant. She was trying to push her hair into some semblance of neatness, and smoothing her dress as best she could after a boat ride in the breeze..

"I thought Ellen pretty," he mumbled, "but..."

"Ellen is very pretty, Commander. Her husband and I are lucky men. We thank you for the compliment," Neville added, in an attempt to make Archibald feel less awkward. "We're free to sail, Archibald. This is the 'special assignment' you wanted. You know what we are doing here, yes?"

"Mrs. Dagleishe showed me her letter, aye."

"Then, let's go retrieve Sir Mulholland. *Minerva* has already hauled her wind." Georges and Ellen were waving from the stern of the departing ship.

"Aye, Sir," said Archibald, now looking like his confidence had returned. "It's nice to be involved." He turned to his First Officer and said, "Set a course for Le Havre, and hoist the Stars and Stripes."

"There are three reasons I had wished to arrive at Le Havre in the late afternoon," said Neville, "although it would now be difficult to do otherwise."

"First, I will be surprised if we are not stopped – more than once, possibly – by our own blockade. Explaining our mission, though it might be a bit awkward, could take some time. Mr. Chapman's letter, here in my jacket, should be of considerable help, of course.

"Second, we need to contact at least one of the ships on my 'chase squadron' for the purpose of passing along my orders. … *an odd thought… I have a squadron, therefore I suppose I'm a Commodore, even though I have no such orders from the Admiralty…* I will also leave those orders with the Channel Fleet in case we do not see our own, and to advise them we are out upon the water.

"Thirdly, we certainly want the least bit of inspection of this ship as possible in Le Havre – so we should arrive when any reasonable Frenchman would prefer to be home at supper."

Stork would appear, from Le Havre, to arrive as any eastbound shipping traffic. American ships, if not carrying cargo Britain would classify as contraband, or who had somehow managed to evade the British blockade of the port, would arrive from the northeast. The only French ships sailing to or from the port on a normal day would be fishermen and small coastal traders considered insignificant to the war with Britain.

By the time *Stork* ghosted slowly into Le Havre and threw off her sheets, Archibald had given the full story of events in Baltimore.

"Archibald," Neville said, "I suggest you neither anchor nor tie alongside the quay. They might accuse you of snooping, but not spying, if you do not land. You really don't want to be attached in any way to French soil, if you can avoid it."

"Avoiding the quay doesn't look to be a problem, Neville. There's very little space there, look. Two small coastal traders are in, one French navy sloop of war who, thank the Lord, doesn't appear to be preparing to leave, and another American -- with a familiar name: *Pride of Maryland*."

"That answers our question, doesn't it?" Neville queried. "There's no telling how long she's been here, though."

"Don't panic, my good friend," Archibald commented. "Nobody aboard *Pride* knows anything about us. We might have been amongst the shipping traffic arriving Baltimore as they departed, but nothing more, and they would have had no reason to pay any attention to us. Let's have your boat ready... "Mr. Ristock..." he called out.

Neville and Archibald began their charade when *Stork's* largest boat touched the water. Sound carries well over water, of course, and particularly in the quiet of late afternoon, so they expected someone in the harbor would attest to their unpleasant arrival if it were needed. To the boat's crew, Neville said quietly, "We're just going to put on a little show for the Frogs, men. Don't be concerned."

"Don't look to me for another passage, you French rascals!" yelled Archibald in English, immediately as Marion's foot touched the boat.

One of Marion's large trunks descended on a tackle from above, interrupting the interaction.

"And you can keep your smelly little American rowboat on the other side of the Atlantic," Neville yelled back in French.

A second trunk -- this one Neville's, landed hard enough to be heard across the harbor... just softly enough not to break the boat.

"It is not my ship that smells, *Monsieur*, but you!" hollered Archibald.

"Not so," retorted Marion. "It is neither your little boat nor my husband. It is you, you pig!"

Marion's second trunk thumped into the little boat, almost overloading it.

"Oooh, you coarse fool!" Marion added, "You've almost upset us!" The rowboat visibly wobbled side to side.

"Push away, Cox'n," said Neville to the smirking boat commander. "That's good enough. Take us over to the *Pride of Maryland*, if you please. We'll need help getting these trunks up onto the quay."

Standing visibly at the railing in his civilian 'ship's master' attire, Archibald yelled, "Ove-wire to both of you," when the rowing began. He flipped his hand in the international 'I'm done with you' motion, and turned away from them.

"The *Pride of Maryland* looks to have just arrived, doesn't she, Marion?" Neville queried.

"Yes," she answered, "I see some baggage being carried down the walkway just now. It doesn't have the look of cargo. It looks like personal... It looks like Michael's," she spat. "He enjoys that childish color blue. And there's his second trunk."

"Excellent," said Neville. "All this means we were exactly correct. Mr. Stearns came across on this ship. And Sir William as well? Could Ellen have been somehow misled in Baltimore about Sir William being with Stearns? She said she hadn't actually seen either of them. They had gone before she arrived."

"I doubt she would be misled. What reason would a hotel clark have to deceive anyone?"

"Well, we have choices to make now. How do we follow the trunk? What do we do when we get there?"

"I'm sorry, Neville, but I don't think we can follow the trunk. They've just put it on yon wagon, and the driver is climbing up. It will be gone before we even get to shore."

"Hmmm, so I see. Are you ready for our next act?"

"Yes. Now we're the 'annoying British couple', yes?"

"Yes. Cox'n, heave to under the *Pride of Maryland's* stern, if you please."

"You up there, haloo," yelled Neville to a man he saw on the poopdeck. He could not discern from below, with a low sun reflecting off brightwork and shiny paint, if the man was an officer, an idler, or another passenger.

Neville could see the man bend over to peer down at them, so he yelled again, "Haloo, my good man. Can you assist us?"

"I'm not... just a minute..." he walked away.

The *Pride of Maryland* was not such a huge ship that someone couldn't be summoned in minutes. Another man walked to the rail and looked down. "Hello, what is it? Where have you come from, and what do you want?" He must have noticed Marion just then, because his tone changed. "Oh, hello, Miss. I'm sorry to have spoken rudely. How might I help?"

"Good evening, Sir," said Marion. "It's nice to meet a gentleman. Those rude things out there," she waved her hand toward *Stork*, idling in the harbor with her sails loose and flapping in the light breeze, "have put us off."

"Can you sling our dunnage to shore, my good man? I don't know how we might other..." began Neville.

"I was telling the story, Nigel," interrupted Marion. She looked up again, saying, "these fellows in the boat don't know this harbor, either, and so we..."

"He doesn't care about the men in this boat, Edith. We just need his help to get these trunks," he said, pointing at the trunks, "up there," then pointing to the quay.

"All right, sir. We'll send a chair down for your lady, and you, my friend, may climb the ladder to the quay, over there. We'll get your trunks up."

"Sister," yelled Neville up to him, "not 'lady friend'."

"I see," said the man with more enthusiasm, "We'll be with you in just a minute, Miss." He turned and called forward, "Abrahamson, fetch a bo'sn's chair for a visitor."

The process of hoisting the trunks was not quick. The man – an officer as it turned out – directed Neville to stay on the quay and watch over them, as one after the other was strapped for swaying up, slung over the quay, and lowered carefully to the deck. The moment the third trunk lifted out of *Stork's* boat, her coxswain ordered his men to shove off, and they began their row back out into the harbor.

The men of the *Pride*, who had been doing the work, went off somewhere for several minutes, leaving Neville sitting on a trunk waiting for the third one. It now hung in the air over the quay while the gloom of late evening began to gather over the city. He began to worry about Marion. Where was she, and why was his third trunk not yet lowered? His concern grew until he reached his decision to take some action. The moment he stood to go investigate, he heard voices above, and the trunk began to descend. Marion walked down the gangway on the arm of the man he had spoken with earlier. Neville noticed *Stork* had gathered her boat. Her sails were drawing now, and she began moving slowly toward the ocean.

"Thank you for a most pleasant greeting to Le Havre, Charles, and again for the glass of wine..."

"What's the meaning of this, you scoundrel?" asked Neville as he walked up to the pair.

"Charles, here, simply entertained me for a moment, Nigel, while you got the..."

"Charles, what designs have you on my sister's honor? Never mind, I'll ask her later about your behavior. Call us a carriage straightaway. Come along, Edith, we'll wait..."

"I'm not an errand-boy," interrupted Charles. "You may find your own carriage. You're welcome, and I see why they tossed you off. Edith, it was truly a pleasure to meet you." He turned and walked back aboard.

"The first bit's done, then, isn't it?" queried Neville. "We're ashore. Now we're French, *oui*?"

"*Oui, Monsieur.* Who would you like to be now -- Nicolas? Maurice, Raoul?"

"Raoul, yes. It has a ring to it. And you? You could be..."

"Marie. No question. I like it when you say my name, and Marie is quite close, yes?"

Neville winced. Close, yes; too close to 'Maria', whom he would have married, had she not died in an earthquake – only six years before, as he remembered it. However, since he had not shared the story with Marion yet, he said, "Yes, Marie. That also has a ring to it. Let's go, now. We must find a room or a meal or a carriage. The trunks will not walk away by themselves."

The quay fronted the town. They decided to walk along the quay, now almost deserted at dusk. Activity at the *Pride of Maryland* had ceased. They could see down the streets as they walked one block after the next.

"This quay appears to be only another block long, Raoul," said Marion / Marie, "What is your next plan?"

"Ah, just there, see – the light flowing into the street about three blocks in? That will be a pub or Hotel or something. Shall we?" He offered his arm, and he felt for the dagger he kept in his belt. It was there.

The light grew in intensity as they approached the building in question. They saw two men enter and one leave.

"They do not appear to be the town's professional people, Raoul," said Marion.

"Of course not. We *are* on the waterfront. But someone here will know something. Are you ready to be the center of attention and the talk of the waterfront for the next few days? Is your dagger handy?"

"*Oui*, and yes. I suppose there is no other way?"

"None I know of. Stay behind me." He pushed the door open and they stepped in. The room, of medium size for a waterfront tavern, held only about eight men and the barkeep. The tables and benches were of rough wood, and the bar itself not much more than a table. A small fire crackled peacefully in the corner. One man at a table of four in the corner looked up, down, and quickly up again. He nudged his mate, who looked at him, and then followed his gaze to the door. Others noticed, and the room went quiet. The appearance of a middle-class man, as Neville had dressed himself to be, would have been a rare sight there, except possibly when a ship had just come in. The entrance of a woman such as Marion had probably never happened before. Knowing all eyes were upon him, Neville saw no reason not to be bold. "Good evening, gentlemen. We've just come in by ship," he announced. "Can anyone direct us to a hotel – or a carriage?"

The room remained quiet for a moment; then one of four men at the corner table said, "I didn't see no ship. Last one in was that Yankee at the quay. What you doing here?"

"Another Yankee ship, kind sir," said Neville. "She just dropped us off and departed. Is there a hotel near?"

"*Oui*," said another. "Two streets over. We could take your lady there." He grinned a two-tooth grin. Two men at another table stood up, and the barkeep nodded at them. They left without saying anything.

The four began to stand. The barkeep said, "Marcel, no trouble tonight," but it didn't appear to slow Marcel, who began to swagger toward Neville and Marion.

"Pour me another ale," said Marcel over his shoulder. "I think I'm going to be thirsty tonight."

"Two streets over, you say?" asked Neville again, hoping some talk might calm the situation. These were not small men.

"Only for the lady. You're of no use to us. Stand aside." Marcel reached his hand out for Marion's shoulder, but before it touched her, Neville's dagger flashed from his belt and stuck through it. Marcel began to howl, and Neville shoved him backwards across the closest bench. Two of the three remaining men turned their full attention to Neville now, rather than Marion, changing their approach to a threatening, stalking pattern.

The third man made the mistake of going for Marion. Her dagger also came out in a flash, slicing his hand. Even before his scream of pain, she kicked him hard in the left knee, and he bent forward, issuing a small screeching noise. His face was closer to hers now, so her free hand – now a tight, bony little fist – jabbed him hard in the throat. He went to the floor with a gurgle, blood streaming from his hand. She turned her attention to the remaining two men who were circling Neville. "Which shall I stab first, Raoul?" she asked him calmly.

Still trying to comprehend what he had just seen, Neville replied, as nonchalantly as he could muster, "The bearded one there is closer, don't you think, My Dear?" He also decided it might be a good moment to ask his request differently: "I'll buy each of you a glass of wine, if you'll direct us to the hotel and a wagon for our trunks... but not Marcel or that one," wagging his blade toward the man on the floor. "They were quite rude."

"There," said one of them. "Them two as is sitting there is our wagon men." He pointed to the two remaining men at the more distant table who had neither left nor joined in. They were watching closely however, and Neville knew they had greatly enjoyed Marion's performance.

Marcel had run out the door by this time, dripping blood as he went. The man on the floor had gained a sitting position, and now tried to stand while holding his hand to staunch the blood.

"How much for two, barkeep?" asked Neville.

"*Quatre-vingts centimes*," the bartender answered.

Neville and Marion were both still holding their daggers out to keep their attackers at bay. Neville fumbled in his pocket for a coin. He soon found a *franc*, and tossed it to the bartender, indicating he expected no change.

Seeing Neville paid as promised, the two backed off, holding their palms up, pulled the floor-sitter to his feet, and returned to their seats.

The daggers were returned to their places. Neville turned to the 'wagon men'. Marion began rubbing her red knuckles.

"Haven't put mine away for the night yet," said one. "I'll take you. It's out back."

"All right," said Neville, "but it better be a horse and wagon out back, and not more of Marcel's friends. I'll stay close to you."

There was, indeed, a horse and small dirty hay wagon in the little courtyard behind the tavern, and no threatening men. The driver, his friend, and Neville were together able to load the three heavy trunks, and the wagon began clattering its way through the dark streets of waterfront Le Havre.

"I will give you this advice in exchange for your lady's good show," said the driver. "I am sure Marcel will come to me tomorrow to ask where I have taken you. I won't tell him unless he wants to get rough, but then I might. I won't get myself hurt for you. You should leave town, or change to another hotel, perhaps, and not say where you are going."

"I understand. Do you know of two men – passengers – who came off the *Pride of Maryland?*"

"Yes, there were two."

"Did you carry them somewhere?"

"No, Raphael took them. He suggested two of our finest hotels, but I do not know which they chose, and I have not seen Raphael since."

"Are you worried for him?"

"Oh, no, no. If they paid him too much he will be drunk now... tomorrow, maybe."

"What are the hotel names, please? Another *franc?*"

"*Merci. Hotel du Mer* and *Hotel le Pont Noir*. But like I said..."

"*Pont Noir?*" Marion exclaimed, but stopped there.

"Why, Marie? Do you know it?" asked Neville.

"No, I'm sorry. I'll tell you later, Raoul."

"Here you are," announced the driver. The ride took longer than Neville had hoped, but finally they arrived at another tavern. This one had a 'Hotel' sign out front, and it appeared to be far nicer than Neville had expected.

"Will you come for us tomorrow?" Neville asked the driver.

"No, but I will send my friend – the one who helped us load the trunks. Then I can say I don't know where you went. And Marcel is too stupid to connect my friend and I in this. His wagon is nicer, anyway. It has seats." Marion stood to the side, brushing straw and a bit of dirt from her dress.

Unloading went quickly, and they were early enough to get some venison stew to eat, and a glass of acceptable red wine. The room was clean. "Marion," asked Neville once inside the room, "you recognized one of the hotel names, did you not? Have you been here before?"

"Not here, no. But it is the same name as the hotel in Marseille where I stayed, and where we met with Georges... where Mr. Stearns followed me. 'Pont Noir' will be the place. That annoying man will be there; no question of it. Such a predictable, bumbling man."

"And what was that other thing... "

"What other thing, Neville? I'm too tired for guessing games."

"You knocked that big man to the floor before I could even deal with the others. Where did you ever learn to do such a thing?"

"Ellen. She's quite good."

"Ellen, too...? Sweet little Ellen?"

18 - "Hotel du Mer:

Morning, Day 1."

The hour was late by the time Raoul and Marie had checked in to the *Hotel du Mer* and had their dunnage carried up. Still, they were up as early as they could, very shortly after sunrise. It had been a most enjoyable night, with their two bodies wrapped tightly together, warm and comfortable. But it was also a very short night. They were too tired for lovemaking, and had no time in the morning for anything but getting to the business of rescuing Sir William Mulholland.

"We cannot simply go to the *Hotel Le Pont Noir* and check in, hoping Georges and Ellen might discover the same thing and come to visit us," said Neville. "There is no possibility whatever that Mr. Stearns would forget either of us, or not recognize us. You, he fancies as his future lover; I stabbed him with a sword in his silly duel a few years back."

"And, this time, he would not hesitate to cry out," she said, and continued: "If Georges and Ellen discover the *Hotel le Pont Noir*, what would they do? And when might they arrive? They had still to find a smuggler to carry them across the Channel. They must be at least a day behind us, and then only if everything went well for them."

"First, we must confirm that Sir William is here. We still don't know it for a fact. I propose to go down to the street and find a boy whom we can send in to inquire at the *Hotel du Pont Noir* desk."

Marion finished her preparations for the day while Neville went out. *I won't stand in front of this hotel waving like a fool*, thought Neville. *It would be just as well the boy doesn't know where I have come from.* He walked a couple blocks off the hotel street, there finding another *rue* busy enough to have a few early wagons on it. Three older boys were playing at something near the corner of an alley, so he went there.

"Anyone want to earn fifty *centimes*?" he asked. He realized they were gambling; there were coins on the stones, and dice.

"I need some money. These boys cheat me, I think," said one darker boy, rising to stand. The other two scooped up the money and ran off, laughing.

"Do you know the *Hotel le Pont Noir*?" Neville asked.

"I am Jacques," said the boy, staring at him.

"Hello, Jacques." *A different culture,* thought Neville. *Egyptian? Business is not possible unless he introduces himself?* "I am Raoul," he said. Jacques tipped his head to the side, as if to say, 'I'm listening'.

"Your name is Jacques, really?"

"No, it is Jabir, but here in France they call me Jacques."

"I see." Neville dispatched Jacques to inquire at the desk for Stearns and his friend, handed him twenty-five *centimes*, and agreed to meet on the same corner in half an hour. He returned to his hotel for his morning coffee. Marion had not yet come down to the hotel lobby, so he went straight back. Jacques returned at the agreed time for the rest of his money, provided the requested information, and walked away.

Marion had yet to appear in the lobby, so Neville took the stairs – two at a time – and gave a quick couple raps on the door before entering. "Marion, are you alive?"

"Don't be rude, Neville. I'm trying to get into costume for the day. I must appear well-to-do, but not so much as they'd want to chop my head off… why are you grinning like a chimpanzee?"

"They're here," he announced.

"Who's here, and does it have anything to do with my costume, or breakfast, or some chimpanzee? I hope it has to do with breakfast."

"They're at the *Hotel le Pont Noir*… Mr. Jackass and Sir William. We've found them!"

"Wonderful! Now, can we go to breakfast?"

"You're not excited?"

"Of course I am, but I'm hungry, and we can do nothing in an instant. I'm ready to go. Think, while we walk down, about what we **can** do, and we'll talk about it over some eggs."

The hotel dining room was unoccupied, save one slouching waiter. He took their order and departed for the kitchen.

"I must go out to see if I can make any contact with Georges' friends, Neville, and you must stay in the room. I know it is difficult to sit and do nothing, but there is nothing you can do now. You have confirmed Sir William is here, but you have no clothes to wear for standing in the street watching the hotel…"

"And I can't burst into their room and demand Sir William's release, or call the *gendarmes*…"

"No, you must wait while I make contact with the anti-Napoleon forces here. They could help us overpower Mr. Stearns. Georges gave me only one name here in Le Havre. He said the man is a harness-maker, but I don't know where to find him.

There is otherwise no hope for me to find any connection to people I met during my visit with Georges several years ago in southern France. I must be very careful."

Marion went out. She came back for lunch with Neville, as they had agreed.

"Nothing, Neville. I'm sorry," she reported, "Maybe I'm just not meant to be a spy."

19 - "Smuggled Into France: Day 1"

"**G**eorges, how long has it been?" Ellen asked when they had their first moment of quiet aboard *Minerva*.

"I am thinking two years, maybe? You look wonderful, Ellen. I think marriage agrees with you. How is Joseph?"

"Quite well, the last I saw him. He is gone too much. What is your plan, Georges? They will take Sir Mulholland to Paris, no?"

"What else could it be? They will make a spectacle, and then they will accuse him of all sorts of things before they send him to the guillotine. I doubt they will use him for a trade unless the British have captured someone very important to Napoleon."

"You heard me say our Mr. Stearns is the one who has taken him, yes?"

"Yes, I heard. Why does he do this? Forsooth, why would I ask? I know this man. Of course, he is still trying to show what a clever spy he is. He thinks he will be a hero to the USA if he can do something wonderful for their French allies. I know you Americans are not getting along well with the British now, but Mr. Stearns may not even care."

"What are we doing here, then? How can we hope to free Sir Mulholland?"

"Mr. Stearns would never be permitted to parade him into Paris. It must be the French military who do this. Therefore, there must be a handing-over place where Mr. Stearns gets his reward and the French take our man. Our best hope is to free him before the handing-over occurs. Then it will be just Mr. Stearns against us. I know he is a big man, but we are several. Once the French have Sir Mulholland he may be lost to us, but maybe there is still hope. I have friends. If nothing else, we can take Mr. Stearns."

"We are late, though. Neville and Marion should be there soon, because they can sail in directly, but how do we go? "

"The way I always go – very quietly in the back door," said Georges. "To sneak in the back door, we must find smugglers, and very quickly. I see you have a pretty dress on now."

"I didn't remember you as the flattering type, Georges… no offense meant."

"I am French, *non*? Should I not compliment a beautiful lady? But I must confess, my observation is business. You are very pretty, and we may need some honey to catch a sneaky bug. Here is what I think we should do in Seaport…"

"**I** am not sure we can trust this captain, Georges," Ellen said to him in the pub in Seaford a few hours later, "and I don't like the way he looks at me."

"Oh, you certainly must not trust him, Ellen. He seems most scurrilous. But he is willing to leave right away; and by that, I mean almost immediately after dark. I suspect he has already business arranged somewhere on the French Coast, and we are just a little more pocket money. We may be in France almost as quickly as Neville and Marion. But keep your wits about you, and your knife handy. You are carrying it, aren't you?"

"Of course, Georges. If I am around you, I must assume there will be a surprise soon, *n'est-ce pas?* You have taken this passage many times, yes? When do you think we will arrive in France?"

"Just when there is light enough to see the coast. We should already have passed through the blockade fleet in the dark. This captain knows their ways. He will not want to have a disagreement with the rocks, however."

"I'm going below to change now, then. This dress is perfect for travel. It will fit in a very small bag – in a space smaller than my farmer's trousers and shirt, I hope."

Ellen returned to the deck in half an hour, changed into rough clothing in order to appear as George's errand-boy. "What do you think, Georges?"

"I liked the other better," he answered, "but this will serve. Let us go over this again. I have given the captain my desired destination. It is about 10 miles from Le Havre, where the cliffs have fallen at Valleuse d'Antifer. It is a mile west of a small peninsula - the Pointe de la Courtine - between Le Havre and the next small town of Etretat. I have had no opportunity to arrange a 'good, assisted arrival'. We will be more on our own than is usual for me, but it is my country, *oui?*"

"*Oui.* Do we go straight for Paris?"

"Í have thought much about it. It would be good to go around Le Havre to the Paris road, and then back into Le Havre. We might see a likely coach on the road and make plans to overturn it; but if not, we go in to see if he is still there in Le Havre."

"That sounds like a long way to travel."

"It is, and we would need to do it quickly. So, I think we go as directly into Le Havre as we can. Mr. Stearns will be at some fancy hotel, where he will do his handing-over – as we discussed, and there is exactly where we should expect to find Neville and Marion – and, hopefully, Sir Mulholland."

"Yes, we need him back. Mr. Stearns we can sort out later."

"So, if we are separated, we shall each make our way to the harbor, learn what we can about the arrival of the *Pride of Maryland* and her passengers, and move forward from there, yes?"

"Yes, and it looks like it is time to go. My thoughts will be with you forever, Georges."

"And mine with you, Ellen." He leaned over and they kissed quickly on each cheek.

The ship's second mate walked up to them. "You see it there, my friends?" he asked, referring to a great schism in the towering white cliffs. He delivered the rest of his speech in a hard, flat tone: "We will not wait for you. Even you, girl," he said directly to Ellen. "We will row you in, and you will get out of the boat, no matter what happens. We won't keep you. We won't help you. We don't know who you are. We like our heads attached to our necks."

The smuggler's ship did not take the chance of anchoring, so the men rowing the shore boat knew their friends would leave them if the French navy appeared. The launch splashed, the rowing crew boarded, and a rope ladder was thrown down. Georges and Ellen threw their satchels down into the boat, and Ellen climbed down, followed by Georges.

"Shove off," said a man, quietly, from the stern. The rowers made surprisingly little noise, in Ellen's memory, all the way to the beach. The beach had nothing on it. No pier or dock, or any such thing; only a clear area to land a boat on thousands of white pebbles. They heard someone shout, though – at some distance to the east. They could not determine what the man said. He shouted again. Georges jumped out when the boat scrubbed land, and threw his satchel to higher ground. He then worked his way around to the other side of the boat to help Ellen disembark, but before she slid out into the water, they heard the sound of a musket ball skipping close by on the water. It was followed immediately by the sound of the exploding powder that sent it. The sound echoed first from the trees inland, then from the cliffs of the Pointe de la Courtine, and lastly, from the cliffs to the west; then more softly from each again. Another shot followed. This time, the musket ball struck the launch, throwing instant panic into the boat's crew. Someone ashore actually knew how to handle a musket! The sound echoed 'round the little beach again.

Ellen threw her legs over the gunwale to slide out into the water, but Georges threw her back in. The boat crew, not wishing to remain, threw her back out, pushed them both off with their oars, and began rowing to sea. Ellen did not release her hold on her satchel, but did she get a hold on her dagger. She slashed at the closest oarsman, but completely in vain. His oar struck her lightly beneath the right arm; enough time for her to grab it and twist. The launch left Ellen and Georges standing in two feet of water, but short one oar. A third musket ball ricocheted off the water and whined harmlessly off the water into the trees.

"To the trees, Ellen, as fast as we can!" spluttered Georges. They began splashing, and then running, up onto the strand. Georges grabbed his satchel on the way, and they dashed across the sand and pebbles into the woods beyond. The launch became the target of the musketeers on the other side of the little bay. Two more shots were fired, with the noise echoing once and again for each before the bay went quiet.

"The distraction is good. Let them shoot at the boat as long as they can see it. We must hide quickly," said Georges. "They will come looking for us as soon as their target is gone. They might be military, but are probably police or some coast guardsmen."

The smugglers' ship could easily be seen from the wood, but it had now moved out of range for muskets, removing the reason for any more shooting. The ship began raising more sail to leave. "Where do we hide? This wood does not look to be very large."

"No, the map I had showed most of this area to be working farms. Let us leave the wood, where they will spend most of their time looking, and lie in a farm ditch. Bring a few branches to cover yourself. Here, I see a light there – and some smoke – to the west. They will also go inquire there. Let's walk in a line perpendicular to a line from the woods to the light – out into the flat field, there, where there is nothing of interest. We must lie down before they come out of the wood."

Ellen and Georges walked a good half mile out into the wheat field, to a place where a small hedge and a ditch separated it from a pasture. Nothing – no shrub or rock or weed – stood more than three feet high, but the hedge continued the length of the field.

"Perfect," said Georges. "Here. Lie down and I'll put your branches and your brown satchel over you. I'll go just there, where I can put my face between those rocks and see out a little. Take a nice nap."

Nap? thought Ellen. *My heart is thumping so loud those men must hear it. I hear them coming through the wood now, making a huge noise.*

"They've come out," whispered Georges, "They are but two, and they're going to the farmhouse where we saw the light… the farmer has come out; he's waving his hands. They are looking in the barn and behind it; now looking out here and around, but I don't think they'll bother. Wait, they're coming this way."

"Why here?"

Georges remained quiet for a minute, and finally said, "Not here, exactly, just nearby. The road must be in this direction. Stay very still, now."

Closer they came, until their boots could be heard on the stony ground. One began talking. "I'm sure I saw someone get out of that little boat, Henri," he said, "and we found that oar. Why else would they have come in?"

"To pick someone up, maybe? They buy some good wine for England, mmm? Whatever. Forget it, Gaston, I'm done for tonight. We can look later if you want, but right now I am ready for my breakfast. We can tell the army to watch for strangers on the road, if you want."

"No, Henri, I won't go near those buggers. The last time my father…" They soon crossed the ditch without jumping, and not far away, by following a farm lane. With their backs now to Georges and Ellen, their voices could no longer be understood.

"We must wait a while, still," said Georges… "All right, let's go." *No time has passed,* Ellen thought, suddenly realizing she'd fallen asleep the second the danger had passed. It had been a long night, and an exciting chase… "Ellen!"

"Yes, yes, I'm awake now. Ow, there's a pebble stuck in my side."

"Yes, quite uncomfortable, I must admit. Now you must wait for my foot to be awake. This whole part of the coast is good for smuggling to Paris, so it is well watched. But, on the other hand, I have connections in the area, if we can reach them. We can't travel in the day, though. I think we should go back into the wood. Those two will not be back, I am sure, despite what they said. Did you bring anything to eat in your little case?"

"No."

"Me, either. Maybe there are a few berries or nuts."

Georges and Ellen began to move at dusk. "Some light is good. We can see, and anyone watching us can't really tell who or what we are," said Georges. "This road goes toward Le Trilleul, only about a mile away; from there to Le Havre. The moon has waned further, and there will be no traffic at all after dark. There are guard points, but they never change them; I know how to go around. The land is flat, Ellen. We can easily walk another five miles to Saint-Martin-du-Bec – before midnight. I can find a ride in the morning. Or, if you are up for it, we could walk another five miles into Honfleur, which is right alongside Le Havre. I have better connections there."

"I think we should walk the ten miles rather than wait another night," said Ellen. "We've had a good rest in these woods. Maybe you can find some food in Saint-Martin-du-Bec?"

Fortified with bread and cheese from a supporter of the Napoleon resistance in Saint-Martin-du-Bec, Ellen and Georges walked on beneath a canopy of stars broken only in small places by black puffs of cloud. The dim light of stars and the small moon were quite enough for them to find their way without danger of stepping into ruts or puddles. Georges easily directed them around two army barricades. They worked their way through the dark streets of Honfleur until they found a street name Georges remembered, and then down an alley to a stable behind a large green house.

"The sun will be up soon," said Georges, "so I should be able to make contact with a man here who can find some kind of ride for us."

"It's not far now is it? We're on the edge of the city, yes? Can we not simply walk?" asked Ellen.

"Easy for you to say, my dear. You are obviously in excellent condition. My feet hurt, and my old hips are complaining of all the walking. Besides, we don't know exactly where we're going. The man whose house to which this stable belongs is one we can trust. We can't stay here, though. He is not that brave – or foolhardy, maybe – but he knows where we can stay while I send out inquiries."

"The light in the house just came on, Georges."

"I see. I will wait for him to make his tea before I go to the door. One should be polite when he has his hat in his hand."

20 - "Hotel du Mer: Afternoon, Day 2"

Marion returned to the hotel after searching the area unsuccessfully for a harness-maker. Its clean and spacious lobby was a comfort after her exploration in the rough alleys of the old city. She noticed Neville sitting at a table in the corner of the dining room. She walked over to him, and he stood to seat her. "You look as if you've had a rough time of it, Raoul," she said.

Neville leaned over to her and whispered, "Hold your thought please, Marion. I have been here for fifteen minutes, and we may have something. We must listen to the men at the next table. I cannot catch all they say, but I believe they are anti-Napoleon, and only speak so loudly because they think I am a foreigner."

The waiter came, took her order for a glass of wine, and left. "But they're not talking, Neville, just eating. What am I supposed to hear?"

"They stopped when you arrived. They don't know if you are also a foreigner. Let's talk about selling rum – in English. We should encourage them to believe we are both foreigners."

Marion launched into a discussion of the Stillwater Rum Trading Company's business. There was no need to make up stories. The men at the next table certainly did not care about her business, and probably did not speak English. What did it matter if they did? Neville actually found her dissertation interesting, as well as being impressed with his fiancée's business acumen. "We should also spend a few minutes with our plan to actually sell rum here," she said, "We can't stay for days and days and do nothing. We can't look as if we are on holiday."

"We had this discussion in Jamaica," protested Neville. "I can't be married to someone who trades with the enemy!"

"Oh, pooh, Neville. We are an American company."

"Ah-ha. Now I know why you were in Baltimore for three months."

She blushed, Neville noticed. Embarrassment or annoyance?

"I didn't hide it from you," she said. "At any rate, it's not a time for that topic. I've just had an idea."

Marion rose and took a step over to the table of possible anti-revolutionaries. She said, with some urgency, but in a quiet voice, "*Monsieurs*, I need some help. My father was supposed to come in here, and I thought he was to be on the American ship in the harbor. He is coming to find a harness-maker who specializes in fancy-work for the rich. I know we can't speak very loudly about things for the rich, but that's not what I'm looking for... it's my father. If I could find this harness-maker, maybe I could find him. Would you know such a man? Could Emperor Napoleon have taken him for some reason?"

The question caused an amusing reaction. All five men immediately looked cautiously about, making an excellent imitation of a flock of wary pigeons. Two of them stood up, gave Marion suspicious glances, and walked out. One of those still seated leaned toward her and said, in a voice just above a whisper, "One must be very careful these days. The eyes are everywhere. Men have disappeared simply for being suspected of saying things against one of the Napoleons. Meet me out back in fifteen minutes. I would hate for such a beautiful woman to lose her father." The remaining men then left the room.

When Marion and Neville met the man behind the hotel, he was cautious, but willing to talk for a few minutes. "Can you give me a description of your father? I did see another pair of foreigners here a few days ago."

Marion gave him a description of Mr. Chapman at Whitehall, and then added, "There are two Englishmen at the *Hotel le Pont Noir*, I know, but neither is my father. Do you know the harness-maker?"

"Yes," said the man, "He was at the table; the first one who left."

"I saw no one who looked like a harness-maker," she said.

"It is Sunday, *Mademoiselle*. We are dressed for church. I am surprised you are not."

"Sunday?" she queried, with an honestly surprised look on her face. "We have been travelling. I suppose we have lost all track of time." *And I have found the men I need*, she thought. I suppose I can ask a name. If they don't know it, they don't know it. "Do you know a M. Georges Cadoudal?"

A flash of fear crossed his face, but he said, after a pause, "I may have met such a man, but not here. I really must go now."

"Wait, *Monsieur*. Are you sure he's not here – in Le Havre – today, and looking for two or four people?"

The man paused again, for at least a minute, and studied the faces of both Marion and Neville. At length, and after looking guardedly about, he said, "I doubt it, but I will ask the harness-maker. *Au revoir.*"

"Wait, where would I find…?" Marion began. The man did not wait to be detained a second time, however, and vanished around the corner of the hotel.

"Well, Marion, you're all dressed, we have made excellent headway today, although we have no idea if anything more will happen. We've had our lunch, and supper is some time away yet. Although you have suggested we do something with your idea of selling rum, I just cannot leave the situation with Sir William alone."

"I agree. The rum must wait. I can set up a return trip. But what can we do when we cannot even get our eyes into the *Pont Noir*?"

"That's it, Marion! It doesn't have to be *our* eyes; just somebody's eyes. Somebody who will come tell us what they see. Where is our Jacques friend? I think we could trust him."

"I'll go back out. I'm still dressed for the street."

"No, we can both go. We'll be just taking a walk, but we can talk to boys we meet, yes?"

After walking a zig-zag pattern through a few of the tawdry streets, and asking a few boys they met along the way, they concluded that Jacques was not to be found today. "We just choose another one, at random, Neville?"

"Yes, I suppose so. Choose one who is not such a ragged muffin that the hotel wouldn't allow him in. He won't be welcome for long without a purpose, but a neater one might get to see the lobby before he's out on his ear… the little monkey in the gutter there, perhaps."

"You can't see I've got a job?" asked the boy when Marion asked if he'd like to earn a few *centimes*.

"I am sorry," she said. "I didn't recognize it. What are you about?"

"Feathers, Mademoiselle. Me and me sister have got a pillow business. I brings home all the pigeon feathers I can find, and she stuffs her pillows with 'em. We're doing well, we are. Try Louis over there. He ain't got no business."

They passed on Louis, who looked like some sort of refugee, and walked 'round the corner. There, of all surprises, stood Jacques.

"Marion, this is Jacques. Jacque, please meet my lady."

"I am not Jacques," he said, "And I do not know this man, but I am very pleased to meet you," he said, grinning a brown-toothed smile at Marion.

"I've made a mistake, then. I'm sorry," said Neville.

This boy was very similar to Jacques, with the same black hair, flat nose, and twinkling eye, but slimmer and a bit shorter. "I am Ragab, the brother of Jacques," he said. "Jacques has taken a wagon to the waterfront, and he must walk home. It will take him some time. You can call me Roger." He obviously had no idea of any connection between the pair who'd had sent his brother to the waterfront with a donkey wagon and these two. He offered no other information.

Neville glanced at Marion, and she gave a slight nod. "Would you be interested in earning a *franc* or two?" Neville asked Roger, "The work is very easy. Just watch a doorway for us, and report what you see… maybe you will need to follow someone."

"Someone dangerous?" Roger asked.

He's perceptive. "Not particularly. He might be angry if he finds he is being followed, but he's not a murderer or a government agent of any kind," Neville answered.

Roger agreed. They gave him a description of Stearns, more detailed instructions about watching and following, and paid him some money. When he left, they returned to the *Hotel du Mer* to kill some time. Neville condescended to discuss the business of selling rum to the French navy. He still disliked the idea, but immersed himself in the discussion, knowing it would pass the time quickly. Marion also talked him into a few hands of a simplistic game of cards she had enjoyed since childhood, and, in those moments when they found themselves alone in the room, some whispered conversation about what action they might take to free Sir William.

At about 2:00 p.m., they heard a louder-than-normal conversation at the hotel door. "No, you cannot come in," the bellman said to someone outside. "Begone. You have no business in here."

"But I do," the visitor said. Neville recognized the voice as Roger, and jumped for the door.

"Hold on there, bellman. I think your visitor is a messenger I am waiting for."

Roger peeked cautiously into the door; he broke into a smile at the sight of Neville, probably with relief that his pay would continue.

"Well why didn't he say 'messenger', then," groused the bellman. "He would have been announced, rather than making a 'to-do' of it."

"I'm sorry, bellman," Neville said. "Here's twenty *centimes* for your trouble. I'll tell him what to do next time."

"Hmmpf," said the bellman. "Take him in there," he added, pointing across the lobby to the baggage room, "until you're done with him."

"I'll not go in there, myself," protested Neville, "and neither will my lady."

"Out back, then, into the garden, if nobody else is there," the bellman huffed. "And he can leave by the alley." He turned and walked away, still grumbling, "…can't have street rubbish walking about loose…"

The three adjourned to the garden. All were surprised to find it in mid-autumn luxury.

"This must be some gardener's hobby," said Marion. "It's lovely."

"Yes, it is," agreed Neville, and quickly turned to Roger, "Why have you come? Is there something afoot?"

"But I think no," said Roger. "Your man went out…"

"Out? Out where?" queried Neville, now curious, and possibly excited about something different than they had seen for over a day.

"No place, Monsieur… just out. He did walk for a while to the north, and then to the west, and then he did walk back through the buildings to the hotel. Just a walk, I think. No shop, other than the *tabac*… Just a walk."

Neville cooled for a moment. The insignificant event had given him new concern. "Roger, will you do another thing this afternoon, please? Wait until you think it is tea time in the dining room there, and then go in to see if M. Stearns has come down to eat. If he is with someone, come back to tell us what the other man looks like, all right?"

Roger left by the alley.

"Your idea is excellent, Neville, and I have another one. Let's take a glass of wine at this little table here in the garden and play another hand of my card game. It should be warm enough until the sun drops behind that tree."

Roger dropped by again at about 4:00, causing the bellman further annoyance because Marion and Neville were in the garden and difficult to find. "I make a pretend at the *Pont Noir*, yes?" said Roger. "I say I have a message for a man in there…"

"What name, Roger? What name did you use? Not M. Stearns!"

"No, no. I am not *stupide*. I know he is not supposed to see me. I ask for the banker from a mile away. I know his name because…"

"Good, Roger, very good. Was the hotel serving tea?"

"No, *Monsieur*. The French, they do not drink much tea. But it was dinner-time. M. Stearns, he came down the stair just before they tell to me there is no man for my message and I must go away. No tip. He gives me nothing. Your man, he is with another man – tall, like you, and thin, but he looks sort of tough, with very long legs… and some hair that is white, here," he said, touching his temple.

"Thank you for your ambition," Neville said to Roger. He dug a few coins from his purse, and paid Roger twice what he had asked. "You will check with us in the morning, yes?"

"*Oui, Monsieur. Merci, merci,*" said Roger, and shuffled away.

"Neville, this is the first eye-witness account we've had that Sir William is actually here!" said Marion when Roger had gone. "The description certainly sounds like Sir William. It's proof we're not chasing a wild goose, or just silly Michael Stearns!"

"I agree, Marion, but it also tells me we cannot rely only upon having them watched by Roger. It's too slow – too delayed; and it is not always easy to understand this Egyptian speaking French... we must watch the hotel ourselves somehow."

"Yes, but as I said before, we cannot go into the street dressed like we are, and just stand around waiting all day. We would appear most suspicious... enough to attract the police, I should think."

"We must ask, then, what else can we do, or what else can we wear?"

"Both, I think. We should find some better costumes; they need to make us less noticeable on the street whilst we find some other place from which to watch."

"Ahhh, yes, yes. Windows across the street... but there are no hotels across the street."

"Can we rent a room? It doesn't look to me as if this street is very active. Even a vacant building would suit us."

"We would have to be very careful. If Mr. Stearns has been there for almost a week now, and looks out his window at all, he might notice a light in the evening where there had been none before."

"Yes, so we need an occupied building with one open room. And, we need to open our trunks and see what clothes we might employ to make us look more like those people we see on the street... so we can start our search in the morning."

"I'm not sure I have much here that is rough enough," said Neville. "How about these?" He held up a pair of brown trousers.

"Yes, it should do," she said, "They seem to wear just any old thing. I know I sound spoiled, but I have many choices. Most of these street people probably don't, so they don't concern themselves with any styles. We should make it a point to wear trousers that don't match the blouses... that sort of thing." She went back to pawing through her trunk.

"I suppose, but it's not necessary to appear as farm peasants or fishermen. We could be more… urban; clark and housemaid, for example."

"Oh, yes. Good thought. Oh, you might like this," she said, grabbing a couple articles and stepping behind her dressing screen.

He heard her rustling about behind the screen for a moment, but then she stepped out, wearing only her underthings. She held an outfit up to the side. "What do you think? Should I try it on?"

Neville's reaction was immediate. The sight of his scantily-clad fiancée and lover produced immediate excitement within. He threw his trousers on the floor and took three quick steps across the room to her. Pushing her outfit aside, he slid his hands beneath her filmy blouse, ran them up her bare back, and pushed her body against his. Her reaction was equally swift. They kissed a long, warm kiss while his hands caressed her back, and then down, pushing her pantaloons out of his way so he could feel her buttocks.

"My turn," she said, and began to unbutton his blouse. He did the same with his trousers. In a single minute, the two were pressed against each other again, feeling the warmth of each other from thigh to shoulder, and all their clothing was piled at their feet. Marion turned him enough to push him so he would fall backward onto the bed. He wriggled another couple feet into the center of it while she followed. Without waiting for further play, she mounted him. He grabbed her buttocks and pulled her hard onto him as they slid smoothly together, and he then ran his hands up her back and pulled her body down; pulling her firm breasts down to his waiting tongue. He circled the tip of it around each nipple and she pulled away again, sitting upright to display herself to him. She put all her weight down in his center, and began pulsing, in every way she could imagine, to urge him toward the inevitable climax of their union.

Only a few minutes later, after the initial urgency had passed, they lay pressed warmly together with their hands still slowly exploring each other's body. Neville said, very quietly, "I know this doesn't seem like the time, Marion, but we know Mulholland is there. Is it not more important now to watch?"

"It might be," she purred, "but you are the one who said nothing will happen at night. I don't mean here. I mean at the *Pont Noir.*"

"Yes, you're right. Now it's my turn, then." He rolled over on top of her naked body, feeling his excitement return straightaway.

21 - "Smuggled Into France, Day 2"

The inhabitants of the little green house in Honfleur were kind enough to provide a place where Georges and Ellen could lie down for a few hours to nap. Georges had made a strong request to be awakened by mid-morning, at the latest, and by ten o'clock they were under way toward Le Havre.

"This is a stroke of luck, is it not, Ellen? Not only was our friend in a generous mood, but he has given us the perfect disguise."

"It is a good thing, Georges, of course, but I think we are doing him a favor to deliver this wagon back to the waterfront – and not having to deal with this donkey. Get on, you ass." Ellen flicked her whip at the stubborn animal pulling the wagon. "We save him at least half a day of travel. Why would he have a tinker's wagon, anyway?"

"I don't ask such questions. I assume it was to help someone else go the other way. Mind your manners, boy, or I'll have you fixing shoes for a week," he joked. "This will be it."

"What is *it*?"

"This street is the hotel street. They were all lined up here back when the harbor was busy with shipping. Everything from dormitories for the poor travelers to fine hotels. Most are closed now, you see? Some have two or even three families living in one small room. Napoleon is not the savior for our country he pretends to be."

"There – this one's open, the *Hotel du Mer.*"

"I see. We shall continue along the street toward the waterfront, where we will dispose of this wagon, and take the time to see everything along our way. It's quiet now. Nobody will bother a tinker going to work. Here's another, the *Hotel du Emperor Napoleon.* Pfft."

The next block had three closed rooming houses, and the one following, a single hotel, the *Hotel le Pont Noir.*

"Do you see this, Georges? Does it mean anything to you?"

"Yes, the same name as in Marseille. I think it is where Mr. Stearns would be."

"I'm sure it is. What do we do now?"

"First, we determine if Mr. Stearns and Sir Mulholland are here. Then, if they are, we find an older boy to take this wagon to its place, and we begin watching. Drive around back of the next building, boy."

"Don't push it, Georges. I'm hungry, and I have the whip."

"Sorry. I can't believe Marion and Neville will not have found this place, as well. Where are they… somewhere here, watching? I saw a boy on the next corner. I'll have him go into the hotel and inquire. Oohh; my legs hurt when I climb down."

Georges limped out to the street to find the boy he'd seen. He seemed to straighten himself up as he walked. He walked more normally for a few steps, but then went back to a pretending a limp. He returned in a very short few minutes with a dark boy of fourteen or fifteen years ambling beside him.

"Ellen, this is Jacques. He says he can drive the wagon."

"Don't you have the cart before the… donkey, Georges?"

"You would think so," Georges said, "but Jacques, will you tell my boy what you just told me, please?"

"Your papa, he tell to me that he will give me money if I go ask in the hotel for a *Monsieur* Stearns and if he is alone."

His French is worse than mine, thought Ellen. *He is Turkish, possibly, or Egyptian?* "You don't want to go? I have another coin," offered Ellen.

"Oh, no. It is not the money. Your papa, he is generous. But I don't need to go, because another man; he ask me to do the same only this morning."

They're here!

"When I go to the man at the hotel desk," Jacques continued, "he is a very grouchy fellow. He told to me they should come ask themselves… but then he told to me that your M. Stearns is in his rooms; and another with a long English name what makes him to think of the Dutch."

Mulholland, for sure.

"Your friends are there, *oui*. You have a surprise for them?"

"*Oui, Oui.* A man and a woman, yes? Well dressed? Where do we find them?"

"A man, yes. He tell to me his name is Raoul. I cannot do business with a man I do not know his name. He is well dressed, but I do not see a woman, and I don't know where to find them, *Monsieur*," Jacques said, turning to Georges and spreading his hands. "I meet him in the street, maybe three blocks there." He pointed south. "I could help you find them."

"No, it is all right. We thank you for your help, but we need more for you to take this wagon to the waterfront. We will pay you for it. The donkey is very stubborn."

"I have also found a room in a small house on a back street where we can stay for a day or two and plan," announced Georges, when Jacques had crossed the court and climbed into the wagon.

"Raoul?" Ellen asked.

"I would like to believe he would not announce himself as 'Captain Burton'," Georges smirked. Jacques 'cluck-clucked' and snapped the whip at the recalcitrant donkey, and the thing brayed, but began to move. "The owner has agreed to supply breakfast and something for dinner."

"*Oui*, Georges, thank you, but also, if you possibly can, a basin of water to wash my face. What do you think Neville and Marion are doing? We know now they have discovered Sir Mulholland?"

"I don't know, but we must find them. They should have been here all day yesterday, and they may have a plan well under way. They don't know we are here. I'm going off again. My connections here should be able to contact them quickly – and quietly. I suspect they are in the *Hotel du Mer*. But we must also keep a watch on the front door of the *Hotel le Pont Noir*," suggested Georges. "If Neville and Marion are doing the same, or are disguising themselves to go in and take Sir Mulholland out, we will see them. Mr. Stearns is not expecting us, and certainly the hotel staff is not, but we are expecting Marion and Neville. We will spot them, even if our enemies do not. The question is, how do we watch? We can't just stand in front."

"We're not tinkers any more, I suppose," said Ellen. "There goes the wagon." The contraption was clattering down the street. "The damned donkey seems to behave better for Jacques. Hmpf… I could go on the street as some sales boy. What can we find for me to sell? News sheets? Vegetables? Flowers? Shoe shine?"

"This isn't London. I don't see customers here for shoe shines and flowers… you could try news sheets. They are quite the rage now, with the war going on. It's not like we actually want customers. I could ask one of my associates to buy a stack of the *Mercure*."

"While you're away, I will go explore the hotel area to see where I should take my papers in the morning. Maybe I can just wait in some nook to watch through mid-day."

"A good idea. I doubt we have to worry today. Even if the *Pride of Maryland* came in the day before yesterday, and Mr. Stearns sent a message to Paris first thing the next day – yesterday – he will not have any response yet."

22 ~ "Hotel du Mer, Day 3"

"**O**h!" said Marion with a start. "Neville, wake up. It's almost light. We must get on if we are to find this room today."

His hands sought her immediately, to feel her softness; her smoothness and warmth. He pulled her close to feel her naked body next to his. "Last night was heaven to me," he whispered. "Let's not get out of bed yet. We could…"

"It was heaven for me, too, Neville, and I would love to stay another hour or two, wrapped around you, you naughty thing, but you haven't even married me yet… and we have something important to do. How do you say it? 'Duty calls'?"

"Oh, you would say 'duty'. All right, let's go. He caressed her bare chest again, gave her one more long, warm kiss, and then began to rise. "We can't ignore breakfast this morning, though. All that… exercise… has made me very hungry."

"And me," she agreed. "This costume should work. Oh, wait. We'll have to change after breakfast," she said with a wink. "They'll never allow street people in the dining room. What's come under the door, there?" she asked, pointing to a scrap of paper on the floor by the door.

"Someone's slipped it under the door while we were… busy," he said. He picked it up and unfolded it. "It's a bit of a note. Not many words, but it tells us of great joy. Here, you read it."

Your friend has arrived

We will be in touch

"They're here, Neville! This is our best news in three days!"

"Yes, here. But where is 'here'? I say we get on with today. If we can get our own plan, we'll be much more ready to act once we're in contact with Georges and Ellen."

"I can see only four buildings that might serve, Marion," Neville said. They stood in an alcove at a corner near the *Hotel le Pont Noir* after having had their breakfast, and then dallied in the room for half an hour while changing clothes.

"The last building might not have much of a view, either, because of that tree," said Marion.

"You're right. I hadn't even noticed the tree. Finding a building is the easy part. Finding someone to speak with about a room may present a problem."

"We must find our way 'round the block to get to the rear alley of the buildings opposite the hotel. I would not want to be standing across from the hotel if Mr. Stearns goes out for his walk, or risk the chance Stearns will look out his window and see us," said Marion. "We must stick to the back entrances; visit from the alley."

Wearing their costumes, they found a room soon enough, notwithstanding that it took most of the day to find the building manager. Neville paid him two weeks' rent, and he took another half hour to find a key.

"This room is disgusting, Neville," Marion said. "What is the smell?"

"Over there, in the corner. I think it is a pile of old potatoes. I will throw the muck out, and the smell won't be so bad. We can burn a candle."

"Well, I won't lie with you here, you can count on that. And I had hoped there might be a little… relaxation." Marion winked at him, pushed herself against his body and gave him a warm kiss.

"The thought is incredible," said Neville, "and I would have thought it would be me making such a suggestion, but what can I say? I agree the place is disgusting." He kissed her again. "Let's go to work then, if we can't play. We should set up watches. Neither of us can stare out the window all day and remain vigilant. What do you say to two hours apiece?"

"Aye, aye, Captain Burton," said Marion.

He kissed her smiling face again, pinched her bottom, and said, "All right, then, you're on duty. I will deal with the potatoes."

"This day has dragged terribly, Neville," Marion announced at about 6:00 in the evening. "Nothing has happened at all."

"I am painfully aware, my dear," he answered. "I suggest we hold on until about ten, go back to the hotel for some refreshment, and we'll find something to do there." He smiled his best wicked smile, and ran his finger up her bare arm, around the nape of her neck, and around to her lips.

"Your suggestion is acceptable," Marion responded, "but you are putting pressure on the wedding date, to be sure. I can't believe anything will happen here in the middle of the night – well, not here, anyway – and we haven't seen Georges and Ellen yet, so we can't put much of a rescue plan into operation. Mr. Stearns shouldn't be taking any walks; it's not a nice part of town."

"And if Napoleon has sent his troops, I'd wager they aren't so diligent they wouldn't stop at some *bistro* before nightfall. But we must be back on watch before sun-up."

They watched until almost ten in the evening, but not longer.

23 - "Sweet Tomatoes (Day 3)"

Early in the morning, Ellen returned to a place she had found on the street corner nearest the hotel entrance. There she placed a bundle of papers on the curb by her feet, took one sheet for each hand, and stood up to look around, all while doing her best to look nonchalant. She did not position herself directly across from the hotel, since it was not on the corner where any intelligent news boy would stand, but two doors down. She could easily see anyone who came or went. At this time of day, there were few people about.

"What am I to do if I see Mr. Stearns come out?" she'd asked Georges.

"I am going around the area to see what help we might have, so you will be on your own for a while. Leave me a sign; let's say, a news sheet on the door of the building across the street. It looks to be empty. Then follow him. We'll meet back at the house at noon, or as soon after you follow him and he goes back in."

A man – a baker, perhaps – came ambling down the street. He bade her good morning and took the paper she handed him. "I haven't seen you before," he commented. "What's happened to Richard? Oh, this is the *Mercure*. Well, all right." He paid for his paper, and ambled away.

Richard? She wondered; but not for long. "Oi!" shouted a young voice a block away. A small boy hurried toward her carrying a stack of newspapers. "My corner!" he yelled when he had crossed half the distance. "My corner. You get lost. Find some other place." He waved his hand as if shooing away a dog.

Ellen waited for him to come closer. She had no interest in raising a great ruckus; calling attention. "What paper have you got?" she asked.

"*Le Moniteur*," he said. "It's better than the drivel you have. And you're not even from 'round here," he added. "You sound like you're from the Loire or someplace. No wonder you don't know, but no matter, it's my corner, and you can shove off."

"I'm not leaving. We can sell both papers, people can take a choice."

"They ain't gettin' no choice," he said. "They're buyin' mine." He dropped his papers and squared off to her.

"But…," she began.

He shoved her backwards by the shoulders. She dropped a few papers.

"No 'but'," he yelled. "Sod off, you foreigner."

By purely bad luck, two things happened at exactly the same time. A policeman appeared from around the corner just as the boy shoved and yelled. No policeman could resist involving himself in a scuffle. He blew his whistle and hurried over. Out of the corner of her eye, Ellen saw a man emerge from the front door of the Hotel le Pont Noir. She was positive he was Michael Stearns. He came out with another older boy in a rumpled uniform: the hotel bellman, who appeared to be giving directions, pointing down the street.

"What's going on here, boys, and what did you call this one, Richard?"

"He's a bloody foreigner from the Loire," Richard said. He turned to Ellen, and with a sneer, added, "You see? He knows whose corner it is. Bugger off."

"Maybe you should come with me, boy," said the *gendarme*. "We don't like foreigners 'round here. We used to get a lot of 'em from the ships, and they were always trouble. Bring your papers and come with me."

"Ha!" shouted Richard as Ellen followed the policeman away.

"Button your lip, Richard," replied the *gendarme* over his shoulder, "or I'll bring you along."

Good luck appeared soon, however, just two blocks away. Ellen and the *gendarme* were met at the corner by Georges. "What is this?" Georges asked, "Where are you taking my assistant?"

"He's got himself crossways with the news boy on the corner back there. Richard says he's a foreigner. They were havin' a dust-up in the street. We can't have it – or foreigners, neither."

"Well, I'll take him, if it's all the same. He's not from 'round here, no, but he's a great help. I'm very sorry for this nuisance. He won't do it again. Here's a *franc* or two for a glass of wine for your trouble." Georges didn't wait for the policeman to protest, but grabbed Ellen by the ear and led her away, chiding her as they went, "I told you to stay and wait for me before you got up to your tricks. You were supposed to just sit there…"

The policeman watched them go, shrugged it off, and went looking for a more serious criminal.

Once out of the *gendarme's* sight, Ellen slapped Georges' hand away from her ear, "Ow, Georges; no need to be so rough!"

"Had to make it look good, right?" he said. "Now what?"

"We simply must keep an eye on the hotel, but not this instant. Mr. Stearns just stepped out while that repulsive little urchin began his pushing and shouting, and the policeman appeared. Mr. Stearns is out and about right now, though, and we don't know where he went because of the little paper-selling snot. But he's alone. Sir Mulholland did not go with him. Should we charge in to the hotel now?"

"We've been thoughtless, Ellen. We haven't made any plan for action at all – only our plan to watch, so I'd say no; we would be careless. *Merde!* We must decide on a plan of **action**."

"I can go back on the street with something else later; maybe turn my shirt inside out or borrow one from somebody? Tomatoes, perhaps. At least I'd have something to throw at that little tramp."

"Ah, yes. A good idea, tomatoes. I must go see what my friends would do to help. When I return, I will bring some bread and cheese, and maybe some wine. You can bring your unsold tomatoes, yes?"

"Unsold? Pffft. I may throw them at you."

Ellen returned to the street again by early afternoon, this time a block the other side of the hotel, with a basket of mistreated tomatoes. Richard was no longer there, anyway; undoubtedly done selling the day's news. She continued watching for the next couple hours, but Mr. Stearns never appeared, either at the window or in the street.

24 - "Menage a Cinq"

"**M**arion, we've done it again!" blurted Neville. The previous evening he had opened the curtains enough to let in the light of a new day even before the sun rose. The exertions of the night, however, had proven too powerful for him to overcome... on schedule, at least. Marion had urged him to yet another surge only an hour before, but now morning had definitely arrived.

"Done what, Neville?" she murmured, more like a purring cat than his accomplice in spycraft.

"Overslept, dear. It's light out. I'm afraid I am still concerned that they could go off in the night; we must stay in the room after this and watch more closely. You are far too much of a temptation for me... and maybe Georges will show up."

"What?" she cried. She sat straight up. "We must go," she said, swinging her legs out of bed. "The time is getting shorter. Some sort of gaol-wagon could be here at any time."

"You are correct, of course," said Neville. "Today we must take action whether Georges and Ellen appear or not. Let's get on."

After they had dressed in their street costumes, Neville grabbed the basket containing a few bits of food they had found the day before, and the two headed for the ground floor.

"We have no cover of darkness, so we'll just need to be careful," Neville said outside. They walked around the block to get behind the buildings opposite the *Hotel le Pont Noir*.

"It's clear, go ahead" said Neville. "Oop, oop. Stop." Neville held his hand out across Marion's chest to stop her from stepping out to cross the side street. "There is a shoving match between two paperboys, and a *gendarme* is coming. Just wait a minute." They heard the *gendarme* blow his whistle, and could see the three talking together for a minute before one of the paperboys went off with the *gendarme*. "All right, it's clear now, let's go."

"**G**aahh, here it is. We've only spent yesterday here, Neville, and the thought of spending more than today is simply horrible."

"I think that's irrelevant, Marion, because we're not going to. We absolutely must take action today. We must do something other than watch. If Mr. Stearns sent a message when he first got here, there should be a response very soon – today, even – if there will be one at all. Maybe you should go out again to look for the harness-maker – to see if we can find Georges."

"I disagree. The note said they would be in touch. How do they contact us if we aren't there? They know where our room is," argued Marion.

"There wasn't another note this morning. I agree to wait; not have you go out. I don't like it when I can't see you. I'll go 'round the block and back to check our room for notes at noon and three... and six if need be, but no more. We must act!"

"All right, then; let's go back to our hunting game again. What's Stearns' brilliant idea? If we think it's simply to show off to his American spy cohorts, what's he going to do with Sir

William? Just hand him off? What more could he do? What does he get out of it?"

"I'm not sure, but we must act quickly. It's your turn."

"My turn?" queried Marion.

"At the window. It's been two bloody hours already."

She went to the window and looked out; "Is it not possible to clean the glass?" she asked. "It is disgusting, and there are a hundred dead flies here on the sill. I'm not sure I could recognize my mother through this. Oh, the paper boy from this morning is back; I'm sure it's him," she said. "There is something familiar about him... Ooh -- the curtain across in the Hotel just fluttered. I really think I just saw Mr. Stearns. A man in the street is walking – no, limping - this way. He has stopped at the tomato boy and they... no, he said something, but now he's moving on... nothing more, sorry."

Marion was still on duty when the man returned. "The old man is back. He has groceries now," she reported. "He stopped at the boy, and the boy has gotten up from the curb... I think they are... they're coming into this building..."

She had the attention of Neville now, who hadn't seen anything, but had apparently heard the door below. The two of them sat very quietly looking at the door, hearts beating as the footsteps came closer; and then a knock...

"Do we call out, or open the door, Neville?" Marion whispered.

"Pull your knife and stand aside. You say it is just the old man and the tomato boy?" Neville pulled his knife as well, stepped forward, and opened the door.

The two visitors stood grinning like court jesters in the hall, but said nothing. One held a basket containing a loaf of bread, hard cheese, a couple apples, some grapes, and a bottle of wine.

Their other visitor, the tomato vendor, carried his basket of tomatoes, as if coming for a social visit. Astoundingly, there was no immediate recognition, but the stupidity lasted only about half a minute.

"Ellen?" said Marion from behind Neville, "and Georges? How could we not know you? Come in. You look very tired… and dirty, and… foreign."

"And so tired," said Ellen. She fell into Marion's arms.

"So am I," volunteered Georges, "but I believe we have little time to act."

"We agree, Georges. We assume Mr. Stearns sent a letter to Paris the moment he came in. If so, and Napoleon received a letter, and decided to act on it – which I suspect he probably would – then there should be an army detail here soon; maybe today. Have you heard from your contacts?"

"Yes, we have, and I hope we'll have a little help from them, too. I expect the army detail will be delayed at least a day, although we can't count on it."

"Do you have ideas, then? Have you made any plan you would have enacted even if you did not find us?"

"*Oui, oui.* Here's the plan we came up with: We think our best …"

25 - "Siren"

"We have noticed something we can use, Georges," said Marion. "Every day at 4:00, the bellboy is sent to the *boulangerie* for the evening's bread."

"Oh, yes," said Ellen. "I also noticed that he leaves, but I didn't notice the time. I certainly smelled the bread when he came back about a half hour later."

"Four is the time, then: we go in when the bellboy leaves. We'll have half an hour at most, and we don't want anyone to know what happens, or the army will mount a manhunt. We want them to think Mr. Stearns is an idiot who wastes their time."

"We have a couple hours for you two," said Georges, indicating Neville and Marion, "to pack your trunks for leaving, and for Marion and Ellen to dress for tea."

"I'm the distraction, so I'll stay in my street clothes," said Neville.

"There he goes, Marion," said Ellen. "It is time for our play-acting. Jacques is going in now. You be careful, Georges. Mr. Stearns is not a small man." As soon as the bellboy turned the corner to the west, Marion and Ellen crossed the street directly to the front door of the *Hotel le Pont Noir*. Jacques opened the door for them very politely on his way out.

The desk manager had not left his post after Jacques had delivered the note, since he had obviously seen two beautiful women entering. He may have thought the lack of a carriage odd, but it didn't show. He was too busy watching his visitors.

"May we dine here, sir?" asked Ellen.

"*Oui, oui! Certainement!*" responded the clerk, "This way." He walked them to a table in the dining room, and seated them at a table by the window. "Do your men come to join you?"

"Not today, monsieur. It is quiet this afternoon, is it not?" asked Marion. "May we have a glass of wine each, please? Pinot Noir would do fine, thank you."

"*Oui, oui,*" he said. "I will tell a waiter, but will be back. I must deliver a message to one of my rooms." He left hurriedly.

"Waiter, Marion?" whispered Ellen, "We didn't know there was a waiter at this hour."

"I don't think there is. We'll see. Don't worry about Mr. Stearns, though. I am sure I can handle him. I can lead him wherever I want, I'm sure of it," she said, "He would never in life avoid me."

"What if they don't both come down? We meant the note to imply that his visitors have arrived – that someone has come to take Sir Mulholland."

"Yes, but he may wish to receive his reward before handing over his hostage. If Sir Mulholland does come down, remember – Mr. Stearns has no idea that either of us knows him."

"Here they come down – both of them," Ellen said.

Marion could feel her heart racing now. She made an effort to breathe regularly. She watched Stearns step down as far as the last step, but then stopped and looked expectantly around the room. He obviously didn't see what he expected, turned and said something to Mulholland, and then walked across the room to the front door. He stopped there and looked out. Only five feet from Marion and Ellen, he hadn't seen them. He wasn't looking for women.

Close enough, thought Marion, "Michael Stearns, is that you?" she asked. Stearns jerked around to look in her direction. He saw the ladies, but momentarily returned a blank stare; confused. They were not what he had expected to see.

"It is you, isn't it, Mr. Stearns?" asked Marion again, "What on earth are you doing here?"

Stearns' reaction may have been blank, but he was recovering. Behind him, on the other hand, Mulholland's dull, unhappy eyes went round with recognition, but he managed to stifle any outburst.

"What am I doing here?" he asked, directly facing Marion. "Tobacco sales, of course." His 'cover story' came out automatically. "What are *you* doing here?"

Down at her side, as best hidden from Stearns as she could manage, Ellen tipped her hand horizontal to the floor, palm down, and wagged it back and forth; a signal to Mulholland not to do anything rash. A smile crossed his face; he stifled that, too. Stearns was now obviously fixated on Marion, as he had been for years before.

"Rum sales, same as last time," she said. "How could you do that to Father?" she asked suddenly, in a loud voice.

"Not so loud, Marion. We needn't make a scene. Certainly not at the front door, when I am expecting an important guest."

"Important guest? Forsooth! Was Father not important?"

"Step outside for a minute, then, and we can discuss it as loudly as you like." He turned to Ellen. "I'm sorry Miss Aughton. It appears we are to have a private discussion. Please meet my business associate, Mr. Mulholland, from London. Might you entertain each other for a moment, please?" He looked around the room for a waiter, but saw none.

"Certainly," said Ellen. As Marion and Stearns opened the door to have their discussion outside, they could hear Ellen begin, "From London, Mr. Mulholland? The weather will be quite unpleasant there soon, I should think…" The door closed.

Marion began her planned tirade, "I mean to tell you, Mr. Stearns, what I think of your actions in Jamaica…"

"In here, then," he said, looking around. "This gate leads to a nice quiet courtyard behind the hotel. We can talk there." He led the way down the narrow path to a place where it opened into the courtyard. There he suddenly doubled over when struck in the belly with a stout club. Three men pounced on him, a second man deftly slipping a black hood over his head. When he yelled, "Marion, run!" the first man knocked him on the head with the club. He went down, and his attackers tied him. He made no more noise. The remainder of the abduction was quiet and efficient. Marion returned down the walk to the street with her heart racing again, and her hands shaking. She opened the gate just as Neville entered the hotel door twenty feet away.

By the time Marion reached the door and went in, the desk manager had just left Ellen and Mulholland's table, with Neville right behind him. Two more glasses of wine sat on the table, and the manager seemed unaware of any danger. She watched Neville follow the desk manager behind his counter. When he suddenly realized Neville had followed him, he reached for something under the counter. Neville had expected such a move; he knocked the clerk's hand aside, grabbed him by the collar, and shoved him through a door behind the counter into the hotel's little counting-room. The door closed.

"Good afternoon, Sir Mulholland. Is there anything in your room you must take with you?"

"No. My, it's good to see you two! Did I just see Neville?"

"You did," said Ellen, "but it's time to go, before the bellboy returns with the bread."

"Bread?"

"Please come with us. We'll cross the street calmly and enter a yellow building with an ugly green door; the one I pointed out a minute ago? Up to the third floor and knock on the brown door, all right? Georges expects you. We'll be right behind."

"Ellen, I know Mr. Stearns wrote to an aide of Napoleon when we first arrived. I expect a cadre of soldiers to come for me any time… today, possible. I expect that is what he is looking for."

"We expect the same, but we most go now."

Mulholland turned without saying more, and opened the door for them all. They crossed the streets in twos, with Marion last to enter the door of the yellow building across the street. Before she closed it behind her, she saw Neville leave the *Hotel le Pont Noir* and the bellboy appear around the corner with his daily bread.

"I am so pleased to be done with that place," said Marion, "The smell was horrid, and I kept expecting a line of rats to emerge."

"They did," said Georges, "did you not see Napoleon's goons arrive?"

"Yes, and it worries me, because I haven't seen Neville since."

"You said you saw him exit the hotel…"

"I did. What are they doing down there now?"

"Their commander went inside five or ten minutes ago, and he's coming back out now," reported Georges, he being the only one exposing his face to the window. "Oh, the desk clerk is with him, so Neville didn't kill the fellow, at least. He's waving his troops to come to him. No, not all, just three. They're all going back in, now."

"He'll probably have them search the rooms."

Three unexpected knocks at the door made them all jump. Ellen, closest to the door, asked in a quiet and polite voice, "Who is there, please?"

"Raoul."

"It's Neville, Ellen, let him in," said Marion, getting to her feet. She walked to the door and threw her arms about him the moment he entered. "We think they're searching the rooms now."

"They're back in the street now," said Georges, "looking up and down like a herd of deer." He slowly removed his face from the window. "I don't want them to see me and know they're being watched. We'll just have to wait for the next move. They can't very well search. I doubt they have ever met either Sir Mulholland or Mr. Stearns. They would have only the clerk's description. And only then if they believe him."

The next move came in five minutes, when shouting could be clearly heard. "Who will pay the bill, hah?" the desk manager shouted twice.

"Ho, ho!" chuckled Neville. "They must be leaving. Look again, Georges."

"Yes, they are. The clerk is waving a paper at them, and they are just thumbing their noses. That's the end of it. What did you do to the clerk, Neville?"

"I was gentle. I held him down to tie his hands and feet, and I stuffed a rag in his mouth. I also stole this, so it would seem a proper robbery." He held up a small bag of money from the till.

"And what about Mr. Stearns, Georges? What is to happen to him?" asked Neville.

"The ladies would not allow me to have him killed, so my friends will just take him away. They will carry him to another city, well away from easy access to the sea... one of my men knows a small town in the forest east of Clermont-Ferrand. They can keep him for several days and then dump him there with no money or papers, ha, ha. I wish I had suggested no clothes, as well."

"Outstanding! I suspect the French government will not bother to read any more of his letters."

26 - "Return to the Sea"

Evening, *Hotel du Mer.* "You know I am more than anxious to leave immediately," began Sir William Mulholland, "I've done enough sitting in little ship cabins and hotel rooms to last me the rest of my life."

"We know, we know," said Ellen, "but we still have some travel ahead of us, and Georges and I, if not the others, are almost asleep on our feet. We need some time to rest."

"And I don't see any reason you can't go for a walk here, now, as long as it is nowhere near the *Hotel le Pont Noir* – or the *boulangerie* at three or four in the afternoon. Give us a couple days to rest. Then we can go," added Marion.

"Would any of the boys report us to the manager of the *Pont Noir* for a few coins?" asked Neville. "Is it a concern, Georges?"

"A good thought," Georges said. "I will put out word for Jacques and Roger to let them know we have a little something more for them if such a thing never happens."

"But my French is terrible," said Mulholland. "What if I go for a walk and get lost?"

"I've had better sleep than the others," volunteered Neville. "I'll go with you. I can do with stretching my legs."

The next day they rested. The second day they took time preparing for travel. Neville and Marion had to pack their trunks, but Georges, Ellen, and Sir William had almost nothing. With the 'pressure off', they enjoyed a lazy tea in the afternoon and told their stories of travel and arrival in France. They also sent Jacques to see if the *Pride of Maryland* remained at the quay.

"Jacques reports our ship is still there," said Neville.

"When does she sail?" asked Mulholland.

"He couldn't get a straight answer. They wouldn't talk to him. We must assume she will still be there tomorrow and will take us at least out to the Channel Fleet, though," said Neville. "Why would she not? There is nobody chasing us."

"I agree," said Georges. "We shall all leave together early tomorrow. This will be an easy trip for you to go home."

"Georges, you're not going?" asked Ellen.

"I haven't decided. I will know more tomorrow," he said.

The five gathered for an early breakfast. Finished eating, Neville threw down his serviette. "The bread here in France is wonderful, but the rest of a French breakfast is no to my liking. Give me a proper English cooked breakfast any day. I'm looking forward to crossing the Channel. The trunks should be down by now. I'll go see to their proper loading. As soon as it's done, I'll come back in for you, and we'll be off."

The other four remained chatting at the table while Neville went to check on the loading. Outside, the carriage house court was empty, except one saddled horse that looked as if it had just come in. *What's this about?* he wondered. *Oh, maybe our man is loading in the street behind.* He walked out of the walled court to look. *Ah, here it is. But, where's our man gone? The reception clerk! He's called our man off to some silly chore, I'd wager. Now, I've got to go get him back on this.* He began his walk back into the courtyard, from where he would enter the hotel.

* * * *   * * * *   * * * *

While Neville was walking from the courtyard to the street, Marion suddenly jumped up from her chair – causing Georges and Sir William to start politely standing. She waved them to sit. "I've just forgotten something I want to carry, not leave in my trunk," she said. "I'll be right back." She walked out of the dining room, heading for the hotel's rear door to the courtyard. *Neville will probably be annoyed with me about this – having to open the trunk again...* She opened the door to the courtyard, stepped out, and closed it behind her. In the corner of her eye, she sensed motion. A dark figure lunged at her from behind a rose bush beside the door. Just before his hand pushed a sweet-smelling cloth onto her face, she recognized the dark blur as Mr. Michael Stearns. She tried to yell, but the hand was too tight. She thought he said, "Come with me, dear." She tried to kick, but her limbs were feeling sluggish. Her arms didn't seem to work... all went black.

* * * *   * * * *   * * * *

Neville rounded the corner from the street where the wagon was parked. What he saw in the courtyard at first confused him, but not for long. A large man had just thrown some sack over the horse that had been waiting. The sack hung across the horse in front of the saddle, and the large man was setting his foot in the stirrup to swing himself up. *That's not a sack, it's a person. It's a woman. It's Marion's dress! It's Marion! Who would…?*

The man swung his leg up and over the horse, and jerked the reins to turn the horse to leave through the only opening from the courtyard to the street – the carriage door behind Neville. Recognition occurred at the same instant Neville made a running jump for the man: Michael Stearns. Neville got hold of Stearns's coat with both hands. The buttoned coat did not slide off, and Neville's weight dragged Stearns free of the horse. The two fell in a lump in the courtyard. Stearns was not damaged, or even befuddled, and leaped to his feet, literally tossing Neville to the side. Marion hung precariously over the horse, head down. The horse did not stand still, but fidgeted nervously at the sudden activity.

Neville and Michael squared off to fight. They began circling each other for the inevitable clash.

"How did you get loose?" asked Neville.

"Georges' friends are not quite what they seem. They were willing to let me go for my money. I told them I had a lot of it back at the hotel, but the manager would have it all locked up when I didn't show up – and he surely wouldn't give it to them without me; at best he'd keep it all for himself – so they brought me back. The hotel clerk was willing to give me my things as long as I paid the bill."

Michael's hand had found a stick of firewood. He swung it as a club, but Neville dodged. In addition to avoiding Michael, Neville's eyes were glancing about for a weapon of his own. Nobody came to the door to help. The firewood stack along the carriage house wall was the most likely source of something he could use. They continued to circle.

"And how did you find us here?" Neville asked. Mostly to buy some time, he pulled out a new knife he'd bought before leaving England. Short and easy to hide, it may have been good for a bar fight, but was almost silly for a fight such as this. They both started when Marion finally slipped from the horse, dropping head-first to the cobbles. She remained motionless, but neither could drop their guard.

"Finding you was not a problem. You think you are so clever, but you stay here. As soon as I saw the hotel, I knew you would be here. There is no other fine hotel in the area. I just didn't know if you were gone – or alone. But again, you are too slow… ha, ha, ha. And too slow with such a little knife. You are a buffoon. This is a proper knife." He pulled a 12 inch blade from his belt.

Marion awoke, but was obviously confused. She attempted to push herself up to sitting. Blood ran down her face – probably from a cut on her head. Neville wanted badly to go to her, comfort her, bandage her. But first, he wanted to beat Stearns with a very large stick. So far there had been very little noise; not enough to get any attention.

"Where's my hauler?" Neville asked.

"You certainly have a lot of silly questions. I paid him to go get me some bread for my travel."

The two had circled to where the firewood pile was now behind Neville. He noticed an old set of fire irons leaned against the wood pile beside the carriage house door. He picked a small split log from the pile as a better defense than his little knife.

Stearns lunged. Neville deflected the lunge with his split log, and slashed at Stearns' arm. He missed, but moved another foot closer to the fire pokers.

Stearns did not slow down. He lunged again. Neville tossed his knife aside and grabbed another piece of split wood. With one, he deflected the knife again; the other he threw at Stearns' feet in the hope he'd stumble over it. Stearns hopped nimbly over it, and Neville threw another, and then a third, in the hope of providing Stearns poor footing.

"You can't even defend yourself without a sword. Throwing sticks, ho, ho."

Neville glanced toward Marion, noticing that she was now striving to get to her feet. She had not yet gained the composure to cry out. Following Neville's glance, Michael also looked over, becoming aware that he must make his big effort to dispatch Neville and run before Marion sounds an alarm.

Stearns' next slash stuck in the end of Neville's stick, and while Michael wrenched it loose, Neville hit him hard on the arm with another stick. Neville pushed him backward and continued to move as if he were just trying to get a better angle. He threw another stick a Michael's head.

Neville's left hand reached for the fire pokers when Michael ducked. When Michael looked back, the poker was swinging at his head. The sound of the strike was as much a 'splat' as a 'thump', and Michael went down on one knee. Blood spurted from his face. His knife hand, now supporting him from the ground, gave Neville an excellent target for a heavy split fire log. Neville kicked the now-knifeless Stearns backward to a sitting position on the cobbles beneath his fidgeting horse. Marion began stumbling toward the hotel door. Neville picked up Michael's blade, and began to approach his opponent.

With a great leap, Michael jumped up onto the horse. Displaying his excellent horsemanship, he reined the horse around to paw the air in Neville's direction. With his bloody face a mask of anger, he yelled, "I know where you're going!" and rode off.

Neville tossed the knife aside, letting it clang across the cobbles. The sound apparently reached inside the half-open door to the hotel, because by the time friendly faces appeared, Neville was holding Marion, and they were both shaking. Marion began to cry softly, but as she regained more of her sense, her crying stopped, and she began getting angry.

"What happened, Marion?" Ellen asked.

"Mr. Michael Stearns happened," she answered. "The man must be insane. He tried to kidnap me. He held a cloth with something sweet on it over my face, and I went insensitive. When I woke up, they were fighting. I guess I fell off the horse on my head, too, see? It really hurts."

"Ellen, will you take her inside, please?" Neville asked.

"Georges, your friends let him go. He paid them."

"I am sorry, Neville, but it happens. They may take my enemy's money for some favor, but they will not come after me, or sell me out. Money and patriotism are two different things."

"He said he knows where we're going. How could he... because of the hauling man, I suppose. Here he is now, with Mr. Stearns' bread. We'd better question him."

"I told the man who wanted bread that the trunks were bound for the waterfront," said the driver. "I meant no harm or offence. I just made conversation, and I went for bread."

"Keep the bread. He gave you the money for it, *oui*?"

"What now, do you think, Sir William?"

"There is nobody really looking for us now, is there?"

"No," said Neville, "Mr. Stearns said he even paid his bill at the *Pont Noir*. Unless Stearns stirs up some hornet's nest somehow, nobody should bother us, but I still think we should go quickly."

"Yes," said Georges, "You are still foreigners who should keep to a low path, but nobody knows you. There is nothing wrong with foreigners heading to the port to *leave* the country."

"Stearns may try to uncover my activities," said Georges, "so I should go with you. It is not easy to identify a man you can't find."

27 - "The Cliffs of Etretat"

"Don't be too self-conscious. We are just average American business-people going back to the harbor to catch our ship home. All right, 'average' and 'American' don't seem very 'average' here, but I think that's how we should act," said Georges. "We look a bit odd on a hauling-wagon, but it makes us a bit more humble. We will be watched, yes, but it shouldn't arouse the authorities."

The hauling wagon rattled through the quiet streets of Le Havre, laden with three men, two women, and two large trunks, progressing with no apparent urgency, for the next half hour. Portions of the water came into view, and the shore-birds were more prevalent – mostly gulls. Neville felt his heart beating faster. He told himself to be reasonable about his feelings, but he gripped Marion's hand tighter and tighter, until she pulled it away.

When the quay came into view, the entire wagon-load exhaled; but not cheerfully. No ship remained at the pier. Even if the *Pride of Maryland* wasn't there. They had each secretly hoped there would be some American ship. But there was no ship there at all.

"She's there," announced Neville. He pointed to a sail about two miles distant, just then about to disappear behind a point of land to the west. The hauler stopped his wagon and, before any of them were ready for the question, He asked, "She's sailed, citizens, where now?"

It was Sir William who answered – in English: "A good pub."
Neville translated.

"**W**hat do we do now?" asked Marion. They had moved from the
wagon to a little bistro they'd found on the waterfront facing the
street along the quay. Their wagon sat in the street behind. She
looked to Georges for an answer.

"It's a great view of an empty quay," said Ellen, "And the sea
beyond. I think we should try one of their wines and enjoy the
view for half an hour. I think I know what's next."

"What's that?" asked Mulholland.

"Walking," she said, "More walking, like Georges and I did on
the way in."

"We must shift to our 'Option B', if you remember it," chimed
in Neville. "We have a wagon. We can ride. 'Option B' takes us to
some small town on the coast where we can commandeer, buy, or
steal a small boat and sail out to the Channel Fleet. We've done it
before, right, Georges?"

"Yes, we remember 'Option B,' said Georges, but Ellen is
right. There's more walking, and my hips are just getting over the
last. We still have three problems," he added: "one, there are those
trunks in the wagon; two, the driver may not wish to take us; and
three, we will not look at all like locals. We will arouse suspicion."

"There's a fourth problem," said Neville. "Everyone duck for
a minute. Don't look out the window. Down low, ***now***!"

"We might look strange to the barkeep, but it is more
important Mr. Stearns does not see us," whispered Neville beneath
the table. A fleeting shadow passed over the table. "There he
goes." The shadow did not hesitate. Neville waited a minute

before saying, "Take a peek out the corner of the window, Ellen. See if you can tell he's gone."

Ellen sat up and looked out. "Yes, I can see the back of him two doors down. He's not stopped."

They all sat up. "Having him looking for us makes us look even less local," said Mulholland. "He can identify all of us, and lead the authorities to us."

"He could, but does he even know who the authorities are? Would they believe him?"

"The *gendarmes* would certainly come running if he made a big disturbance," said Georges, "if only to keep the peace. And if he's walking the streets looking for us, he might find the wagon. We must take it and go."

"Go where?" asked Neville.

"Etretat, very near where Ellen and I came in, is still our best option, I think," said Georges. "I can't trust my contacts at this point, either."

"You see? More walking," said Ellen.

"And the trunks?" asked Marion. "I really would hate to lose all my things. Could we ship them?"

"Excellent idea. We'll have the wagoneer take them to a shipping agent with a note. I'll write a letter instructing them to be shipped, whenever a ship is available, to your address in Boston, Ellen, if the idea suits? Yes? They can be shipped wherever you like later, Marion – Baltimore or London. You won't have them soon, but someday."

"Quick, Marion, we must take out some traveling clothes and our carry-bags while Georges writes, change here in the loo or some back closet, and then be off," said Neville.

"This is a lot better than I had hoped for," said Georges. "The wagon-driver has agreed to cart the trunks to a shipping agent."

"So for now, they are lost to us?"

"Yes, of course... you have what you put in the sacks, though. And, I found a livery with a donkey for sale. We may be walking, but we aren't carrying bags. See? All on donkey's back. And I think he could carry Marion, too, if her head begins to bleed again."

"Better than our trek in, right Georges?" queried Ellen.

"Verily, it is lovely," answered Neville, "The only thing we need is rain; we could have mud."

"Cheer up, Neville. We should be there by tomorrow morning. We're better to walk this afternoon, and into the night, if need be, so we don't attract attention. We have no schedule. We can sleep in some stable as long as we like, unless the farmer finds us and runs us off with his pitchfork. Here's the road east, now."

"East? Where are we going, Georges?"

"I suggest again, Etretat. It's only sixteen miles, the slope down to the water from the cliffs is quite reasonable, and there is fishing done there."

"So, we'll find a boat, then."

"Yes. There are other towns closer, but most are within this Le Havre harbor; within the city's defenses. You may choose another, if you wish."

"No, you are right. We should not expect to sail out of Le Havre harbor. Do you really think we can make up costumes that won't arouse too much suspicion?"

"Ellen and I have survived perfectly well with what we have."

"I'm sure of it," said Marion, "I can smell you from over here."

"Sorry. Yours seem a bit… clean and tidy; and rather fancy for travelers, but once we are in town we will no longer be 'travelers'."

"We'll be conspicuous on a fishing boat, though," said Neville.

"Yes, and there were watchers when we came in. Someone shot at us."

They walked into the darkness, but they reached the edge of Etretat before the hour was late. "There wasn't a building outside the town, Georges. Now we're in town, and there's still no stable," commented Marion. "Where do we take our nap? Do you see any likely place?"

"These huts, maybe. I think they are for fishing gear. Let's look for one with nothing in it. I would think being empty would imply no fisherman will bother us in the morning."

Georges proved correct regarding the lack of disturbance in the morning. Ellen, Georges and Mulholland slept well past dawn, but Neville rose early, and was soon joined by Marion. "Marion," said Neville, "would you please go into town and find the *boulangerie* and any other *marché*. See if there are things we might eat. Georges knows the people better here, but I think you might be a more… expected… sort of a shopper. Here are some of my remaining French coins."

She gave him a kiss and went off down the slope toward the town center. When she returned, the others were awake. All were pleased with bread, cheese, and bit of cooked lamb she brought back, and they turned their thoughts to obtaining a boat.

"The town is beautiful," Marion said; "very picturesque buildings… it's a very old town, I think. The white cliffs are dazzling, with arched rocks at the ends of the harbor, and a little river coming down on the far side. The people are cheerful enough to say 'good morning'. I saw several fishing boats on the beach and there are more up the river, I think. I saw two come out from there, at least."

"Georges, I think you should be the one to find a boat. Your clothes are closer to those of the fishermen, and your language best, of course," said Neville. Georges finished his bread and departed for the strand. He returned in an hour.

"I asked a couple fishermen if there were any boats for sale, and they both pointed to a larger thing near the end of the strand. They told me the old man who owned it died, and he has no son to use it. It is not in very good condition, they said, or someone would have bought it months ago."

Neville accompanied Georges back to the strand to look it over. "I would not want it for my boat if I were fishing every day, but it should serve our purposes: one short passage out to sea. We will need to find the widow, though, and pay her something for it so we can get the sail, and maybe the oars."

28 - "Diligent"

"**I**t's time to go," said Neville to the others early the following morning. "The tide will be high soon. Georges, would you do us the favor of walking down the main street and finding us a loaf of bread and some cheese while we get the boat ready? We can't be certain we'll be picked up today."

"I will, for sure," said Georges. "There's nothing I would like more than going for a walk. Does anyone have a few more *francs*?"

"Yes, here," said Marion, digging in her purse, "Don't forget the wine."

While Georges was gone shopping, the others carried what little they had left down to the beach. They found the high tide had the water lapping at the stern of their little craft.

"This is good," said Neville. "She's too heavy for us to move her very far." *And I'm sure she couldn't handle much being moved around on land.* He didn't want to express much of his concern about the boat's sturdiness. "The tide still has some to rise," he said. *Leaving this boat to sit in the tide day after day has done her no good.* "Let's put our things in, and I'll see to sorting out the sail."

"Here's Georges already," said Marion, not twenty minutes later, "and he's carrying things."

"I had luck with me," said Georges. "The little store you visited yesterday morning had everything I wanted, and the young girl who waited on me was not in the least curious. Shall we begin pushing?"

"You will all have to get your legs wet, I'm afraid," said Neville. "I admit I've become spoiled, with eight or ten men to let me step up from the strand and then shove us off, but we must have some water under this little thing if we're putting in this many people."

With their great effort, they dislodged the old boat from the sand and slid it into the water. It finally floated, with its bow on the sand and everyone in except Neville. He gave his last shove and jumped over the gunwale. Mulholland swung out the oars, actually looking forward to a bit of exercise other than walking. He rowed ten feet from the strand, then twenty and thirty, and he kept on while Neville raised the frayed sail.

"Nobody seems to care about us," said Georges, surveying the beach.

"Thank the Lord we're not being shot at like the last time, eh, Georges?"

"Verily. I hope we find a reasonable captain out there, too; one who doesn't think we should be hanged immediately as spies."

"Isn't this beautiful?" said Ellen. "The great white cliffs and those arches at the ends of the strand are wonderful, indeed."

"Yes," Neville agreed, "But these great white cliffs choke our wind for sailing. Within the harbor, we should have calm seas and little wind, but it may come up quickly once we get farther out."

"Should I keep rowing, then?" asked Mulholland.

"Only at your pleasure for exercise," said Neville. "The sails will push us, albeit slowly. We have no rush; we have all day to sail out where we can see our fleet. I can't push this contraption too hard though, or we may rip the sail or break this old mast. Save your rowing for later. We may need it."

"Time for bread and cheese, then," said Mulholland. "I'm quite hungry."

They bobbed on, farther and farther from the beach, for an hour, before they began to feel the stronger breeze flowing through the Channel. *There's more wind than I had hoped for,* thought Neville, *and I can't say I like the looks of the sky.*

As if reading his mind, Marion asked, "Captain Burton, could we really not just sail across the Channel to England?"

"I'm not sure this old thing could take the abuse. To be honest, I hope we find a ship soon. You notice we have bigger waves now? That's because the tidal current is flowing west strongly, and the wind is from the west. So the wind pushes the waves up steeper." In direct response to Neville's explanation, an even larger wave struck hard on the bow, and all of them clearly heard a sharp 'crack'. Neville looked up to inspect his mast, but it held, with no sign of a crack.

"It wasn't a ripping noise," said Mulholland. "The sail is still together."

"Oh, my dear," said Ellen. "I think it's this. There has been some spray over the edges, but this water here seems to be coming from that crack. I didn't notice whether it leaked there before."

They all looked to the seam Ellen indicated, and her statement did seem likely. Just a small trickle of water emanated from the crack, but it was obvious. "Do we have something to bail with?" asked Neville.

"Yes, our little wine cups," volunteered Georges, holding it up. "The girl at the store had only two of these little iron things. It was either these or drink from the bottle. She looked at me strangely when I asked for them; what kind of Frenchman would have no wine cup, even on holiday?"

"We'll hope for no more damage," said Neville, "but we must combat these waves to get farther out where we might see sails."

Five swells later, they were hit by another wave large enough to throw cold spray over the whole boat and cause another cracking sound. Neville's crew looked at him with concern as he sat in the stern with one hand on the tiller and one on the main sheet. They saw him grimace.

"There's more water coming now," announced Ellen.

"Start bailing, then," commanded Neville in his best voice of good cheer. "It can't be long. We'll make it." *And I would certainly not like to drown my fiancée.*

Georges and Mulholland took the first shift at bailing. The cups were small. Not much water went overboard with each flip of the wrist. "I don't think we are keeping up with it, Neville," said Mulholland. "These cups are just too small."

Another 'crack' made the stream perceptibly larger. "Ellen, please put your foot on the cracked board and give it a push. Does it feel firm?" queried Neville.

She turned to get a better angle, put her small foot against the board above the crack, and pushed. It moved. "No, Neville, it's… it's… sort of spongy."

"Everyone look around very carefully for sails, then. Look for a little piece of white that doesn't move like a wave or one which has square corners like those only man would make. If we don't see a sail, I feel I must return to the beach for our safety. I've had one shipwreck this month, and I don't care to go in the water again."

They all stared in different directions for a minute; then two. "Nothing, then. We return to shore."

"Look, there, Neville. A ship is coming! There, look," said Ellen, pointing to the west.

They all turned west and stared.

"Yes," said Marion at length. "I see it. It's not far off shore. There, Neville, you see?"

"I do, now, yes." He loosened the main sheet so the sail would fly loose with the wind, then tightened it up just enough to steady the little craft. He no longer attempted to make it move, just hold it stable while waiting for the oncoming ship.

They watched quietly as the ship grew larger, floating silently toward them on a following breeze, and stemming the tide easily. "Oh my," voiced Neville. "This is a bit of a sticky wicket."

"Since when did you begin speaking sports terms, Neville? What's wrong?" asked Georges.

"This ship is not one of ours – a small two-masted brig, not a Channel Fleet ship. She's French, friends. We're out of the frying pan into the fire, I'd say. I'll try turning for shore, but there's no thinking to run away from her in this little boat if she wants to catch us. We can't put too much stress on this old boat, or she'll go to pieces beneath us."

Neville could see the ship's features better as she approached. "I think she's some sort of coastal defense boat; a guard boat. She's armed, although not with much. She must just hop between the little harbors when her captain thinks the Channel Fleet is elsewhere. He's probably gotten good at it. We should claim we've come out on a holiday sail and have run into trouble because we don't know what we're doing."

"But of course, you do, Neville," said Marion.

"Don't tell **them**, or they'll hang me for a spy. And remember, we should all talk for Sir Mulholland as much as we can. He's one of our two American visitors. Can you be an American, Sir William? Ellen could be your… daughter?"

"She has definitely seen us, Neville," said Mulholland, "She's coming straight on, now."

"And we're not getting closer to shore as quickly as she's approaching, are we?" he responded.

In another fifteen minutes, the French brig came alongside. Her sails were aback and her sleets flapped lazily in the calmer breeze just inside the protection of the great white cliffs. Ellen, still sitting in the bow, threw the little boat's painter to a man in the chains. The fishing boat literally began to come apart as it scrubbed up and down against the side of the larger vessel.

"Welcome! Come aboard," said a familiar voice – in English. "I can scarcely believe our luck – we've been looking for you for two days now," intoned Mr. Michael Stearns. "That's not much of a ship you're commanding, there, Captain Burton."

Stearns' had his right hand wrapped in some sort of bandage. His face bore the diagonal red streak of a fireplace poker, giving him a more sinister appearance than normal. *He would probably be grinning if his face didn't hurt so much.*

"Mr. Stearns. You seem to have the lives of a cat. Take them to safety, and just shove me off to drift," said Neville.

"No, no. You come aboard. You would find your way out of that predicament, too. I am looking forward to presenting you to the French Navy. Not as much fun as presenting Sir Mulholland to Napoleon's aides, but enjoyable, nonetheless. We'll head back to Le Havre now, and get things rolling as soon as we can in the morning."

The ship's captain strolled over to greet the group. *His uniform is not standard French Navy,* thought Neville. *It must be as I thought – some coast guard.* "Welcome to my ship, the brig *Diligent, Monsieurs et Mademoiselles,*" he said. "I am *Capitain* Sully; charmed to meet such ladies. You look a bit wet and cold. Please hurry below." He bowed to Marion and Ellen, and to Stearns, he queried, "What do you wish me to do with your guests?" They were surrounded once upon deck by three guards armed with pistols and a few sailors with large knives in their belts.

"That one," Stearns said, while pointing at Neville, "you may lock in your brig. As you can see by my hand and face, he is dangerous. The others may stroll about as they wish. They aren't armed, and they certainly have nowhere to go. Keep an eye on the men, but I assure you, the ladies are harmless."

"Ladies, please accept my invitation to dinner in the captain's cabin," said Stearns. "He will have one of his men show you where you can freshen up. Interesting costumes, by the way."

"You won't try to drug her again, will you?" asked Neville. Sailors pushed him away. As he went toward the hatch, his experienced eye surveyed the ship, and reached some very interesting conclusions. There would not be much time to do anything with the information, however. Even as he walked, sheets were being hauled and the helm thrown over to begin *Diligent's* return to Le Havre, which was not far away by sea.

No sooner did the brig manacle clack shut than Neville heard an alarmed commotion above.

*　　*　　*　　*　　　　*　　*　　*　　*　　　　*　　*　　*　　*

"This seems a strange situation, does it not, Mr. Cadoudal," asked Mulholland. The two had been left alone, and so had wandered to the poopdeck out of curiosity once another sail had been seen – and then identified as British. They leaned on the aft rail.

"It is. They've just left us alone. Mr. Stearns is a bit daft, is my opinion. Did I ever tell you of his visit to Marseille a few years back?"

"Yes, you did, and I'll agree with your assessment that he's more than a little odd. Anyway, I wish I had a glass of scotch whiskey right now, while we watch the show."

"Or a good cognac, yes. They have obviously decided the ship behind us is British. Why do we head away from shore?"

"It's the wind, of course, from the west. We can't go direct into it, and the cliffs are just there, to our starboard, so we have no choice but out into the Channel. The *English* Channel, I might add. Even the French don't call it the 'French Channel'."

"Oh, yes, I know these things, but I am no sailor, and so infrequently on a ship I don't remember. Look there, just to the right of the sail. Forgive me for not pointing, but do I not see another sail?"

"Yes," said Mulholland, "I would say it is. Say your prayers. We may be re-captured. I would love to go below and tell Neville, but I think we must save our visits for a time when we might give him something more than just a little information. He must hear all this yelling, anyway.

"Now I think there are three, and they are coming on quickly. The first sail appears to be a smaller ship, with shorter masts – harder to see; but it must be ahead of the other two."

"I think you're right, Georges. Can you make out what they are saying there by the steering wheel?"

"I think I have most of it. They had expected to reach the safety of Le Havre in five hours, even with having to tack into the wind, but now, with the British ships in the way, they are considering chasing out into the Channel to evade."

With nothing better to do, the two remained at the stern rail watching the British ships grow steadily larger. An hour later, Georges gave another report based on his eavesdropping: "They think there are two frigates and another, faster ship chasing us. The two frigates are fast, but they cannot come so 'close to the wind', as they say. They must go farther out into the Channel. The little one comes straight at us, you see?"

A flurry of activity began forward. "What is this now, Georges?"

"We are tacking. The captain is turning the ship from northwest to southwest. He must think we can run straight to Le Havre from here. He thinks maybe he can outrun the little ship behind us?"

Diligent changed her attitude from one tack to the other. She has been heeled to larboard, but now to starboard, and her speed had increased with a steady breeze.

"What does our follower do?" asked Georges.

"She's turning, too. Maybe she has what they call 'the weather gage'. She can follow, whatever we do?"

"Yes, yes, you are right. No, look. She is still there in the middle of her turn. Her sails are flapping, if I see right. Still flapping, yes? Something is wrong?"

They watched for several minutes, and the minutes grew longer, until they were convinced. *Diligent's* crew was apparently also convinced, for they heard a muted cheer rattle around the ship. "Something went wrong on the little ship. She is no longer getting closer. We are leaving her behind. We have gone from re-captured to just captured, just as we were before," said Mulholland.

"*Merde!*" said Georges. "Shall we see if we will be allowed something to eat?"

The two walked forward and down the main companion stair to the ship's galley area in search of food. The smell guided them, and they soon came to a place they understood to be the kitchen.

Georges asked a man there if they might have something to eat, and was surprised to find his request granted. Advance notice of 'guests' had apparently been passed down, and they were handed two wooden bowls of some sort of oat-based gruel that actually contained small pieces of meat. It was hot. They took it to one of the trestle tables in the small dining area. There they were alone. "I assume the ship's men are either above, sailing the ship, or asleep," said Mulholland.

"Yes, I assume so. What is this now?" Considerable commotion began above for a second time. The ship's motion changed again, and it heeled to the other side. "We've tacked again? Why would we make such a maneuver? I thought we were close to Le Havre."

They returned their bowls to the cook. Georges thought to ask whether he would be allowed to take one to the man in the brig. The cook handed out another bowl, complete with a spoon.

"Let's go visit, shall we, Mister Mulholland?"

They found the brig with little difficulty on such a small ship. Neville was shackled with a clumsy ring and crude lock on his leg to a sturdy beam, and sat leaning against the hull. It wasn't a little cell, just a space designated for keeping prisoners. "How is it here, Neville?" Georges asked.

"I'm out of the way, ain't I?" he joked.

"Here's a bowl of dinner. We had ours. It wasn't bad, and it came with a spoon, you see? I thought maybe that clumsy old lock might be picked."

"Thank you. I'll try it later. What's going on above?"

"We were being chased. They were sure it was British. Something happened, though, and it quit chasing, so we tacked for Le Havre."

"I prayed we'd have more time to mount a mutiny."

"Exactly how do we mutiny?" asked Mulholland.

"Look around for me. I think this is no navy vessel. There just aren't enough people. We saw three guards when we came aboard – no platoon of marines – and barely enough men to sail the ship. If the weather turns worse, they may call all hands to sail, leaving only three guards, the captain, his first mate, and maybe two others to deal with. They could be held at bay with a swivel gun while we surrender to some British ship. Look to see if there is a swivel gun, and where it is. If I can pick this lock, then I will come running when I hear all hands called."

"You make it sound so simple. We shall be your scouts, then, and get you word of it all. Enjoy your porridge. Cheer-o."

The two then climbed back to the deck. Squinting into the late afternoon sun, they saw more sails. These sails were not behind *Diligent*, but forward, and now on the larboard bow. "We've tacked back out into the Channel," said Mulholland. "We've been cut off by British ships again."

"So it appears. Are there ships behind?"

"No."

"We have lost the others then, and this is a new group, coming at us from the west?"

"Yes, brilliant! If this new group chases us offshore, maybe we will cross the frigates that were following, and once again, we may be re-captured."

"Unless the frigates went to the aid of the small ship which was catching us," said Georges.

"Either could happen, I suppose. We must pray these ships forward will not have similar troubles."

"Do you know this thing called a swivel gun, Georges?"

"Yes, there's one there. That tiny cannon on the rail near the steering wheel. They use it for signaling and for shooting at crowds of men. It's a vicious weapon when used in such a manner."

"I see. We didn't carry such a thing in the horse guards. He's right about the men. There's almost nobody to be seen, except those playing ape up there."

"And where are Marion and Ellen? I have come to the opinion that your 'lady soldiers' are a force to be reckoned with. They are probably Neville's secret key to a mutiny," said Georges.

"I'm sure they are. They could each disable a man before he knew he was in danger. They have a great element of surprise."

"We have more to watch than those ships now, don't we?"

Not much worth comment happened for most of the afternoon, however.

"It looks to me that four ships have spread themselves out across the bay between us and the harbor entrance to Le Havre. I'd say our fate has at least been delayed. We'll not be going in there soon," said Mulholland.

"No, thankfully. The fifth ship has apparently been assigned to chase us, though. She has been coming closer, but I think it's because she comes in on an angle from the west. Now that she's gotten more behind us, she doesn't seem to be getting closer. I think she's just another ship like this one. I think your question about our ladies has just been answered," Georges continued. "Do you smell that?"

"Oh yes. I just caught a whiff. A roast of beef, possibly? Mr. Stearns is making a show for his pretty visitors, and I am sure the captain is not complaining," said Mulholland.

"He is French, is he not?" queried Georges. "Why would he complain about the company of women? Their dinner will be better than ours. Shall we check in with Neville? It's been three hours. We have seen much, and nobody seems to care where we go; we know where Mr. Stearns and *Capitain* Sully are."

In the brig, Georges and Sir William reported what they had been observing: "The one ship following is not catching us at the moment, Neville, and we continue on a course to the northwest. It is getting much colder up there watching, so we may sit down here with you for a while. It's not bad here, at all. Oh, and your fiancée is fairing well at the moment. You should smell their dinner!" Georges kissed his gathered fingertips.

"Excellent. And I may look like I am chained here, but I assure you I am able to leave whenever I wish. We should stay here. Let the French endure the cold. We will have no trouble knowing when the ship takes another tack, and we will certainly not miss 'all hands' being called."

Georges and Mulholland went above for another observation before dark which, in this latitude, began about 5:00 in the evening. The chase had continued with great boredom by the time the sun set.

"It seems we have come on deck at the right time," said Mulholland. "Captain Sully has come up. What is he about?"

"He has just given some orders," said Georges, "and a man is coming for us."

"Excuse me," said the man when he arrived by them. "Will you stand over there, please? I must light this light?"

"Lighting a light so we can be followed seems strange to me," said Georges. "Doesn't it you, Sir Mulholland?"

"It certainly does. Some trick, perhaps?"

"It may be, but it's too dark to see anything now. Let's go below where it's warmer." They reported the incident to Neville, who made no sense of it, but he asked that they go topside each hour and report any more such strange things. They went up again in another hour.

"What's different, Georges? It seems darker. The stars are out, and we have the moon rising."

"It's the light, Sir. They've come and wrapped something on it. Why would they do that?"

"I think I see the strategy. They lit the light. Now they have wrapped it, and it's dimmer. They may wrap it once again, and then, as a final step, they will douse it. Think about it. It would look from the following ship as if we were sailing farther and farther away, and then we've gone over the horizon. By what means, who knows... extra sails or magic? Sailors are superstitious creatures. But we are gone. Then the ship tacks... left or right? How can your pursuers follow? They will have precisely half a chance to get it right. We will see them in the morning... or we won't."

They were below again, keeping warm with Neville, when *Diligent* tacked over from northeast to southeast. They knew it by the noise, and the tilting of the deck to the opposite side. The stronger rush of water past the hull changed sides, as well.

"They've made a choice," said Neville. "I think it's what I would do. Our chaser may go the other way, thinking that if it were the logical thing, then this captain would do the opposite to lose them. We'll know in the morning. Where have they offered you to sleep?"

Georges and Mulholland looked at each other. "They haven't," said Georges.

"As I would expect. Choose a warm plank. I'll see you in the morning." He rolled away from them and put his face down on his arm. In two minutes, he lay peacefully snoring.

"How does he do that?" queried Mulholland.

In the early morning, Georges woke to a lack of sounds. The quiet itself caused him to wake; not the noise of men running or the noise of the sea pounding the bows, but the quiet.

Georges was the first awake. He licked his teeth, circled his feet, and rubbed his back. The ship had little motion. He thought first to wake the others, but decided not to. The sun was already up. A general glow and a few slim rays of light found their way down the companion stairs to this lower deck. He would go on deck and see what was happening – or not happening. He stood stiffly, stretched, and hobbled to the stair. From there, he hauled himself upward, feeling far older than his years, into the light of day, where a glorious sight greeted him. The sky was blue and almost cloudless. The wind was light and the sea very calm. But his joy was to see Marion and Ellen upon the poop deck watching the scene. They'd both been provided with warm blankets to wrap themselves. Despite the presence of Stearns a few feet away, Georges walked to them, and gave each a small bow and the customary French kiss on each cheek. He was probably unaware of Stearns' particular distaste for him, though he would most likely have understood if he'd wasted enough of his time to pay attention to the man.

"You slept well?" Georges asked the two ladies. "I smelled your dinner, and can only imagine the wonderful taste of it."

"Yes, Georges, we slept well, and the dinner was excellent. I pray they found something for you."

"Oh, they did. I didn't mean to sound envious. Is this not a beautiful morning?"

"It is, for sure, but we appear to be in the middle of nowhere. There is no land to be seen in any direction. The British ship is still behind us, though."

Georges surveyed his surroundings. The blue of the water and the blue of the sky melded in a surreal picture of natural beauty, save the tiny obstruction to the east which was the mast and sails of some ship.

"Not catching us up?" he asked.

"Doesn't seem to be," said Ellen, "but we haven't been up on deck here long."

"This calmness is unusual for this bit of water – between the English Channel and the Atlantic Ocean – but it happens. I've been out here when…"

"Georges, where's Neville?" asked Marion.

"He's below, where it's warm, dear. Don't worry at all. We got him some food and slept by him last night. All is well. Do you suppose we could talk privately for a few minutes?" he said quietly. "Marion, could you get me a tankard of coffee to set our innocent 'Oh-what-a-nice-day' appearance?"

"Yes, I suppose I could," she said, and left.

Georges noticed Mr. Stearns' attention falling fully on Marion's departure. "Ellen, I will tell you now what I can. You relay this to Marion, and I will tell you both the remainder when she has returned… We are going to stage a mutiny." He looked her in the eye.

Ellen stared back with a steeled countenance, "What a lovely idea," she said. "I look forward to the experience."

Georges explained the expected situation and the signal for it before Marion returned.

"Oh, thank you so much," said Georges, and took a careful swig of the hot, brown liquid. "You two are our secret force. Prepare yourselves for physical combat. Keep any weapon you can with you, and find a person of authority to be near when the situation looks probable. Neville will appear, as if by magic, when he is needed.

"I am so pleased to see you this morning," he repeated more loudly. "Thank you for the coffee, Marion." He went below.

Mulholland was just rousing when Georges arrived in the brig. "Come along, Sir William," he said. "Let us go find our morning gruel. And if we are very lucky, maybe a little more of this." He handed his coffee mug over to Sir William, who took a few swigs and then passed it on to Neville. They returned shortly with three bowls, but no coffee, and they ate, sitting on the hard deck.

"Our ladies are in good spirits this morning," Georges reported to Neville. "Marion found me the coffee. While Mr. Stearns was distracted by Marion's going off for it, I spoke briefly to Ellen. Our pursuer is still there. Last night's maneuver didn't fool him."

"A good captain, then," said Neville. "I should like to know who he is. But I liked Captain Sully's trickery; I'll have to remember it. I suspect there was too much moon for it. There's naught for wind this morning, though, is there?"

The ship herself answered Neville's question. The foremast, near where they sat, creaked. She leaned for a second or two before standing up, and then returning to quiet again.

"No," said Georges. "It's quite beautiful, really."

"But it might be starting to get back to normal. Where are we, do you know?"

"I don't exactly, but I estimate we are off the Cherbourg Peninsula. I think I heard the name mentioned, too."

"Shall we go up and stand watch, Sir William? Without the wind, it's quite nice on deck, and growing warmer with the rising sun."

Light breezes persisted for another three hours. The ship moved enough in that time for the Cherbourg Peninsula to become visible to their southwest. The English ship continued to follow, but in the light winds, did not increase in size. "We'll evade this one, too, and head back for Cherbourg, or maybe 'round Ushant for Brest," Georges heard Captain Sully announce to his first officer, "We'll give all this rabble over to the authorities there."

"Nothing we didn't expect, is it?" said Mulholland to Georges.

By mid-morning, the breeze had picked up considerably. Georges and Mulholland noted that most of the on-watch crewmen were sent into the rigging or were hard at work hauling on halyards, braces, or sheets. The activity of a major sail adjustment seemed to take about fifteen minutes, but there was more to it. Another fifteen minutes of smaller activity followed as the captain fussed over his sail trim to achieve the utmost speed possible. The men remained at their stations for this latter stage, as well. The sound of water rushing past the hull increased measurably after the sail trimming, and it soon became apparent that they would leave their British pursuer behind unless he, too, made some significant sail changes.

Marion and Ellen appeared, and strolled arm-in-arm back to where their compatriots stood.

They passed their 'good mornings'. "Today's the day, I believe," said Mulholland, "Have you chosen your stations?"

"I've chosen mine," said Marion. "Or, rather, he's chosen me. I will be quite close to Mr. Stearns. I have no chance to do otherwise; but I shall lead him near one of the guards to increase the surprise. Despite the hospitality Mr. Stearns has arranged with Captain Sully, I think it's time he received a good old-fashioned beating." Her eyes were twinkling with the thought.

"Such savagery, Miss Stillwater," commented Mullholland. "It becomes you, verily."

"We will hope the main deck guards are near each other," added Ellen. "If they are, I can start Marion's take-down of Mr. Stearns, and then go for the second guard. We're quite looking forward to a little exercise."

"Equally radiant, eh, Mr. Cadoudal?"

"*Oui, oui*," said Georges. "Cheerfully ferocious. I will be near the Captain. I see he carries a short sword in a scabbard that can easily be 'picked'. I don't wish him harm, but if I take his weapon, he should stand down quickly."

"The third guard is mine, then," said Mulholland. "I hope I remember all my training with the horse guards. It has been some time. Be clear on this, my dears: your actions will start the fun. We will not act until you feel you are in place and give the first blow."

29 - "Mutiny"

Georges and Sir William lounged at the stern rail for another half hour, while the breeze continued to strengthen.

"We don't want to run straight below and confer with Neville right after the ladies have left us. We might be suspected of something," said Georges.

"But we ought go soon," said Mulholland, the time for our call of 'all hands' may be coming before too long. The rising wind seems to be related to the gathering of clouds, and the waves are growing larger. I also think our pursuer is gaining. Captain Sully may think so, too. He has raised his glass in her direction three times since the ladies went below."

"All right," said Georges, "I'm cold enough. Let's go down." They made a show of hugging themselves and rubbing their arms as they descended the main companion.

"I have noticed that this ship is colder than most navy vessels," said Neville upon their arrival.

"Really? We are quite pleased to come down out of the wind," said Georges.

"Yes, it may be better than up there," said Neville, "but it's chilly, nonetheless. A navy ship this size would probably have seventy men aboard, while this has but thirty-five or so; there's just not the body heat. What have you seen?"

"We think the ship chasing us is closer, and we think the captain thinks the same. The wind has picked up quite a bit…" .

"Yes, I can hear the wind from down here. It has more to go before they will call 'all hands', though. The ship will have more movement when the waves grow even larger. It seems a bit darker… clouds?"

"Yes, some seem to be gathering."

"A couple hours, then. Oh, our chaser – does she seem to be coming straight for us, or is she moving somewhat toward France?"

"We hadn't paid particular attention, I suppose," admitted Mulholland, "but I would say slightly toward shore. We could see two masts, right, Georges?"

"We could, indeed, now that you mention it. Why?"

"She's cutting us off from land. This ship may not be able to go in to Cherbourg if our navy stands between."

"Ah, yes. Lovely."

By noon, the British ship had grown somewhat larger. She was now in silhouette off to larboard, putting itself in a better intercept position in the event *Diligent* continued her run for the port of Cherbourg. Captain Sully studied the situation carefully, and consulted with his first officer.

Georges could catch pieces of the conversation, and he passed what he heard on to Mulholland, "They are coming to the conclusion they can't beat our navy back to Cherbourg. Captain Sully also knows *Diligent* is not the equal of a fully manned sixteen-gun British navy ship, which is what he guesses our pursuer is. Even if he had the guns, he doesn't have the men. He dares not fight. I keep hearing the word Ushant."

"Sailing northwest would be his logical alternative; to sail out 'round Ushant, turn south in the Atlantic and run, as close in as she dares, for Brest. It will take another day, and the risks include encountering another British squadron, and the Atlantic weather. He should be one very concerned captain at this point, ha, ha!" chuckled Mulholland.

"And he doesn't even know what we have planned."

"We should get ready. The wind is getting stronger, and the waves have grown, just as Neville expected." *Diligent* was, indeed, beginning to shoulder aside larger and larger waves, throwing spray far abeam.

"Our ladies must think the same. They've come up, you see. The annoying Mr. Stearns has come with them, as you would expect. Oh, it hadn't occurred to me until just now… Stearns must still see Ellen as Marion's handmaiden," said Georges. "She was somewhat out of character when we all met in Marseille, but I expect they have not encountered each other in any other situation. I further expect that means he will take even less interest in her doings."

"Oh, yes. I remember your report. He reacted poorly, if I remember. He looks as if he is trying to convince them to go below, and they are pretending to enjoy the excitement of the blow."

The lookout above bellowed, "On deck, haloo! Sails, Ho!"

"A lookout?" said Georges. "I hadn't noticed we had one."

"Neither did I, but I suppose it would be silly to be without."

"Where away?" yelled Guillaume, the first mate.

The lookout pointed west, not east or north. "Three points starboard," he yelled down. Captain Sully raised his glass. "*Merde!*" he shouted, after staring for a full minute. "Call all hands,

Guillaume, and tack for the North Atlantic. We are beset with British buggers."

"That was sudden," remarked Mulholland. "We're not in place, and Marion and Ellen could begin any moment."

"They will watch for our readiness, I think."

Guillaume bawled, "All hands! All hands to station!" Someone began blowing his pipe. The slapping rumble of feet on deck began and, on this small vessel, they felt the shudder of the ship as thousands of pounds of human bodies began climbing the ratlines.

Georges sauntered closer to the captain, and Mulholland scanned the deck for his target guard. He spotted the man halfway forward, near the boats, and began moving slowly toward him. Thinking it seemed wrong, he turned after a few steps to look back to where Georges stood near the captain. He saw his error. The guard near the boats was Ellen's target after she toppled Stearns. Mulholland's target slouched on the opposite side of the main mast; the size of the trunk almost concealed him entirely. He glanced at Marion. He could tell he had confused her by his actions, so he turned back for his intended position and waved at her cheerfully.

Four steps later, their attack began. Time seemed to slow to a crawl for everyone involved. The combatants first put on their best acts of nonchalance, every one feeling like a cat crouching, setting his feet for the pounce, positioned precisely where they have agreed. The moment Mulholland leaned against the mainmast bitts, he saw Stearns go down. Ellen had kicked his knees from the rear and stepped aside while Marion thumped him hard in the chest. He went down hard, indeed. Mulholland heard the thump of his head on the deck. He glanced around the mainmast to his right. His target hadn't noticed Stearns' mishap yet, staring off into the distance, apparently trying to see the line of British ships that caused the pandemonium.

Sir William glanced at the ladies again. Ellen had left Stearns where he fell, to Marion's tender-loving care. She turned for the closer of the two guards, who stood at some crossroads between amused and dumbstruck to see the big stranger on his ship trounced by a small woman. Mulholland would like to have watched Marion's next move, for he saw Stearns struggling to get to his feet, and Marion's dagger coming out, but he couldn't spare the time. As Mulholland stepped around the bitts, Marion punched her next target – the guard – hard, at approximately his diaphragm. Mulholland saw the guard doubling over, and Marion's knee coming up, when his own target noticed the movement of it, and reached for his musket. Sir William struck his arm hard with a belaying pin he had plucked from the bitts with his left hand. The guard howled with the pain of it, and Mulholland drove his right fist hard into the guard's face, sending him sprawling on the deck. He slid to strike his head against the base of the rail, and Mulholland picked up the man's musket.

He raised the musket to point at Guillaume, who now saw the danger. The howl from the guard had alerted everyone. Mulholland wagged the musket in a manner that advised Guillaume to move over near the sprawled guard. He could also see the surprise on Captain Sully's face – not yet at Georges, who already had his sword half withdrawn – but at the treatment of his guard by the 'harmless' Mr. Mulholland. Recognition that his sword was being stolen was second, and he grabbed for it, only to receive a badly cut hand as the tip of the blade slid free. Guillaume sidled to the rail beside the guard. Sully turned to take a swing at Georges. Georges smacked him hard across the neck with the dull heel of the blade, and Sully fell to the deck clutching his throat. The spectacle was far worse than the reality. Sully appeared to have been murdered, with blood flowing from throat, though the blood was in fact from his sliced hand.

Neville appeared, as if from the air.

* * * *   * * * *   * * * *

I hear the call for all hands, thought Neville, *and I hear the pipes. It's time to move.* He pulled open the clumsy lock he'd picked the day before, removed it from the ankle bracelet, threw the things aside, and jumped to his feet. *Ouch, I'm stiff.* He rubbed his back, and walked briskly to the companion stair. Reaching the point where his head was above deck level and he could see activity, he immediately realized that things were going according to plan. Somebody howled in pain. There was Stearns, down on the deck. Sir William was punching a guard in the face. Georges was drawing the captain's blade.

He moved stealthily for several paces, but paused for a moment to be sure Marion would be safe. Stearns was rising, obviously in a rage, but he did not fully stand before Marion plunged her dagger into his right shoulder. *Gads,* he thought, *that's where I stabbed him with my sword in our duel.* "That's for Father," Marion screamed at him. She withdrew her dagger with a nasty twist, and then punched him in the throat with her hand still clasping the hilt of the dagger. He gurgled and went down again. "And that's from me, you turd." Blood ran through Stearns' fingers from the gash in his shoulder.

Ellen's guard knelt before her, his nose bleeding. Marion was turning to deal with the next guard – who stood open-mouthed. Neville ran for the helm, smiling, and no longer concerned for his fiancée.

The swivel gun was exactly where Georges and Sir William had said it would be, loaded and ready.

At the swivel gun, Neville turned its open mouth forward. "Ring the bell, if you please, Sir Mulholland. A dozen times will do. Then take your musket and step to the stern. Georges, go to the stern, as well."

Although they gave him curious looks, they obeyed cautiously, before they realized why they had been ordered so. A dozen men were dropping from the sky, sliding down stays, halyards, and braces, to the defense of their captain.

"Move forward," Neville ordered the French.

"Marion and Ellen, move aft," he yelled at the top of his voice in English; "Now!"

A man grabbed at Ellen as she began to walk aft, but she fended him off with a punch to the face. He staggered back a few paces, but recovered and moved toward her again. Mulholland's musket fired, and the man dropped to his knees, and then flopped backward to the deck, blood spurting from his chest. Ellen and Marion ran the last twenty feet to safety behind the swivel gun.

The first sailor from above who landed abeam of the helm was met with the point of Georges' short sword and herded forward. The second met a similar fate at the point of Ellen's dagger, and the third was knocked on the head with the butt of Mulholland's musket.

"Drag that man away," Neville ordered the next two men to alight. Others who descended by rope were further forward, and their well-meaning efforts were for naught. They now all stood in front of the swivel gun. "Drop your weapons," he ordered, "Your captain has only a cut hand."

"Boy," Neville yelled to a runt of a thing in the middle, "Collect all the weapons and stack them here at the mainmast. The rest of you stand back. Landsmen, throw off sheets, and topmen go aloft. Furl everything, and don't come down, upon your peril."

"Boy," Neville yelled again, "bring me all pistols and two swords." He turned to Sir William. "Marksman Mulholland, will you be good enough to take charge of the pistols? Miss Stillwater, will you select a half dozen expected miscreants to be tied to the mainmast. I suggest the large and threatening types and any who appear to be officers of any description. Make Mr. Stearns the first. We'll tell them they are to come when called or Mr. Mulholland will shoot them dead on the spot. They've seen him do it. Are you ready, Sir William?"

"What good sport!" he responded.

Captain Sully was recovering. Guillaume had found some cloth to bandage his hand and stem the flow of blood.

"Captain," said Neville, "I should like to hoist a white flag. Have you one handy?" he asked (knowing the flag of French royalty prior to Napoleon had been white with a gold *fleur-de-lis* – and had probably not been destroyed).

Sully nodded.

"Haul Napoleon's colours and hoist the white one upside down, if you please."

"Sit!" Neville yelled to the ship's company forward. "Guillaume," he then said to the first mate, "will you go forward, please, and have your men set a single jib. It will become most uncomfortable if we do not. You may tell them we will wait to be captured."

An hour and a half passed before the first ship arrived. It wasn't their pursuer from Etretat, but one from the offshore fleet with the advantage of running before the wind. The 12-gun schooner *HMS Crafty* came roughly alongside, grappled itself on as though *Diligent* might run, and sent her men storming aboard. Neville stepped back from the swivel gun. And went with Georges, Marion, Ellen, and Sir William to gather together in a small group at the stern. They placed their weapons at their feet, and raised their hands in surrender.

"Who's in charge here?" demanded a gruff lieutenant. He had at least accurately identified the mutinous group. "Was this a mutiny?"

He seemed surprised at a response in English. "I am," said Neville, "Captain Burton, HMS *La Désirée*. And you are…?"

Commander Spencer couldn't stifle his laugh. "Ha, I'm sure you are. You smell even worse than you look. I'm Commander Richard Spencer, whatever that means to you. Who are these, your whores?"

"You just crossed the line, you skinny pig," said Neville. He dropped his hands and advanced. Seven muskets were cocked and raised in his direction. He stopped only two feet short of Spencer's pock-marked face. "Did you miss that I said **Captain** Burton? Are you as dense as you appear? We just handed you a prize. And might I add, **this** lady," indicating Marion, "is my fiancée, **that** one," pointing at Ellen, "is **Mrs.** Captain Dagleishe of HMS *Galatea*…"

"*Galatea*? What's she doing here, then? *Galatea* has sailed for the Caribbean."

"Ohhh…" cried Ellen.

"And **that** one," said Neville, continuing and pointing his finger then at Sir William, "is a senior staff member of the Navy Office in Whitehall, who was kidnapped by **that** one." He pointed at Stearns, tied to the mainmast bitts. "Whatever you do, don't let **him** loose, no matter what he says. You had best put a muzzle on, too, unless you wish to be set before the mast." Neville had moved much closer, and now had his face in Commander Spencer's. "If you don't find your manners very quickly, I **will** have you flogged 'round the fleet."

In the face of such certainty, Spencer backed down somewhat. "Take them to the mess," he said. In a low voice, he added to Neville, "You'd better be right, old sod, or you'll be swinging tomorrow."

"You'll be first," said Neville.

Transfers filled the half hour following. Sir William and his rescuers were moved rather roughly onto *Crafty*. The women were treated far more carefully, lest their words carried any truth. *Diligent* received a prize crew, in exchange for Stearns and a few French prisoners who were moved aboard *Crafty*. Given the increasingly rough state of the seas and the lack of any better place on such a small ship, the escapees from France were allowed to wait for *Crafty's* captain in the general mess – with a marine guard – rather than on deck.

Neville noticed Captain Sully was allowed to walk free. He had no problem with it. The man had undoubtedly given his parole, had an injured hand, and had just lost his ship. When Stearns was led into the mess, however, Neville exploded.

"Remove that man from this cabin!" he shouted at the marine sergeant who escorted him down the stair.

"Why, Captain Burton," Stearns queried, "would you be so rude? Do I not deserve…"

"Out, Sergeant. Now! I don't care where you take him; just don't leave him here, or there will be bloodshed. Oh, by the way, did you hear what he just called me? **Captain** Burton. He's not wrong."

For the sake of peace, it appeared, the sergeant led Stearns away, but Commander Spencer arrived five minutes later, in a state close to furious. He yelled in Neville's face, "You will not be giving orders aboard this ship, no matter what you claim your rank to be! My sergeant is to do what I order him to do!"

Neville stood from his seat on the bench and calmly responded, "That man, Commander, is dangerous. He has followed my fiancée from Jamaica to Baltimore to France, kidnapped a senior British official in the process, attempted to collaborate with Napoleon himself, and threatened to expose dozens of French patriots who, every day, pass valuable military information to Britain. All I am asking you for is the civility to keep him under guard and somewhere apart from the rest of us. I am sorry your sergeant happened into the middle of this, and if you wish, I shall apologize personally."

"I shall arrange it," said Spencer. "I have more to do than discuss accommodations with you." Spencer turned quickly to leave.

"I have one more suggestion, if I may?" Spencer turned back slowly. "This had better be good. I wasn't aware I was taking suggestions."

"I assume you will be most pleased to be shot of us as soon as possible?"

"Let there be absolutely no question on that," answered Spencer, "What is it?"

"Do not send *Diligent* immediately off to Plymouth, but keep her at the ready. We could be sent off with her when all this is done, whether we are in irons or not, with no loss to your squadron. If you choose not to hold her, please send this with her to the semaphore station at Plymouth." He handed Spencer a scrap of paper, on which Ellen had somehow managed to find the materials to write a short note.

Spencer's curiosity did not allow him to take it without reading:

Attn: Navy Office, Whitehall; R. Chapman

Sir WM free. Aboard Crafty in Channel. NB, etc.

Spencer refolded the note, turned with no expression, and left. Stearns did not return.

"He's not too friendly, is he, Neville?" asked Marion.

"I'm afraid not. He has me seeing red, but on this ship, as little as it is, I know he can do whatever he wants. We must just wait patiently now."

Thumping and yelling soon began above.

"What is it now, Neville... all the noise?"

"They're casting *Diligent* free. She has a British prize crew aboard, and will be taken to the prize court at Plymouth. Whether she will wait for us or not, I don't know. I assume we will now sail to wherever the squadron commodore is, and offered up to his care. I have made enough of a nuisance of myself for Commander Spencer to be very anxious to have us off this ship."

"You have, Neville. Yes, very good," said Mulholland. "The higher up the chain of command we get, the better the chance I know someone. He didn't say who it is, did he?"

"No."

They heard the call to dinner above in another hour, and they were herded into a corner while the men came down to eat. Two of the petty officers were kind enough to bring them each a bowl. Since it wasn't boys who'd been sent, Neville suspected the real objective was to get a better look at the ladies. The petty officer smiled a lot. Marion and Ellen did their best to smile back and give their thanks.

Shortly after dinner, commands began flying above, followed by the sound of sails being furled. The ship's motion worsened. Under way, with the pressure of the wind holding her steady against the seas, she moved smoothly. Without the sails, however, she wobbled at the mercy of the confused seas. They had lessened from six to four feet in the calming winds of late afternoon, but certainly weren't dissipated.

Lieutenant Spencer descended the companion stair shortly after the commotion ceased and announced, "Time to go see Captain Bissett. Please follow me."

The five followed in a line like sheep, with Sir William at the lead, Ellen and Marion next, and Georges and Neville at the rear. Mr. Stearns was being herded along behind. He now sported a pasty complexion and a clumsy bandage on his bloody shoulder.

Stepping up on deck, a number of British ships were immediately visible.

"She's found the fleet, I see," observed Nevillle to Sir William. That big one there I recognize. She's the seventy-four *Courageux* -- Captain Bissett, as Commander Spencer just said. *Courageux* sat rolling sluggishly in the waves a cable away

The schooner's largest boat, still only an eight-oar launch, waited on the lee side, lurching and pitching like a wild horse, and thumping dangerously against the schooner's hull. It calmed somewhat once filled with eight rowers, a coxswain, and six passengers, but it still bobbed perilously.

This end of the crossing from the little *Crafty* to the ponderous 74 was the easy part. Here, there were no more than a couple steps on a rope ladder and a little hop down into the rowing boat. The men would accomplish it at their peril, but with a little caution and the patience to wait for the rise of one craft against the other, the transfer was simple enough. The process was similar for Ellen and Marion, but they were assisted by many hands. Marion shot Neville a very displeased look following the experience.

The accommodation ladder of the 74, at the other end of the crossing, however, appeared to extend from the little boat into the sky itself. Even under *Courageux's* lee, the waves were two to three feet. *Crafty's* Commander Spencer scampered up the ladder first, and was ceremoniously piped aboard. The men were all fit, and had no injuries (except Stearns), so other than the fright of the endless climb, they had no difficulty. The women were afforded the courtesy of a bo'sun's chair which, when all was done, may have been a more frightful experience. Once strapped in and lifted off the rowing boat, they were free to swing helplessly to and fro. Marion had twice to fend off the big ship's side with her feet in order to avoid being badly bruised, and once again, her arrival on deck was met with many hands. The same followed for Ellen.

At the top, Neville found Spencer in conversation with a tall officer, whom Neville assumed to be the ship's First Lieutenant. Neville had followed Georges and Sir William, and he found the other two standing by the rail under a marine guard. Marion was being escorted to join them. Ellen would soon be fondled by her 'assistants', and Stearns had yet to come up.

Stearns also came aboard by chair because of his battered hand. To Neville's amusement, he swung more ponderously than the women, and smashed hard against the hull once on his way up. Spencer began talking excitedly to the first lieutenant and pointed their way repeatedly. The lieutenant asked a question. Spencer pointed east, to where *Diligent* bobbed cheerily. *Ah, marvelous. I hadn't noticed. He's unsure enough of us to keep Diligent handy.*

Courageux's lieutenant walked across the deck to where they waited under the curious eyes of hundreds of sailors. "Ladies and gentlemen," he said. "I am First Lieutenant Napier. Please follow me." They did as they were bid. Neville said nothing. They descended the companion stair and were again 'parked' to wait in the general mess.

Marion huddled herself up against Neville, and although he felt the behavior somewhat improper aboard a navy vessel, he wouldn't push her away. "Neville," she whispered, "they had their hands all over us, leaving and arriving. *All* over us, I tell you. I am mortified."

"Come with me," ordered Lieutenant Napier, before Neville had a chance to respond with anything more than "I'm sorry, dear." They followed him up one deck and straight aft from there into the captain's outer cabin. "Please sit," said Napier.

Mr. Stearns was then ushered in. He was asked to sit on the opposite side of the cabin. Marines stood guard of the entire affair.

Lieutenant Napier crossed the room to a door aft – the captain's personal cabin – knocked three times, and returned to his position standing beside a large desk. The portly Captain Bissett emerged shortly, took a measure of his guests, and sat at the desk. "I haven't much time for games, Commander Spencer. Why have you brought me these people?" he asked.

"We took them off a French coastal guard boat," he began. "They had apparently taken control of it by mutiny."

"I wouldn't call it muti…" interjected Neville.

"Wait your turn!" commanded Lt. Napier.

"I suppose he may be correct, Sir. Not mutiny, but a coup. They are not French, except the heavy one, there, and so were probably not part of the ship's company. They all speak English."

"Who do they say they are?"

"That is the crux of it, Sir. This one here claims to be a British Navy Captain."

"Captain Neville Burton, Sir. Frigate *La Désirée*, now lying Portsmouth," announced Neville.

"So you may say, *Captain*, but *La Désirée* is not 'lying' anywhere. We saw her just these three days past in the vicinity of Le Havre," chimed in Spencer. "Why would she be sailing about without her captain?"

"An emergency, Sir. And the others of my squadron? *Stork*, *Admiral Mitchell*, and *Alacrity*? Did you see them, as well?"

"Now you're not just a captain, but the commodore of a squadron? But yes, they were there also."

"That will be enough, Commander Spencer. I'll ask the questions. And whom do you pretend to be?" he asked Mulholland.

"I am Sir William Mulholland, advisor to the Admiralty."

"Sir? And a bit far afield, aren't we, ha, ha?" snorted Bissett.

"You asked. I thought Commodore Hood to be the commodore of this fleet. Where is he? He knows me."

"Well, I'm sorry, then, Sir, because his flagship, the *Centaur*, has sailed in chase of a French Squadron that stood from Brest a few days ago. I am the Commodore of this squadron dispatched to blockade. But it seems you might have known that, too."

"What about *Galatea*? Captain Joseph Dagleishe is a particular friend of mine," said Neville, "and this lady here is his wife."

"Oh, ho! This gets better and better. I'm sure he would like to claim her, ha, ha. But *Galatea* has sailed for the West Indies."

"If you know so much, why doesn't his wife tell you where he is now?"

"Because I was abducted by the scoundrel over there," he said, pointing to Stearns, "shipped to America months ago, and then back to Le Havre as a hostage for Napoleon himself. Mrs. Dagleishe has been the key to my retrieval."

"Not true," said Stearns. "He's a willing participant in a plot to provide British navy information to the French. And they're dangerous. You see what the fictitious Captain Burton has done to my face. And that ungrateful wench stabbed me here in the shoulder. I was trying to catch..."

The rest of them all yelled at once:

"Liar," yelled Marion.

"Falsehoods, all of it," barked Ellen.

"You disgusting twaddle," said Mulholland.

"Stuff his mouth, Captain. He's daft," suggested Neville.

"Enough! Enough!" yelled Lieutenant Napier at the top of his voice. "One more outburst and I will have you all wait in irons."

Stearns sat smirking while the cabin went silent. There was a rap at the door. "What now?" mumbled Captain Bissett. "Come," he yelled.

Another lieutenant stuck his head in and asked, "Is there any message for *Thunderer* before she sets sail for Cadiz, Sir?"

"*Thunderer?*" queried Neville. "The seventy-four?"

"Yes, of course, the seventy-four. Stay out of it."

"Call for her Lieutenant Watson. He can identify two of us. I beg of you," said Neville.

Napier looked down at Bissett quizzically. Bissett looked back, paused a moment, and gave the slightest nod. Napier looked over at the lieutenant in the doorway, and said, "Please fetch him."

"And finally – this man and this woman," said Bissett, referring to Marion and Georges. "We might as well hear their stories. Ladies first; go ahead, miss."

Marion glanced at Mulholland, and began, "We... ahh... I... I am Marion Stillwater, daughter of Chester Stillwater of the Stillwater Rum Trading Company, a primary supplier of rum to the British Navy in Jamaica, and I am Captain Burton's fiancée. I have also been a friend of Miss Aught... Mrs. Dagleishe for several years." She stopped there.

"Nothing in your story explains what you were doing aboard a French ship, Miss Stillwater, or why you have another name for the other lady present, or why you were in France," said Napier. "Were you in France? Nobody has said."

"Of course, we were in France, you dolt," said Stearns. "I told you I was chasing the traitor there."

The shouting began again.

"Out," yelled Bissett. "Lieutenant Napier, send them out to wait on the deck. Keep that one here," he said, referring to Stearns.

The marines quickly pushed the group of five out the door and bade them sit at the foot of the mainmast. "Keep it quiet," the sergeant said.

"What's he going to do with Mr. Stearns, Neville?" asked Ellen.

"He's going to ask a lot of questions, I think, and if I'm not wrong, he'll discover our Mr. Stearns has finally gone 'round the bend. He won't have a story without holes big enough to drive a coach and four through."

Stearns remained in the captain's cabin for another twenty minutes before being ejected. A marine escorted him from the cabin down the companion stair. He gave them a funny little wave as he went by, smiling. "Ha, ha!," he yelled, "I've told everything."

Neville could see a boat arriving from *Thunderer*, but could not make out anyone he knew aboard it. As it approached, it came under the lee of the ship, and Neville could no longer see it from his position sitting on the deck. They waited. Lieutenant Napier appeared again, and bade them re-enter the captain's cabin.

"We're sorry for the outburst, Commodore," said Neville. "Did Mr. Stearns present compelling evidence?"

"The man's gone daft, I think," said Bissett. "I'm not sure I can trust anything he says. I'm told *Thunderer's* First Lieutenant has come aboard, so we'll soon see if there's anything to **your** story."

The sentry knocked at the door frame, then held it open for an officer to enter.

Neville's childhood friend stepped in, squinting for a moment in the lesser light of the cabin, knuckled his forehead to Commodore Bissett, and said, "First Lieutenant Danial Watson of *Thunderer*. You called for me, Sir?"

"I did, aye. Can you identify anyone in this room?"

Daniel looked along the group from one to the other for a moment. "Sir Mulholland? Neville? What on earth are you doing here... dressed like... peasants? Whatever are you up to?"

Neville and Sir William remained silent.

"So you know the two Englishmen here?" asked Bissett.

"Aye, Sir. All my life. I joined the navy with Captain Burton, here, and this gentleman helped us. He knows our fathers. This is Sir William Mulholland. He is a... a senior bureaucrat at Whitehall, is all I've ever known."

"Has he anything to do with the Navy Office?"

"I... I don't know. He's there often enough, when he's not home, I think."

"You know where he lives?"

"Yes Sir, in Bury St. Edmunds, Suffolk, where Captain Burton and I come from."

"So, if he..." said Bissett, and then paused. He continued, "Oh... I see, I think; oh. Sir Mulholland, this Frenchman and these ladies, they... are your associates?"

"Yes Sir."

"Aha. This meeting is over. Sir Mulholland, if you would please stay. Lieutenant Napier, please see to whatever accommodation we can make for these others, but keep Mr. Stearns in the brig."

"One favor, Sir?" asked Neville.

"Go on."

"Can we keep *Diligent* at the ready for a few hours more?"

"Yes, do so. Commander Spencer, you are released. Inform your prize captain."

"What about *Galatea*, Sir?" asked Ellen.

"I'm afraid she did, indeed, sail – some weeks ago," answered Napier. "I am sorry."

Neville stood and walked to Daniel. The two embraced and clapped on each other's backs. "Daniel, you really must meet..."

"Sorry, gentlemen," Napier said. "Take it outside, please."

Daniel had little more time to spend than to meet his friend's fiancée and their special friends Georges and Ellen, accept Neville's congratulation on his promotion to First Lieutenant, and then answer a few questions about his wife Angelica at home in England, before he had to run. *Thunderer* would not wait for personal matters, and it was now Daniel's job as her First Lieutenant to be sure she didn't. He waved good-bye and slid deftly down the accommodation ladder. Neville watched him go, wishing he had time to get to know him again.

Outside the cabin, Neville also had the chance to speak with Commander Spencer. "Don't hold a grudge, Commander," he said. "You did the right thing. There's only one piece of advice I have for you."

"Yes, Captain?" said Spencer.

"Remember, of all things – this event never happened. It's not a story for an evening by the fire."

"Aye, Sir. Never happened." He shuffled nervously from one foot to the other for a moment, and then said, "I apologize for the insult to your fiancée, Sir." He spun on his heel and departed.

30 - "End or Beginning?"

Despite their appearance, *Courageux's* visitors were treated to a sumptuous feast for supper in the Commodore's cabin. They were given the means to wash – at least hands and faces – but there was nothing to be done for them in the way of costume. They were also provided places to sleep that far surpassed what they had endured for the past two days, while *Courageux* sailed northeastward up the English Channel.

Before light, a knock came at Neville's door. He arose in something of a stupor, went there, and opened it. "Marion, what is it? You look concerned."

"The noise, Neville, do you hear it?"

"No, I don't hear anything unusual… Oh, yes… the scratching of rats…"

"Rats, Neville?"

"Sorry dear, not rats. It sounds like the scratching of a hundred rats, but it's just the holystones."

"Holy…what?"

He bent over and kissed her. "Allow me a moment to dress, dear, and we'll go see."

Neville came out of his cabin – or closet, as it might better have been described, held his elbow out for Marion to take, and led her to the weather deck. "You see?" he said. "This happens every morning on a navy ship. We call those rocks they are scrubbing on the deck 'holystones', and the little ones they use in the corners are called 'prayer books'. I think they sound like rats running about over my head. This is how the decks are cleaned and made free of splinters. Here's a place. Sit here and watch a moment. I'll find some coffee." He returned in five minutes with two steaming mugs of brown liquid. Ellen was now huddled with Marion. "Don't expect this to taste exactly like coffee, my dears. We call it 'burnt toast coffee'. It's what we use when the ship has been out for a long time, and stores are low. One gets used to it."

"I've had the experience," said Ellen. "I pushed Archibald to leave Baltimore so fast he forgot coffee. And, being a navy ship, the holystones were at work every morning. Wait until you see what happens next. They come back and slap at the decks with their mops to dry them. But it's quite comical."

"Archibald, hmm?" said Marion. "Joseph has been away a long time…"

"Oh, shush. You must admit he's attractive!"

"Not a cat I'd like on my lap," said Marion. "Ow, no pinching!"

"That's quite enough in public, ladies," said Neville. "We officers are all dashing in our uniforms. It's why we wear them."

"Such nonsense, Neville."

"You see, Marion, there is much to learn about the navy. I look forward to showing you more of it," said Neville. "Is this not a glorious morning?" The sun was rising before the ship, casting a long shadow aft and changing the color of the water from steel gray to dark blue. The morning watch began flogging the decks dry, and with the aid of the rising sun, the planks began to shine white. "*Diligent* will take us to *La Désirée* this morning. We will collect my squadron and sail to Portsmouth. I think I should have *Stork* take Sir Mulholland directly to London, without delay. He has been away too long for the country's safety. You should go, too, for your comfort. I can follow in a few days."

The midshipman who had been assigned as prize captain of *Diligent* came aboard *Courageux* to receive his final instruction. "Whatever you've been told, you needn't convey us to London, Mr. Midshipman," Neville said to him, "but only to our own squadron off Le Havre. They should be easy to find, particularly on this glorious day."

Having sailed eastward while they slept, the morning found them quite close to Le Havre. Ships of the fleet were clearly visible for miles in each direction.

"Oh, wait, Midshipman. I think we'll not need to bother you at all. You'll have a splendid sail directly to Plymouth today. See the sail to the northeast, there? She's my ship, the *La Désirée*. If we can signal her, we can simply transfer ourselves and we'll be in Portsmouth before you make Plymouth."

As it is only about eighty miles from where they set themselves aboard *La Désirée* to Portsmouth, and a fresh westerly breeze to aid them, *La Désirée* and her two escorts *Admiral Mitchell*, and *Alacrity* reached rapidly across the Channel to find cautious safety shortly after dark on the edges of the Spithead anchorage. Returning to their proper assigned locations in Portsmouth would have to wait for the light of the next day. *Stork* did not accompany them. She had gone straight for London in front of a following wind with Sir Mulholland, Marion, and Ellen aboard.

"Whitehall will be expecting Sir William at the very earliest possible, even though he should probably rest awhile," Neville had argued.

"Rest?" queried Sir William. "I've done almost nothing else these past months, except the walk from Le Havre, a bit of rowing, and some excitement aboard *Diligent*. Let's be off!"

"Take the ladies, then. Escort them to my flat where they can rest and change to something fresh. Marion's things are there. It's right where you're going, isn't it?"

"We're not taking Mr. Stearns with us, are we?" Marion had asked.

"No, my dear. I hope never to be on the same vessel with him again. For that matter, I hope never to see him again. I have sent him under guard aboard *Diligent* to be held for trial for kidnapping and attempting to conspire with the enemy; 'acts of war' rather than 'traitor', basically, because he's not British."

Neville spent two days in Portsmouth, discussing the needs of the ships in his 'chase squadron', thanking the men of the ships for their diligence, and attending a couple celebratory dinners in the frigate's gunroom with the squadron's officers.

Admiral Mitchell, the 12-gun armed cutter (Lt. Richard Williams), offered to carry him to London. *Admiral's* small size would make her an effective transport up the Thames, so Neville agreed. There was no thought of taking La *Désirée*. A frigate cannot sail very far up the Thames. The afternoon before leaving, Neville finished reading his pusser's report just as a heavy shower passed over Portsmouth. It rained heavily enough to be heard in Neville's cabin below-decks. Neville was surprised at his instant anxiety, but jumped to his feet to go on deck to investigate.

"Are you all right, Sir?" asked Midshipman Foyle, when Neville came so rapidly on deck.

"Yes, yes, sorry." He looked up to see the sky already clearing after the late-autumn rain. "I just... wondered... about the weather for tomorrow's sail to London, but it looks as if there should be no trouble."

"No, Sir, it should be fine. I'm sorry to hear about your last passage up on *Active*. You must admit the weather was extreme then."

Five days later, Neville, dressed in a proper British captain's uniform, walked in to his flat in London. There he met a pair of ladies who not only looked the part of London society, but also smelled like it. During their following repast at a local dining room, they began discussing their list of questions for a visit with Sir Mulholland the next day.

"Sir William," Neville began once they had all trooped in to Navy Office room four, "some things are still a wonderment to us." Mr. Chapman had joined them for the debriefing. "Do you have any idea how Mr. Stearns managed to commandeer *Diligent*?"

"Yes, I do. Captain Bissett told me that one of the things in Mr. Stearns' possessions is a letter to him from the aide to Napoleon with whom he had been corresponding. I am sure he waved this letter in Captain Sully's face and demanded his help to catch a dangerous foreign spy. That would have been his stick. His carrot would have been the opportunity to have dinner with two lovely young ladies who were being held by the despicable creature… me, that is. Once he offered to pay for some sumptuous supplies for the table, the deal was closed, and they came out looking for us."

"It sounds logical for Stearns to expect results from telling tall tales."

"How is it you did not escape from him in all this time?" Ellen asked.

"At first," said Mulholland, "the captain locked me in my cabin aboard the... what was it...? *Spirit of Concord*, yes... until I agreed to his demands not to interfere with his ship. And where would I go, anyway?"

"Aboard ship, yes, but what about in Baltimore?"

"The Master locked me in again for the arrival, of course, and then Stearns came aboard to collect me with a silly police badge, handcuffs, and a pistol. So, once again I went along – off to his boarding house in Baltimore."

"Yes, we found it straight off, because he chose a place he discovered Marion had stayed," said Ellen. "We think he only missed Marion's departure by a few weeks, and we only missed his by a day or so. Archibald Mewes and I followed the *Pride of Maryland* aboard *Stork*, and we beat you, but not by enough to get Neville's squadron out early enough. But still you remained captive?"

"I knew nothing of Baltimore – or the United States – at that time. I can't say I know much more now. I..."

"You must promise to come visit me in Boston. It's a beautiful place. You could bring my husband," interjected Ellen.

"I had no American money," continued Sir William, "I assumed the people of the United States would still be unfriendly to British government officials, and I didn't even know how to post a letter there. I tried the latter, however, and was rewarded by being locked in my room for two days with nothing to do. I was quite curious as to Mr. Stearns' intentions, and so exercised patience to the utmost. I was just about to throw a chair through a window and be off in the night when he came to tell me we'd be leaving the next day. In all, we were only there a few weeks, and then I was back on a ship, with nowhere to run, until we landed in Le Havre."

"We could deduce most of what followed. We didn't see you out and about."

"No. Mostly, Stearns kept me locked in. He came to get me for breakfast and tea, but he certainly didn't want to lose me at such a crucial point in his scheme. I knew he carried a pistol, and he is a large man, as you know. My French is not the best, either, so what would I announce if I'd escaped? I had to hope Napoleon wanted me for some prisoner exchange."

"What happens now, Sir William?" Neville asked.

"Stearns will be going to trial. Georges, you may go about your business. I would appreciate any help you can give us. We must get Ellen home somehow, and I'm afraid we have a bit of a conundrum for you, Neville."

"Conundrum?"

"Yes. Mr. Chapman tells me he has a mission of a diplomatic nature for which he thinks you would be an excellent choice. I haven't fully reviewed it."

"Exactly who is 'you'? Me, alone, or me and another?" Neville looked to Chapman.

"You, for sure, Neville," said Chapman, "but possibly the others, depending..."

"Has this anything to do with the reason I came to London in the first place, Sir William?" Marion asked.

"I think the time has passed on that, but I haven't been back long enough to be sure. But then there's the Navy, Neville," said Mulholland, in a deft change of subject. "Or, I should say, the Admiralty. They're always looking for ships, and you have a little squadron all ready to go…"

"But then there's me," said Marion, "We can't go on much longer without we are wed. When are we supposed to fit that in?"

"Why not right away?" suggested Neville. "They have plenty of churches here in London."

"Neville, not without Father present, and he's in Jamaica – or at least he was, when he wrote last, about two months ago. And I can't stay away from the business forever, either. I've set up a warehouse in Baltimore, and it needs attention."

There was a knock on the door. Both Mulholland and Chapman spoke loudly, "Enter." Chapman looked sheepishly at Mulholland. "Sorry, Sir," he said.

"Maybe we carry Ellen back to Boston, meet your father, and then arrange to have a wedding in Baltimore? You could both check on your warehouse."

"I would dearly love to attend," said Ellen. "Is there any chance my husband could carry Mr. Stillwater up from Jamaica, Sir William?"

A sentry stuck his head in the door. He passed a message in to Mr. Chapman, who was the closest. Chapman opened the paper, and read the message aloud:

Cpt. N. Burton,

I thought you'd want to know:

I'm told Mr. Stearns has escaped custody. The gaol-van transporting him to London for trial overturned on the Post Road west of the City.

Cmdr. Williams, Admiral Mitchell

Life: what happens while you're making plans.